chocolate

for

two

Text copyright © 2012 Maria Murnane

Published by Amazon Publishing

PO Box 400818
Las Vegas, NV 89140

ISBN-13: 9781611099119
ISBN-10: 1611099110
Library of Congress Control Number: 2012919211

chocolate

for

two

by maria murnane

amazonpublishing

To Alex Carr, Waverly's best friend of all

prologue

I shot straight up in bed.

My hands were sweating.

My pulse was racing.

When I realized where I was, I pressed my palms hard against my eyes and forehead.

Was it just a dream?

After a few moments I regained control of my breathing, then removed my hands from my eyes and slowly looked to my left.

The side of the bed where Jake had spent so many nights keeping me warm was empty.

Dazed, I turned my head the other way and squinted at the clock on the nightstand.

It was 5:21 a.m.

Everything was dark except for the soft glow of the sun rising outside my bedroom window.

I put my hands on my temples.

What?

My brain flooded with fresh memories.

The walk in the park...

The ring of trees...

The unexpected question that made me laugh and cry at the same time.

Huh?

I blinked a few times.

Did none of that happen?

I slowly lowered my hands and gazed at my left hand.

It was bare.

Bare?

Was it really just a dream?

I'd never had such a vivid dream.

I'd never had a dream that had left me so utterly confused.

Still half-asleep, I pulled the covers to one side and swung my legs onto the hardwood floor. I wiggled my feet into a pair of slippers and shuffled into the kitchen.

I opened the cupboard and reached for a glass, then held it under the faucet until it was nearly full. I downed the water in a few gulps and slogged back toward the bedroom. Dream or no dream, I was determined to get a few more hours of sleep.

I was three feet from my bed when my brain finally kicked into gear.

Oh my God.

Oh my God.

It wasn't a dream.

I turned around and sprinted into the living room. I skidded to a halt in front of the bookcase, then reached for the top shelf. I carefully pulled down an antique wooden box with an image of a lush green forest glazed on the lid. The box was pretty much the only thing I'd inherited from my mother. Inside I'd kept the few photos I had of her, including one of her smiling in her wedding dress and one of her and my dad holding me as a newborn at the hospital.

She died just a couple years later.

I smoothed my hand over the top of the box, then carefully opened the lid.

The moment I saw it, I felt tears welling up.

I smiled and exhaled.

It wasn't a dream.

Tucked neatly beside the photos was another box.

A small box.

A velvet box.

A ring box.

I reached for it, then slowly opened the lid. Inside was a diamond ring.

I felt my cheeks flush with heat.

It's real.

I'm engaged.

I gently slid the ring onto my finger and held up my hand in the soft morning light.

chapter one

When I woke up for real a few hours later, I half skipped, half floated into the kitchen and made a pot of coffee. As I waited for it to brew, I gazed at my ring again, then slipped into a happy daydream to replay the day before in my head like a movie...

"Keep walking," Jake said.

"Where are we going?" Dry leaves crackled under my flip-flops.

"Shhh...just keep walking straight ahead...you'll see." He kept his hand on the small of my back and nudged me forward. The cool breeze provided a welcome relief from New York City's relentless summer heat.

I coughed and stopped walking. "I'll *see*? Given that I'm wearing a blindfold, that seems unlikely."

He laughed. "I bet I could offer you a million dollars to stay quiet for five minutes, and you wouldn't be able to do it. Maybe even two million."

I didn't reply. I just kept walking.

"Am I wrong?" he asked.

I stayed silent.

"You know I'm right. It's killing you not to speak right now."

I bit my lip.

Then I caved.

"I could do it." I half muttered, half coughed the words.

He laughed again. "I think I've just proved my point. Okay, stop walking. We're here." He placed his hands gently on my shoulders and turned me to the right.

"We're *where*?"

"We're *here*. Let me help you with that." He removed my blindfold, and I blinked a few times. As the light flooded into my eyes, my surroundings began to take shape.

We were standing in a secluded dell loosely framed by a bright circle of flowering dogwood trees, the grass warm and lush beneath our feet. It was a Saturday afternoon in July, so I knew the park must be packed, but somehow Jake had found a private nook right in the heart of it.

"Are you sure we're in *Central Park*? The crazy-crowded one in the middle of *New York City*?" I peered up at the buildings dotting the familiar Manhattan skyline beyond the pink-flowering tree branches.

He nodded. "Yes, ma'am." As if on cue, a few birds chirped overhead.

"But where is everybody?"

He took off his backpack and removed a blanket. "I came across this spot when I was walking through the park a few weeks ago, and I thought it looked like the ideal place for a picnic. A pretty sweet discovery, don't you think?" He shook out the blanket and laid it on the grass.

I smiled. "It's gorgeous, Jake. Magical, even. I didn't think privacy was possible in Central Park *ever*, much less on a Saturday in the dog days of summer."

He handed me a deli sandwich and a bottle of water, then looked up at the sky. "I thought of you as soon as I saw it. Makes me feel like we're on a movie set."

I pointed at him. "Try to remember that when winter hits. You might be cursing me then."

"Will do." Jake had moved from Atlanta about six months earlier to take a job as head physical therapist for the Brooklyn Nets…and to be closer to me. *Sigh.* I still couldn't believe my luck. Not only did he make me laugh, but he always knew where I'd left my phone and never forgot to order my coffee with extra cream and sugar. It didn't hurt that he was make-me-swoon handsome to boot. Even after all this time, I still found myself feeling a little giddy when I looked at him.

I unwrapped my sandwich, which I knew would be carved turkey and Swiss on Dutch crunch with no pickles and extra honey mustard, my favorite. Jake always remembered my favorite everything. "Don't worry. If you get too cold when it starts to snow, *I'll* keep you warm." I gave him a playful smile.

I expected him to tease me back, but he didn't, so I shrugged and took a huge bite of my sandwich.

"Shelter, food, and water," he said as I chomped.

I looked over at him, my mouth full.

"Hmfph?"

"Shelter, food, and water." He gestured to the trees framing our private glade, then at the picnic spread before us and the water bottle in his hand. "That's all you need to survive in the world, right? Isn't that what they always taught us when we were kids?"

I squinted at him as I swallowed. "Come again?"

He shrugged. "Just thinking back to my Boy Scout days. It was all so simple when we were kids, wasn't it?"

"Tell me about it. I remember being absolutely *consumed* the summer before my sophomore year in high school with—I kid you not—whether or not to grow out my bangs. My *bangs*. Please."

He leaned over and brushed a loose strand of hair out of my eyes. "It's not enough, you know."

I smoothed my ponytail with my hand. "Not enough? You think I should grow it longer?"

He laughed. "I'm not talking about your hair. I'm talking about food and water and shelter. It's not enough to get you through life."

"It's not?" I took another bite of my sandwich. *When did he get so philosophical?* It wasn't like him to be so serious.

He started picking at the grass, which I'd never seen him do. Then he looked at me.

"You know how everyone says that if you want to get married, you should look for someone you can imagine...spending the rest of your life with?" he asked.

I stopped breathing.

Oh my God.

I stared at my sandwich.

Oh my God.

"But I've realized that's not true. That's not true at all."

Oh my...God?

I sat there frozen, my eyes fixated on my turkey and cheese, unable to move.

What is going on?

"Waverly, will you look at me?"

Slowly, slowly, slowly, I set the sandwich down and lifted my head.

"Yes?" I whispered.

Now he looked down and started picking at the grass again. "I've realized that if you want to get married, it's not enough to find someone you can imagine spending the rest of your life with."

I swallowed. "It's not?"

He shook his head. "I think to be happy—truly, *truly* happy—you need to find someone you can't imagine spending the rest of your life...*without*."

I opened my mouth to speak, but no words came out.

"My life changed forever when I met you, Waverly."

I gaped at him, still speechless. Our eyes were locked on each other, but—for once—I couldn't utter a sound.

He reached over and grazed my cheek with his fingers. "I thought I had it pretty good before I met you, but then you came along and showed me how much better it could be. So much better."

I smiled.

He cleared his throat. "I know it's been a bit of an...*indirect*...road to get here."

I winced. *Indirect* was a polite understatement, given how many times my irrational behavior and fear of getting hurt had nearly derailed us.

"But looking back, I wouldn't change any of it, because it's forced me to do a lot of thinking." He stood up, and I tried to process his words. *Is he saying what I think he's saying? Is what I think is happening really happening?* The cacophony of my own voice inside my head was deafening. I felt dizzy and was glad I was sitting down.

Jake, however, was standing.

I looked up at him, and slowly, very slowly, he reached into his pocket.

And pulled out a small box.

Oh my God oh my God oh my God.

My eyes welled up with tears, and through a hazy, teary blur, I watched him kneel down before me.

Then he reached for my hand.

"Waverly Bryson, I can't imagine my life without you. I don't *want* to imagine it without you."

I was incapable of speech, so he just continued.

"You've made me so happy, you *make* me so happy, and I want to spend the rest of my life returning the favor."

"You...do?" The words came out as a squeak.

"Yes, if you'll let me. I love everything about you, Waverly. Absolutely everything."

"Even my jokes?"

He laughed. "Don't push it."

I narrowed my eyes at him. "You love me even on those mornings when I talk too much and you—"

He smiled and put his hand over my mouth. "Just let me do this, okay?"

I nodded, tears streaming down my cheeks.

"Promise?" He raised his eyebrows, his hand still covering my mouth.

"Promise," I whispered into his hand.

Slowly he removed it.

Then he opened the box.

chapter two

It was torture waiting for the sun to rise on the West Coast. When your favorite people live in California, those extra hours cast a few raindrops on the *I have exciting news* parade.

I figured seven their time was late enough. Then I remembered it was Sunday. My dad and stepmom would probably be up, and maybe McKenna too, since her daughter was barely a year old, but I knew Andie would be asleep until at least ten.

At 7:01 their time I picked up my phone and called McKenna's cell phone. She answered on the third ring.

"This had better be important," she whispered. "Elizabeth's still asleep. So is Hunter. Hang on. I'm going into the living room."

"Why do you have your phone turned on while everyone's sleeping?"

"I'm a mom now, Waverly. Moms don't ever turn their phones off."

I laughed. "You really think Elizabeth is going to call you *on your cell phone* from her crib? Can she even talk yet?"

"Touché. So, how are you?" she asked in a normal voice. "I'm in the living room now."

"Are you sitting down?"

"Yep, I'm on the couch. What's up?"

I took a deep breath. "I'm getting married."

"OH MY GOD!" she shrieked. Then her voice quickly dropped a few decibels. "Oh, damn it. I hope I didn't wake her up."

"Can you believe it? I can't believe it."

Her voice stayed hushed but bubbled with enthusiasm. "Oh, Waverly, I'm so happy for you. How did it happen? Tell me everything. *Everything!* I'm so bummed that we're doing this over the phone. I sooo wish I were right there with you."

"I know, me too. But we'd probably be doing this over the phone even if I hadn't moved to New York, because I sure as hell wouldn't be driving over the Golden Gate Bridge to your place at seven in the morning."

"You have no idea how much I miss you right now. So, start at the beginning."

I leaned back into the couch and told her the story in glorious, girly detail. The blindfold, the secluded spot in the park, the surprise picnic, and how Jake told me he couldn't imagine his life without me. I recounted that last part to her verbatim, or as closely as I could remember. Honestly, it was all sort of a dizzy-happy blur now.

Her voice cracked. "You're making me cry, did you know that?"

I smiled. "I may cry too. I can't believe how happy I am, Mackie. I don't think I've ever been this happy."

We chatted for a few more minutes, and eventually she asked the question we both knew she had to ask. We'd been friends for too long for her *not* to bring it up.

"Was it weird at all, you know, going through it...again?" McKenna had been there every step of the way through my previous engagement, which had ended most unceremoniously two weeks before the ceremony—when my fiancé showed up on my doorstep, told me he didn't love me, and called the whole thing off. A year later, he was married to someone else. It had taken me ages to get my self-esteem back, and I'd nearly blown things with Jake because of it.

I tucked my legs underneath me. "Actually, it wasn't weird at all. And you know why?"

"Because Jake isn't Aaron?"

I smiled. "Well, yes, of course, but no."

"Because this time it feels different?"

"Yes again…but no."

"Because this time you just know it's right?"

I laughed. "Well…yes again. But that's still not what I was going to say."

"I give up."

"Okay, listen to this. At some point, most women fantasize about hearing someone like him say the words *Will you marry me?* Right?"

"Of course."

"But we dream about hearing them only once, right? At least, ideally?"

"I guess so. I mean, I'd like to hope so. I guess I never thought about it, to be honest."

"Well, that's because fortunately you never had to. Anyhow, we all know that *un*fortunately, I already heard those words once."

"Yes…"

"And Jake knows that too."

"Yes…"

"So he didn't say them."

"He didn't?"

I shook my head. "No. You know what he said instead?"

"Please don't make me guess. I can't bear the suspense."

"He told me how he couldn't imagine his life without me… and then he…"

"And then he *what*?"

I hesitated.

"And then he asked…if he could be my husband."

"That's adorable!"

"I know, right?" I grinned.

"I love him, Waverly."

"Too late for you. Did I mention *I'm* marrying him?"

"You have no idea how happy I am for you."

"Oh, I have an idea, Mackie. I know how much you love me."

"It sounds like everyone loves you these days."

I laughed. "Andie's not going to love me when I wake her up to tell her the news. That I know for sure, but I'm calling her anyway."

"Now, *she'll* have her cell phone turned off. Guaranteed."

"That's the beauty of knowing her landline, my friend."

I told her I'd be in touch with more details soon and hung up to call Dad next.

• • •

After sharing the happy news with my father, I braced myself for a grumpy Andie and dialed her landline. She answered on the sixth ring.

"Someone had better be dead." Her voice was raspy and groggy.

I sat up straight on the couch. "Good morning! I have news."

"Is the news that someone is dead?"

"No."

"Then can you call back at a reasonable hour? Some of us like to go *out* on Saturday night, you know."

I laughed. "I love you too. So much, in fact, that I may even ask you to be a bridesmaid."

"What?"

"You heard me."

"Let me get this straight. You're engaged?"

"I'm engaged."

"You're getting married?"

"I'm getting married."

"Holy hell, Waverly. Let me take the phone into the living room so I don't wake Nick up."

I heard rustling, then the sound of a door opening and closing, then more rustling.

"You're really getting married?"

"I'm really getting married."

"Already?"

"Already? I've known him for almost three years, Andie."

"Really? Has it been that long?"

"Indeed it has. I met him at that trade show a month after I turned twenty-nine. In October I'll be thirty-two."

"You're right. Damn, that went fast. So, spill. How did he propose?"

I regaled her with the whole story, again inventing riveting dialogue where my memory failed, but I didn't care, and neither did she, because accuracy wasn't the point. When I was done, I leaned back into the couch and put my feet up on the wicker chest that served as a coffee table.

"And then I called you," I said.

"Damn, Waverly."

"I know."

"Why did you put the ring in that box?"

I held my left hand up and stared at it. "This might sound silly, but Jake left for a work trip last night, so since he wasn't here anyway, I decided to put it with my mom's photo before I started wearing it, just for a little bit."

I expected to be mocked, but Andie surprised me.

"That's sweet, Waverly."

I scrunched up my face. "You think? I know it's a bit strange."

"Well, *you're* a bit strange."

I laughed. "Thanks. I think."

"Damn, another one bites the dust. You and I were in it together, you know. What am I supposed to do now?"

"Oh, please. Your awesome boyfriend is asleep in your bed right now. Given that you *live with him*, you can hardly play the single card."

She didn't respond to my comment and instead changed the subject.

"So, listen. I know today is all about you, but I have news too."

I tucked my legs underneath me. "Oh yes? Do tell."

"One of the reasons I'm so hungover right now is that my company had its annual summer party last night."

"Since when does your company have an annual summer party?"

"Since yours truly joined the party-planning committee. Keep up."

I laughed. "I've been trying to do that since the day I met you."

"So I was talking to the COO at the party, and he asked if I could help with a company-wide performance audit."

"A what?"

"A performance audit. Basically it's reviewing how we do things across all departments to uncover ways to make us more efficient, that sort of thing. My role would be studying the finances and looking for ways to reduce costs without affecting productivity."

"I forgot how boring your job is. I think I just fell asleep for a minute."

"Do you want me to hang up?"

"Is there a point to this story?"

"The *point*, Miss Bride, is that it's a great opportunity, but I'd have to leave my current position for three months to do it."

"Okay…"

"You ready for it?"

I fake-yawned. "I was ready ten minutes ago."

"Suck it. The team conducting the audit is based in our New York office."

My eyes got big. "No way!"

"Way."

"So you'd live here for three months?"

"I'd live there for three months."

"Oh my God! Are you going to take it?"

"Hell yes. You know I've always wanted to live in New York."

"Where will you stay?"

"They're going to put me up in some high-rise corporate apartment downtown."

"Won't that cost a fortune?"

"I work in corporate America, Waverly. We're all about wasting money."

"Didn't you just say that you were coming here to find ways to cut expenses?"

"*Other* departments' expenses, not mine. Big difference."

"My mistake. That's so cool."

"I know. It's going to be awesome. I can't wait."

"What does Nick think about it?"

She hesitated for just a moment, long enough though to set off a tiny alarm bell in the back of my brain.

"He's not thrilled that I'll be so far away, but he knows it's a great opportunity, and it's not forever, so he thinks I should do it," she said.

I wanted to pry, but I knew her well enough to let it go. If something was up between those two, Andie would only talk about it when she was ready.

Nevertheless, I decided to gather some information via the indirect route.

"I love that guy. Does he know how much I love him?"

"Believe me, he knows. So don't encourage him. His head is big enough as it is."

"He'd better come visit."

"He's already started sniffing out the best fares."

"So, when do you get here?"

"Probably within a couple weeks. They want to get the project going as soon as possible."

"Awesome! I can't wait."

"You won't be too busy spending every waking moment with your perfect fiancé?"

"Please. I mean, he's definitely perfect and gorgeous and all that, but he's no Andie Barnett."

"Well said."

chapter three

Jake was out of town until Wednesday, so I had to spend the first few days of our engagement celebrating without him. It was sort of a bummer that he wasn't around to join me in my state of post-proposal bliss, but I was used to our disjointed schedules and work that kept me as busy as I could handle.

I was still a regular contributor to the daytime talk show *Love, Wendy,* which was as popular as ever. My segment, *Honey on Your Mind,* could certainly be stressful at times, but I'd pretty much gotten the hang of interviewing people on the street about their innermost thoughts and feelings. That allowed me to spend more time on my brainchild, the ever-expanding Waverly's Honey Shop. My quirky line of clothing and products featuring one-line observations about life seemed to have struck a chord with the general public. I enjoyed the entrepreneurial thing, but juggling both jobs was beginning to wear me out. You can drag the girl out of bed, but you can't drag the need to spend nine hours sleeping in that bed out of the girl.

Tuesday afternoon I strolled the mile from my Brooklyn Heights apartment to Waverly's Honey Shop's small office in Dumbo. We'd moved in more than six months before, but it was still pretty bare. There just never seemed to be time to properly decorate, and while I knew it was my responsibility, I secretly hoped someone would take charge and do it for me.

I'd spent the day before at *Love, Wendy*, so I hadn't yet shared my big news with my small but loyal team here. When I opened the door, Paige, my business partner and confidante, was sitting at the conference table with Tasha and Beth, our interns from Manhattan's Fashion Institute of Technology. The table was covered with papers and fabric swatches.

The three of them raised their heads like marionettes when they heard me come in.

"Hi, Waverly," Paige said. "What's shaking?" Her round face was a bit fuller than usual, a side effect of being in her third trimester.

I hesitated for a moment, then smiled and raised my left arm. "What's shaking? Oh, just my hand, just a little bit. It's tired, you know, from carrying this *diamond* around." I fluttered my eyelashes Marilyn Monroe style.

Paige's eyes got big. "Oh my God!"

Tasha leaped out of her chair and made a beeline for me, followed by Beth. Paige struggled as she lifted herself—and her growing belly—out of her seat.

"Let's have a look, then," Tasha said as she reached for my hand. "Are you *kidding* me? It's enormous!"

Beth's eyes grew wide. "Oh my gosh, Waverly, it's gorgeous."

I smiled and fluttered my eyelashes again. "Why, thank you. I quite agree."

Paige walk-waddled over to us and gave me a hug. "Congratulations. I'm so happy for you."

"Thanks, Paige. Can you believe we're *both* engaged now? Who would have thought it was possible? Only a year ago, you were dating assholes of every stripe, and Jake was living in Atlanta!"

She laughed and spread her hands over her bump. "Tell me about it. Life can turn on a dime, that's for sure."

Tasha grabbed my hand again and studied the ring some more, then looked up at me. "Were you expecting it?"

I shook my head. "No clue."

"Honestly?"

"He completely surprised me."

After I finished filling them in on all the juicy details of the proposal, Beth sat down and sighed.

"What a fairy tale. *I* want to get married."

I looked at her and laughed. "Stop it. You're only twenty-four. You're way too young to even *think* about getting married."

She sighed again. "I know, but I'm already sick of dating. Dating in New York is an exercise in torture. It's worse than getting waxed."

Paige gave her a sympathetic look. "Sweetheart, I hate to break it to you, but dating is hard *everywhere*."

Beth picked up a piece of fabric and started folding it. "Maybe so, but men are…*meaner* here than they are in Indiana."

I laughed. "And that surprises you?"

She continued to play with the fabric. "I know, I know. But I just want to find a nice guy and be done with it. Is that too much to ask?"

Tasha nodded. "I agree with Beth. I grew up here so can speak only from my own experience, but on a scale of dating difficulty, New York has got to be in a separate league." She put a hand on Beth's shoulder. "You're just too nice and pure, Midwestern girl. Nice girls like you get screwed here because so many New York guys like bitches."

"I'm not *that* nice," Beth said.

Tasha tilted her head to one side. "Do you still give spare change to people in the subway?"

"Yes." Beth looked at the ground.

"There you go."

"Okay, maybe I'm nice. But I'm not *that* pure," Beth said. "It's not like I'm a virgin or anything."

Tasha tilted her head to the other side. "Pure is a relative thing. Do you think it's gross to sleep with someone on the first date?"

"Yes." Beth continued to look down.

Tasha held up both her hands. "Would you ever sleep with more than one guy at the same time?"

Beth couldn't even bring herself to respond to that one, but the horrified look in her eyes said it all.

"Not at the *exact* same time," Tasha said, looking at me and Paige. "You know what I mean, right?"

Paige and I laughed. "We know," I said.

"Well?" Tasha said to Beth. "Would you ever sleep with more than one guy at a time?"

Beth's cheeks turned a deeper shade of pink. "No," she whispered.

Tasha crossed her arms in front of her and looked at me and Paige. "I rest my case. The guy who lives in the apartment next to me is sleeping regularly with three women."

Beth's eyes doubled in size. "*Three?*"

Tasha nodded. "*Three.* His apartment is basically a revolving door of sexual partners who, from what I can tell, have never been out in daylight with him. Personally I think it's gross, but as he likes to put it, that's dating in New York."

"Wow," Beth said softly. She suddenly looked a bit pale.

The interns walked back over to the conference table, and as I watched them I couldn't help but smile. Their exchange was like listening to me and Andie ten years earlier.

How things have changed.

The thought of Andie reminded me of my other news. I looked at Paige. "Hey, did you hear your crazy cousin is moving here?"

"Andie?"

I gave her a look. "Do you have any other crazy cousins who also happen to be one of my best friends?"

"Why is she moving *here*? Didn't she just move in with her boyfriend?" Her face suddenly got serious. "Don't tell me they broke up?"

I shook my head. "It's a work thing, some three-month project, so she's coming solo." *I hope that's the only reason.*

"When?"

"I think next week."

"Wow, how fun. I haven't seen Andie in ages."

"She's the same. Short. Blonde. Spunky. A little bit crazy."

"Sounds like she hasn't changed a bit."

"Here's to that, and let's hope she never does."

• • •

On the walk home that evening, I pulled out my phone and sent Jake my first text since we'd gotten engaged.

Hi fiancé, it's your fiancée. I love you SO MUCH!!!!
Lots of LOVE,
Your loving fiancée
p.s. I love you so much!

I made a quick stop at the grocery store, and when I got back to my apartment, I nearly collided with a FedEx delivery guy on his way out of my building.

"By any chance, are you Waverly Bryson?" he asked.

I saluted. "That would be me."

He held up a package marked OVERNIGHT EXPRESS and handed me a stylus. "This is for you. I just need your John Hancock."

I signed his little device and eagerly hurried upstairs. I couldn't remember the last time I'd received a package, especially via overnight delivery.

I sliced the packing tape with scissors and opened the box. Tucked on top of something wrapped in pink tissue paper was a small note:

A little gift to get you started.
Fondly, Ava McIntyre

It was from Jake's mom.

I set the card down and carefully opened the delicate paper. Inside was an enormous black leather wedding planner. The letters WM were monogramed on the front.

WM?

Then it hit me.

Waverly...McIntyre.

Uh-oh.

Like I would ever change my last name.

As I flipped through the gilded pages, I wondered what else she might be expecting me to change.

chapter four

It turned out that I wasn't the only one with big news.

A week later I felt my phone buzz on my lap during a meeting at NBC. I couldn't answer it, but I glanced down and was surprised to see a name that rarely popped up on it.

McKenna.

Mackie's calling me?

Unless she was returning a call from me, I rarely heard from McKenna these days. She'd gone back to work a few months earlier and was now juggling an energetic little girl and a high-stress banking job. Throw in a husband and a bumper-to-bumper commute from Mill Valley into downtown San Francisco, and her life was even busier than mine. She didn't have a free minute to breathe, much less call me. Ah, suburban bliss.

I shrugged it off as an inadvertent pocket dial, but then my phone vibrated again, indicating she'd left a voice mail. I listened to the message as soon as the meeting was over.

"Hey it's me. I've got some news, give me a shout."

I raised my eyebrows.

News?

I wanted to call her back right away, but I couldn't. I had to spend the rest of the afternoon preparing for a taping of *Honey on Your Mind* before racing across town to scope out a location for a segment later in the week. By the time I had a chance to sit down and pick up the phone, it was nearly eight o'clock. Exhausted, I poured myself some wine and plopped on the couch. I set the glass down and closed my eyes for a few delicious minutes, then called McKenna at the office.

"Hey." She sounded...weird.

"Hey back. Are you okay? I think that was the first voice mail you've left me in like a year."

"I know, I'm sorry. It's just crazy these days, and I don't want to be that mom on the news who was playing with her *phone* while her kid was playing in the fireplace, you know?"

I laughed. "It's okay, I understand. So, what's up?" I picked up my wine and took a sip.

"I'm pregnant."

I nearly dropped my glass. "*What!*"

"Yep."

"Since when?"

"About a month. I just took the test today."

"Oh my God, Mackie. I can't believe it!"

"I can't either, actually. I think I'm in shock."

"Were you trying? I don't remember your saying anything about trying. Were you drinking? Is this one of those champagne babies, like those toddlers who have siblings in college?"

She laughed. "We weren't exactly *trying*, but we weren't really *not* trying either. We were sort of just, I don't know, going with it."

"Apparently it went."

She laughed again. "Hunter's pretty proud of his little swimmers, let's just put it that way."

"Good God, Mackie, you're going to have another kid who can't even feed itself?"

"Looks like it. Unless we have twins."

I set my glass down and put a hand on my chest. "Don't give me a heart attack. I'm still trying to come to terms with being an auntie of two."

"I'm confident you'll manage."

"So, when's the due date?"

"I'm not sure exactly. I think sometime in February. I'm going to see the doctor tomorrow."

"Are you excited?"

She didn't hesitate. "Yes. A little overwhelmed, but yes."

"What about your job? Are you going to quit?"

"I don't know yet. The juggling thing is hard, but it's a good change from having baby food in my hair all day long. Plus it's refreshing to be surrounded by grown-ups who think about things other than diapers and nap schedules."

"I love naps."

"That's because *you're* the one taking them."

"True. I guess this means you won't be coming out here for any more crazy weekends?"

"Definitely not. I'm still recovering from the last one."

I coughed. "You mean the one last *December*?" To be honest, though, I still reeled a bit myself when I thought about how much alcohol had been consumed when she and Andie had come to visit for Andie's birthday.

She laughed. "I don't get out much anymore."

"Clearly not. Well, Jake and I haven't even begun to think about dates yet, but it definitely won't be before February. I was thinking maybe we'd do something next summer. Probably something really small."

"Out here?"

"I guess, but to be honest I haven't been able to face the idea of making endless to-do lists for the big day. It just seems like so much work to get to the *married* part, which is all I really want."

"You think his mom would be cool with a small wedding? I get the impression that's probably not what she has in mind."

I glanced at the enormous wedding planner sitting—still untouched—on my desk. Before I could reply, my doorbell rang.

"Let me guess, that's Jake," McKenna said.

I raised my eyebrows. "How did you know?"

"Just a feeling. He's still ringing the bell?" Jake had keys to my apartment, and while he used them to enter the building, he was too polite to let himself into my apartment. He always rang the bell, or knocked softly if it was late. I thought it was adorable.

I stood up and started walking toward the kitchen. "What can I say? He's crazy-polite. Always has been, always will be, I imagine. I'm certainly not complaining."

"You'd better not be."

"So I guess I need to run, prego. And I guess I need to start calling you *prego* again, even though I feel like I just stopped."

"Good timing, anyway, because I need to get home and prepare Elizabeth's dinner."

"Are you going to fry up the bacon you're bringing home?"

She laughed. "Hardly. Notice I used the word *prepare*, not *cook*. Warming things up is about all Hunter and I have time for these days."

I set my wineglass on the counter and turned toward the front door. "Hey, as long as your child isn't starving, it's all good. You're talking to a thirty-one-year-old woman who still eats ice cream for dinner at least twice a month."

"Ah, that makes me miss you, my friend."

"I miss you too."

I hung up the phone as I opened the door. "I'm so sorry for keeping you wait—"

I stopped midsentence.

Jake was standing there, a bouquet of white flowers in his hand.

I smiled and put a hand over my heart. "For *moi?*"

He looked behind me. "Are there any other beautiful women I want to marry here?"

I snatched the bouquet and stood on my tiptoes to give him a quick kiss. "You know, speaking of marrying me, I haven't asked you yet if I look any different."

"What do you mean?"

I held my arms out to the side and spun around once, still holding the bouquet. "I mean, I am a *betrothed woman* now, Jake. Do I look any, you know, *different?*"

"How exactly would you look different?"

I shrugged and let my arms go limp. "I don't know. It just sort of seemed cool to think I might look more grown-up or something. So, are you hungry? I was thinking we could order Thai."

He laughed. "Sounds good."

I walked into the kitchen and pulled out a vase. "How about a glass of wine? I just poured myself one."

"I'd love one. You want me to put those in water for you?"

I handed him the bouquet and nodded to the vase on the counter. "Sure, thanks." He turned on the tap as I reached back into the cabinet for another wineglass.

"So, guess who called me with big news today?" I topped off my drink, then pulled a corkscrew out of a drawer and went to work on a fresh bottle of pinot noir.

He looked at me. "Big news?"

"Yep."

He took the vase into the living room and set it on my wicker chest, then kicked off his shoes and took a seat on the couch. "I bet...McKenna's pregnant."

I froze.

"How did you know?" I set the bottle on the counter and walked into the living room, my hands on my hips.

"I'm right?"

I nodded. "How did you guess so fast?"

He shrugged. "I don't know. I just had a feeling."

"I don't get it." I held my palms up. "I've known McKenna since freshman year of college, and *I* didn't see this coming. How do you know these things, Jake?"

He chuckled and shrugged again. "I don't know. I just do."

I pointed at him before turning back to the kitchen. "You're too perceptive. It's not fair."

"It's not fair that I'm perceptive?" he called after me.

I shook my head, even though he couldn't see me now. "No."

"Why exactly isn't it fair?"

I picked up the glasses and walked back into the living room, then handed him one and plopped down on the couch. "You're already good-looking, funny, athletic, and super thoughtful. Now you're beginning to make me think you're an alien or something."

He scratched his eyebrow. "You think I'm an alien?"

I laughed and sipped my wine, then gestured toward the vase. "These beautiful flowers, for example. What are they called?"

"Camellias."

"Never heard of them, but I'm sure you have. And I bet they mean something, right?"

He smiled. "Maybe."

I pointed at him again. "See? How do you *know* these things?"

He laughed. "I don't know. I just do."

"So what do they mean?"

He set his glass down, then leaned toward me and pushed a loose strand of hair out of my eyes.

"The camellias?"

I nodded.

"They mean I think you're adorable," he said softly.

I swooned and forgot all about my little rant.

I set my glass next to his, then scooted closer to him and leaned my head against his arm. "What did I ever do to deserve you, Jake?"

"I think the same thing about you every day," he whispered into my hair.

We stayed like that for a few wonderful moments, then I gave him a quick kiss and stood up. "You do realize that every time you come over here, we order out, right? Please tell me you've noticed that."

He nodded. "I've noticed."

"So you do understand that means I can't cook, right?"

He scratched the side of his neck. "You think that's some sort of secret you've managed to keep under wraps until now? Because I hate to break it to you, but I figured that out a while ago."

I put my hands on my hips. "I just want to make sure you know what you're marrying. It's not like after we say *I do* I'm going to turn into Rachael Ray or anything."

"I know what I'm marrying."

"I also can't sing, and I can't draw either. I have a big mouth, and you already know I have a terrible sense of direction." I counted out the deficiencies with my fingers. "Shall I go on? I'm highly flawed, Jake."

"I love your flaws."

I snapped my fingers. "Okay, then, just want to make sure we're clear on that." I pointed to the phone. "So are you good with pad thai chicken and drunken noodles with shrimp? Maybe some spring rolls to mix it up?" I did a little cabbage patch dance.

He covered his eyes with one hand. "If you stop dancing immediately, I will eat anything."

"Deal."

I placed our order, and as soon as I hung up the phone, Jake cleared his throat.

"So, my mom called today."

I was suddenly a little nervous, although I wasn't sure why. I sat back down on the couch. "What did she have to say?"

"She and my dad want to throw us an engagement party."

"An engagement party? Really?" *How nice of them.*

He cleared his throat again. "Yes...um....this Saturday."

I flinched. "As in five days from now?"

He nodded.

"As in the weekend Andie gets here?"

"I know it's a bit rushed, but apparently it's the only date before Christmas that works for all my mom's closest friends. And as you'll soon learn, she's really into her friends."

I stood up and started walking toward the kitchen. "Where do they want to have it?" Jake's parents lived in Florida.

"Would you call off the engagement if I said...Florida?"

I stopped walking.

A party for us.

With practically zero notice.

All the way down in Florida.

With a bunch of people I've never met.

The same weekend one of my best friends is moving to town.

I bit my lip.

Ugh.

"What do you think?" Jake said.

I forced a smile.

"Sounds wonderful."

He laughed. "Liar."

"Okay, you're right. It actually sounds excruciating. But I'm guessing we don't have a choice?"

"Define what you mean by *choice*."

I pointed at him. "Very funny."

"I promise it won't be that bad. On such short notice, they'll probably just have it at their house."

"Their house? Really? Is it big enough?" I pictured my dad's place, which could fit like eight people on a good day.

Before he could reply, the buzzer rang.

"That can't be the food already." I stepped to the door and pressed the intercom. "Yes?"

"FedEx for Waverly Bryson."

FedEx again?

I trotted downstairs to retrieve the package.

It was from Ava McIntyre.

As I opened the box, I felt a tiny pit in my stomach.

This one was full of bridal magazines, each one marked with dozens of sticky notes.

Oh boy.

chapter five

I was walking home from work that Wednesday when my phone rang. I fished it out of my purse and smiled to see Jake's name on the display.

"Why, hello there, *fiancé*," I said.

"I could say the same to you. I'm just about finished here. Want to meet for a drink? Maybe a little dinner?"

I brightened up. "Now? I thought you were working late tonight."

"I was, but my last meeting got canceled, and I can't think of anyone I'd like to spend my newly free evening with more than you. Though I could stay here and do paperwork…"

"No paperwork! Paperwork sucks!"

He laughed. "You don't have to do anything for the show tonight?"

I shook my head. "Tonight? No. Tomorrow? That's another story. Tomorrow is going to suck."

"Do you realize you just used the word *suck* twice in the span of like ten words?"

"I know, I suck. I'm just frazzled." I gave myself a little tap on the head.

"Meet me at Armando's in twenty minutes?" Its convenient location a few blocks from my apartment, yummy pasta dishes, and generously sized wineglasses had turned Armando's into my and Jake's favorite neighborhood date place.

"Deal. See you there, *fiancé*."

I walked slowly up the hill to Cadman Plaza Park, which marked the end of Dumbo and the beginning of Brooklyn Heights. Summer was still in full swing, and though the heat could be unbearable during the day, the reward was a steady stream of gloriously balmy evenings. Gloriously balmy evenings only occur about once every three years in San Francisco, so I savored every single one here and tried my hardest not to curse the hot, humid days when I was a sticky, sweaty mess.

As I crossed through the park, I happened upon a pickup soccer game. I knew I'd easily beat Jake to the restaurant if I walked straight there, so I decided to stick around for a few minutes to watch. The players, all male, ranged from late teens to gray-templed dads, and judging by the way the ball kept flying out of bounds, their skill level was just as varied.

I took a seat on an empty bench, and soon a ball came rolling my way. As I kicked it back toward the field, I was struck by a vivid memory. Years earlier in San Francisco, after a run across the Golden Gate Bridge, I'd walked by the Marina Green on my way home. Along the way I passed a bunch of guys playing football, all of them clearly having fun and most likely completely oblivious to my presence. At the time I'd desperately wanted to stop and watch, but I'd kept walking, too self-conscious to just stand there by myself. What had I been so afraid of?

This time I sat on the bench, alone, and watched.

I wasn't nervous.

I wasn't self-conscious.

I was just happy to be there, enjoying a beautiful summer evening.

While the guys played their game, I played with the ring on my left hand.

I was happy it was there too.

I couldn't help but think how much had changed in my life since that day at the Marina Green in San Francisco.

I finally felt like a grown-up, and I'd never been more excited about my future.

• • •

I was two blocks away from Armando's when my cell phone rang again. I fished it out of my purse and looked at the caller ID.

No way.

I held the phone up to my ear.

"No way."

"Bryson! How goes it?"

I narrowed my eyes. "Is this a crank call?"

"Awww, you're killing me."

"Davey? Is it really you?"

"Yes indeed, the one and only. How are you?"

I was momentarily speechless. Davey, or Dave, Mason, had been my biggest (and favorite) client back in San Francisco for several years, during my days as an account director at KA Marketing. We'd been pretty close, but then one day he quit, got married, and took off backpacking around the world. We'd lost touch somewhere along the way.

"Caller? Are you there? Waverly Bryson, you're on the air."

I laughed. It was definitely Davey.

"Are you back in San Francisco?"

"Not quite. Take another guess."

"Are you in jail? Is this your one phone call?"

"Ah, still so witty. Try again."

"Are you in the United States?"

"Affirmative."

"LA?" Davey had gone to both undergrad and business school at UCLA.

"Hardly. Wrong coast."

I raised my eyebrows. "No way. Are you saying…"

"You know what I'm saying."

"You're in New York?"

"The Big Apple, baby. Can you believe it?"

"You know I live here now, right?"

"Of course. Why do you think I'm calling? I know quite a *lot* about you, Bryson. See, there's this thing called Google…"

"What are you doing here?"

"Let's just say we have a lot to catch up on."

I bit my lip. "Uh-oh. Please tell me things are still good with Lindsay?"

"Oh yes, everything is great. Actually, she decided to go back to school for a master's in social work, which is what brought us here. She's starting at NYU in the fall."

"That's so great! I can't believe you're in town. It's been ages."

"Tell me about it. I'm an old man now. I'm going to have hair growing out of my ears soon."

I made a face. "Nice visual. So Lindsay's at NYU, but what about you? Have you found a job here yet?"

"Not yet, but I'm looking. A few interesting leads have come my way."

"Oh yeah? Like what?"

"I'll tell you over a drink. When are you free?"

"Come on, Davey, don't leave me hanging." I stopped walking and looked up from the sidewalk. I was about ten feet away from Armando's. "Actually, I think I'm going to have to leave *you* hanging. I'm really sorry, but I've got to run. When can we get together?"

"Are you free tomorrow? How about a drink after work?"

"I'm sorry, Davey, I can't tomorrow."

"How about Friday?"

I shook my head, even though I knew he couldn't see me. "I'd love to, but I just found out I'm spending the weekend in Florida. Long story."

"Okay, how about next Thursday?"

I mentally scanned my calendar for the following Thursday. I knew I'd be booked up all day with work stuff but figured I could squeeze him in after that.

"I could meet you around seven. Would that work?"

"Seven is perfect. Just name the place, and I'll be there."

"What neighborhood are you in?"

"West Village."

I closed my eyes and thought for moment. "How about Bayard's Ale House on Hudson and Tenth? It's a cute pub, and they have food there too. Have you been there yet?"

"Negative, but I'm sure it's great. So I'll see you next Thursday at seven?"

"Definitely. I'm looking forward to it. It's been way too long."

"I've missed you too, Bryson."

• • •

Jake was sitting at the bar when I walked inside the restaurant. He smiled and stood up when he saw me.

"Hi, beautiful." He leaned down and gave me a quick, soft kiss. I felt a spark shoot down my spine. *Mmm.*

I took off my purse and hung it on a hook underneath the bar, then opened my palms wide in front of me "You're never going to believe who just called me."

"Not that collection agency again. I thought you'd worked out an arrangement with them." He handed me a glass of red wine.

I pushed his shoulder. "Such a comedian."

He caught my hand and kissed it. "Who?"

"Remember my old client at KA Marketing, Davey Mason from JAG?" JAG was short for Jammin' Athletic Gear.

"The name sounds familiar. Have I met him?"

I sipped my wine and set it on the bar. "I think you did at the trade show where you and I first met, but only for a second. Anyhow, he was the VP of marketing at JAG for years, but then he quit and basically dropped off the face of the Earth to go traveling around it with his wife."

"And he just called you out of the blue today?"

I nodded. "When I was walking here to meet you."

"What did he have to say?"

"He said he just moved to the West Village because his wife is going to school here and that he wants to talk to me about something. Then we ran out of time because I was meeting a hot date, so we made plans to have a drink next week."

Jake scratched his eyebrow. "A hot date? Is that what this is?"

I leaned toward him and grinned. "I'm hoping it is. What do you think?"

"I think I like it." He gently touched my cheek, which made me feel all wobbly even though I was sitting on a barstool. "But first, we need to talk about this weekend."

I made a sour face. "Do we have to?"

He laughed. "Listen, I'm well aware that my mom isn't the warmest person in the world…"

I picked up my glass. "Ya think?" I'd only met her once, and *ice queen* was more like it.

He put his hand on my shoulder. "No matter how she might act, she's excited that we're getting married. I promise."

"Given the fancy packages I've been receiving, I figured as much." I wondered what she'd think of our no-bling approach to the whole thing. Jake was on board with my desire to keep the planning super low-key, not to mention the wedding itself.

"She can be a little overbearing sometimes, especially in social situations, so I just want you to try not to take her behavior personally." He picked up his beer and raised an eyebrow at me. "I realize that might be a pretty tall order, but I have no doubt you'll be your adorable self and everyone will love you. Just don't overanalyze it."

"I can try." I leaned forward and kissed his nose. "Now can we *please* change the subject?"

"Deal. So, Andie's getting in tomorrow?"

I could feel my eyes brighten at the thought of seeing her. "Yes! I'm so excited that I get to run around this fun city with her for the next few months."

He shook his head. "I can only imagine what sort of trouble you two are going to get into together."

"You mean like going to male strip clubs and that sort of thing?"

"I can't say that's exactly what came to mind, but sure, whatever floats your boat."

I took a sip of wine. "I'm sure she'll drag me into a few shady situations, which I'm fully looking forward to, by the way."

"Just don't get arrested, okay? I don't want to have to bail you out of jail again."

"Very funny. Actually, I don't think it will be anything like it would have been had she come a couple years ago. She's mellowed out a lot since she moved in with Nick. It's like he finally tamed the lion." I set my glass down and cracked an imaginary whip.

"Did you just pretend to crack a whip?"

I laughed. "I guess I did. Apparently I'm fired up to see her."

"Nick has tamed the lion, huh?"

I cracked the imaginary whip again. "Yep. I never thought I'd see the day."

He scratched his eyebrow. "I never thought I'd see anyone over the age of twelve pretend to crack a whip twice in the same conversation."

I grinned at him. "Aren't you *so* glad you're marrying me?"

"Don't push your luck. So, where's she going to live?"

"Some luxury building downtown, I think she said it was on Exchange Place. Corporate housing, completely furnished, probably costs a fortune. I can't wait to see it."

"I can't wait to see *you* dolled up for our engagement party. Are you going to wear a tiara?"

I pointed at him. "Watch it, or I just might."

• • •

After dinner, we left Armando's and strolled down Montague Street toward my place. When I'd first agreed to take the *Love, Wendy* job, I'd pretty much assumed I'd never find a New York neighborhood as quaint as Pacific Heights in San Francisco. But

I was thrilled to be dead wrong. Lined with picturesque brownstones and just enough coffeehouses, restaurants, and mom-and-pop stores to keep it interesting, Brooklyn Heights looked like a stage set. And on a warm night like tonight, it was downright magical.

"Want to check out the promenade?" Jake reached toward me with an open palm.

I took his hand and smiled up at him. "Sure."

We walked hand in hand toward the water, and soon we entered a stretch that faces the bright lights of Wall Street, the regal skyscrapers perched directly across the East River on the southernmost tip of Manhattan. They must have been at least a mile away, but they looked much closer, almost as though you could reach out and touch them.

I pointed toward the skyscrapers. "Have you ever noticed how this view is just like Vegas?"

Jake gave me a strange look. "What?"

"The view from here to lower Manhattan. Have you ever noticed looking at them from here is like looking at the casinos in Las Vegas?"

He put a hand on the back of his head. "Could you be a little more specific?"

I pumped my arms and started walking in place. "You know how when you walk outside of one of those enormous casinos, you look at the casino next door and think *That's like a two-minute walk away?* But then you start walking and walking and walking, and like an hour later, you're still not there?"

"I guess so..."

I stopped fake walking and pointed across the river. "Well that's how I feel about those buildings. It *looks* like you could just jump from here right in the East River and gently paddle over in a few minutes, but most likely you'd end up drowning long before you made it."

He pressed his palm against my forehead. "Are you feeling okay?"

I shrugged. "I'm fine. I'm just making an observation. Have you ever noticed that I like to make observations?"

"Believe me, I have. Have you also noticed there's an express-way below the promenade, not the river? The river's like a quarter mile away from here."

I peered over the railing at the cars flying by below, then patted his arm. "Another excellent point. That makes the journey from here to lower Manhattan even *longer*."

"Okay, then."

"So, do you think you and I will go to Vegas when we're old and gray? You know, wearing matching sweatsuits and all that? Play the slots? Maybe some keno?"

He put an arm around me and gently steered me away. "I think it's time to put you to bed, young lady."

"But I'm not tired!"

"Who said anything about sleeping? This is a hot date, remember?"

I smiled. "Race you there?"

"You'll never catch me."

"We'll see about that." I pushed him away and took off running. I caught him off guard, and he nearly fell over, but he quickly regained his balance and began to give chase. I managed to beat him there by a few feet, but only because my building was so close.

When we reached the front door, we were both cracking up, and I was completely out of breath.

"Good lord, I'm totally out of shape." I put my hands on my hips and gulped for air. "Look at you. You aren't even breathing hard!"

He smiled and shook his head. "That's because I work out almost every day. Sort of comes with my job."

"Are you trying to make me hate you right now?"

He smiled. "I liked watching you run."

I poked his iron stomach. "Be nice."

He reached behind me and gently squeezed my backside, which sent a spark all the way down my legs. "Believe me, it was nice," he whispered.

I stood on my tiptoes and gave him a quick kiss. "*You're* nice."

I unlocked the front door to my building, and as we climbed the four flights of stairs to my apartment, I turned to face him. "Hey, you know what we haven't talked about since we got engaged?"

"What?"

"Where to live. Are you going to move in here?"

"Is that an invitation?"

I laughed. "I mean, since we're getting *married* and all, I guess we should probably live together."

"Yes, we probably should."

I unlocked my front door and gestured to the living room. "My place is bigger than yours, right?"

"Yep."

"And you're pretty much here all the time, right?"

"Agreed." The truth was, Jake had barely unpacked since moving to New York. I loved that.

I held my palms up and smiled. "So…it would make sense for you to move in here, don't you think? Although I do wonder where your clothes will fit. I mean it's not like my closet is all that—" He shut the door behind us and interrupted me. "I don't want to talk about your closet right now."

"You don't?"

He took a step toward me and shook his head.

"No."

I swallowed.

He was staring at me with those blue eyes.

"Okay," I whispered, suddenly feeling like a freshman girl who just got asked to slow dance by the gorgeous star senior quarterback. The only thing missing was a Journey song and braces.

He took another step forward, put one arm around my back, and pulled me close to him. My internal temperature rose twenty degrees.

God help me, he is hot.

He slowly moved his lips down my neck to my shoulder, which was bare but for the strap of my tank dress. Another spark shot down my spine.

I sighed at his touch.

Thank God for summer clothes.

He paused briefly to remove his T-shirt. I put my hands on his chest and nodded.

"Yes, sir, you're in fine shape. I think you need to keep that job."

He smiled but didn't speak. Instead, he led me toward the bedroom.

I didn't put up any protest.

chapter six

The next evening I entered the lobby of a fancy building on Exchange Place.

"Hi, I'm here to see Andrea Barnett?" I balled my hands into fists as soon as the words were out of my mouth. I was getting better, but I still turned statements into questions way too often for someone in her thirties.

The doorman scrolled down his list. "Barnett. She just moved in, right?"

I nodded. "She was supposed to get in today."

He called up to her apartment, and I gazed upward and all around. The ornate ceiling was about as tall as my building. Half a dozen chandeliers gleamed and twinkled decadently above my head.

After Andie gave him the verbal okay, he smiled and pointed to his right. "You're good to go. Apartment forty-eight C."

"Did you say forty-eight?" *How many stories are in this building?*

He nodded. "Yes ma'am. Forty-eight C. Third elevator bank."

"Okay, thanks."

As I rode up the elevator toward outer space, my ears popping, I looked at the buttons and wondered if they were made out of solid gold.

"Finally! Get your butt in here!" Andie practically leaped into the hallway to give me a hug with one hand. Her other clasped a goblet of wine.

I pointed at the glass. "You've been here what, like an hour, and you're boozing it up already?"

She waved me inside. "My company sent over a wine and cheese basket. Isn't that nice? Let me pour you a drink and show you around. This place is sick."

I followed her into the living room and froze when I saw the view.

"Oh my God."

"I know," she said. "I know."

I slowly walked toward the arching floor-to-ceiling windows that stretched across one entire side of the living room. My jaw dropped a bit more with each step I took.

"Holy crap," I whispered.

I could see not only lower Manhattan, the Brooklyn Bridge, the Manhattan Bridge, *and* the Williamsburg Bridge, but most of Brooklyn, JFK airport, the Rockaways, and the Atlantic Ocean, all swathed in the soft orange glow of a nearly full moon. I felt like I was on the Peter Pan ride at Disneyland, gently floating high up in the sky, watching the night lights flickering across the city below.

"Oh my God," I said again.

It was the prettiest view I'd ever seen.

"Tell me about it. I've been staring at it ever since I got here."

When I was finally able to peel my eyes away, I turned around to check out the apartment. A model of corporate chic, it was the exact opposite of my place. I lived in a classic brownstone with dark hardwood floors, crown moldings, and light green and blue walls. Everything here was white, black, and *sleek*. White tile floors. Black leather couches. White bookcases. Black coffee tables. White kitchen counters and table. Black appliances.

"Have you noticed that it's like a checkerboard in here?" I asked.

Andie laughed and handed me a goblet of wine. "I know, it's totally over-the-top. And it's costing an absolute *fortune*. Thank God I don't have to pay for it. Did you see the dogs?"

I followed her eyes to a corner of the room. They landed on two life-sized porcelain greyhounds.

All white.

"You're kidding me."

She laughed. "I've already named them Blanco and Whitey. What do you think?"

I raised my eyebrows and nodded. "How appropriate."

"Let me give you the grand tour." She grabbed my hand and led me through the living room and kitchen to the huge bedroom, which was lined with wall-to-wall plush white carpeting. It had a large walk-in closet, a master bathroom with an oversized tub, and an enormous wood sleigh bed. The bed frame was black, and the bedspread was a crisp white, dotted with specks of black; it looked as though someone had shaken a paint brush over it.

I pointed to the sleigh. "Is that a king?" Andie is barely five-two.

She nodded. "A *California* king. I could fit like six people in there."

"I'm sure someone has. This place is like a movie set. At least you'll have room for Nick when he comes to visit."

"I guess so." She walked abruptly out of the room, which I found a bit odd. I shrugged and checked out the view of the Empire State Building from the bedroom windows.

Good lord. Talk about doing Manhattan in style.

When I returned to the living room, Andie held out her tiny arms. "So, what do you think of my new digs? Not bad, eh?"

"Honestly?"

"Honestly."

"The *view* is unbelievable, but the apartment sort of looks like a drug dealer's crib, don't you think?"

She pushed her blonde bob behind her ears. "Drug dealer? I was thinking more Gordon Gecko."

I pointed at her and nodded. "Actually, you're right. Definitely Gordon Gecko."

She sat down on the black leather couch and picked up her wineglass. "It's on the gauche side of the spectrum, that's for sure, but the view more than trumps the décor, not to mention the lotion-y feel of the remote control."

I coughed. "Did you just say *lotion-y*?"

"You heard me. This place has clearly seen more than its fair share of porn. But it's my home for the next three months, and it's free, and I'm super psyched to be here."

"How much is the rent?"

"I have no idea, but I'm sure it's a *lot*. They rented it for a big executive out of our German office who was supposed to be here for a year but left early for some reason, so I'm sliding into the tail end of that arrangement. Otherwise, God knows what kind of postage-stamp studio they'd have stuck me in." She held her glass up to mine for a toast. "To my brand-new life in New York!"

I looked at her sideways as our goblets touched. *This is temporary, right?*

"So, how's Jake?" she asked.

"He's great. We're headed down to Florida tomorrow for an engagement party, actually. His parents are throwing it."

"Given how you've described his mom, I'm sure *that's* going to be fun." She made a scary face.

I laughed and sat down on the couch. "She's not that bad. But to be safe, I'm setting my expectations low."

She took a seat next to me. "I can't believe you're really getting married. Have you freaked out on him yet?" Andie was well acquainted with my tendency to turn into an emotional basket case under romantic duress.

I sipped my wine and smiled. "Surprisingly, *no*. I am proud to say that I don't do that anymore."

She gave me a suspicious look. "What changed?"

"I'm not exactly sure, but it's like somewhere along the way I finally grew up. And once that happened, I started believing that he really, truly loves me, and that he's not going anywhere."

"Wow, that's great. I'm proud of you."

I smiled. "Thanks. How are you and Nick doing?" I knew I shouldn't ask, but I couldn't help myself.

She waved her hand dismissively. "Let's talk about me later. Back to you. What time do you leave for the airport?"

"I think the car's coming at eleven."

"Nice. Then you have plenty of time to keep drinking." She stood up and grabbed her purse. "Come on, let's go."

I looked over at the porcelain dogs. After two glasses of wine, I was already buzzed, and I still needed to pack for the weekend.

I shrugged.

What the hell?

"Okay."

Andie smiled and clapped her hands together. "Great. Now, chop chop. Let's go take a bite out of this apple. I saw a cool bar down the street that I want to check out."

She pulled me off the couch, and she pushed me out the door.

"Bye, Whitey and Blanco," I called as the latch shut behind us.

• • •

"*This* is the cool bar down the street?"

Andie looked surprised. "You don't like it?"

"No, it's great. It's just that I've been here a million times with Paige." We were at Harry's, a glossy tavern and steakhouse in the center of the financial district.

She nodded. "Brilliant minds think alike."

"Have you seen her yet? She doesn't live far from here, you know."

"Are you joking? I just moved here *today*, Waverly."

"Oops, that was the two glasses of wine I just drank talking. Let me rephrase: Do you have any plans to see Paige?"

She shook her head. "Not yet, but I'm sure we'll get together soon. Sounds like we won't be going out drinking, though."

"Definitely not. She's getting huge."

"My mom said they're going to wait until after she has the baby to get married."

I nodded. "She said she doesn't want to be the poster girl for a shotgun wedding."

Andie laughed. "That sounds like something I would say."

"Totally. You know, now I see her as *Paige* and not just your cousin, but when I first met her, every once in a while she would do or say something that reminded me so much of you that I'd get a little sad."

"Sad? Why?"

I pushed her knee. "Because it made me *miss* you, silly."

She rolled her eyes and turned toward the bartender to order drinks. "You are such a sap. It's really quite embarrassing."

I excused myself to use the restroom. When I returned several minutes later, Andie was still waiting for our drinks.

She mumbled under her breath as I took a seat. "Note to self: Before you sit down at a bar, especially in the financial district, always check to make sure there's a male bartender."

"What's the problem?" I asked.

She pointed to her chest. "*These* are the problem. Boobs. Some female bartenders prefer customers who don't have them, a.k.a., *men*, because they think they'll tip better."

I looked at my own chest. "I don't really have boobs. Maybe I should order the next round?"

She raised her eyebrows. "That might not be a bad idea. I really like this bar, though. It seems straight out of a movie, doesn't it?"

"I agree. It's a Wall Street institution. I bet half the people in here are drinking either straight-up scotch or martinis." I scanned the sea of expensive tailored suits.

"Only half?"

I nodded. "You're right. Probably more."

"I wonder what Harry looks like."

"You mean the Harry of Harry's?"

"Yep. You've got to have quite an ego to name both a bar and a steakhouse after yourself."

"Maybe he named it after his son?"

She shook her head. "I doubt it. I say huge ego. If *you* could name a bar, what would you call it?"

I paused to think. "Hmm, there's a bar on Avenue A and Houston called *The Library*. Every time I walk by there, I think that's pretty clever."

"I like that."

"Talk about a euphemism. Along that vein, I think *The Office* would be pretty good too. Or *The Gym*."

"I think I'd call mine *The Next Place*."

I laughed. "I like that."

"Or maybe *Just One More*? I've certainly been to *that* place a thousand times."

"Only a thousand?"

"Shut it."

I pointed at her. "Maybe I should do a *Honey on Your Mind* segment on this. God knows, people in New York do love their alcohol."

"Speaking of alcohol..." She paused to fake-smile at the female bartender, who finally set two glasses of wine in front of us. Then she picked up her glass for a toast. "Here's to *me*...in NYC."

I clinked my glass against hers. "Didn't we already toast to this?"

"That was just a warm-up."

"Okay, then. This poor city will never be the same."

"So, are you neck-deep in the planning yet?"

I took a sip of my drink and set it down on the bar. "You mean for the wedding?"

She nodded.

"Haven't done a thing."

"Really?" She seemed surprised. "I thought you'd be all over it."

"I'm still trying to come to terms with the fact that I'm engaged." I looked at the pretty ring perched on my finger and blinked. Its novelty still hadn't worn off.

She gave a dirty look to the guy on the adjacent stool whose back kept bumping against hers, then turned to face me and raised her glass again. "And here's to that. The longer *you* wait to start planning, the longer it will be before *I* have to wedge myself into an ugly, overpriced dress I'll never wear again."

I took a sip of my wine. "You really think I have such horrible taste?"

She shook her head. "It's not you, it's the dresses. *All* brides-maids' dresses are ugly. Just like all cab drivers are weird, and all musicians are good in bed. It comes with the territory."

I laughed. "What was that last part?"

"You heard me."

"All musicians are good in bed?"

She nodded.

"Why, exactly?"

She gave me a look. "Think about it."

I thought about it.

Huh?

"You mean because they sleep with so many women?"

"No."

I held my palms up. "Then what?"

She pretended to play a guitar. "They're good with their *hands.*"

My eyes got big.

"We've never talked about this before?" she said.

I laughed and shook my head. "Definitely not. I would remember a conversation like this."

She shrugged. "Well, it's true. And it's not just musicians."

"It's not?"

"Nope. Mechanics, surgeons, any guy who works with his hands. *Amazing.*"

"And to think I've made it this long without possessing this information."

She shrugged. "Live and learn."

"Andie, I never stop learning from you."

"And you never will."

I laughed and picked up my wineglass. "I'm glad. Anyhow, getting back on topic, I was actually thinking maybe I wouldn't do the bridesmaids thing this time."

"For real?"

I nodded. "I just feel like I've done it already, you know? I mean, even though I didn't actually *get married* last time, I just... just don't think I want to do it all again."

"Are you afraid the same thing's going to happen?"

I shook my head. "No, it's not that. It's almost...the opposite."

She finished her drink and gestured to the bartender for another round. "How so?"

I slouched on the stool. "I hope I can explain it right..."

"Try me."

"Because I've only just started to process it like this...I guess...as a comparison...so I don't quite have my head wrapped around it yet..."

She made a *Keep talking* motion with her hand.

I sat up straight. "Okay, here's the deal. With the benefit of *hindsight*, mind you...I now realize that once Aaron and I got engaged, from that moment on, so much of my life was about the *wedding*, you know? The ring part, the dress part, the *getting* married part. With Aaron, that eclipsed everything that was supposed to come after."

"But...with Jake?"

I smiled, my heart doing a little flutter at the thought of him. "But with Jake...I know this may sound really sappy, but with Jake...what I really care about is the *being* married part. Does that...does that make sense?"

She slowly shook her head.

"It doesn't?" I asked.

"That's not why I'm shaking my head."

"Then why are you shaking your head?"

"This is a *wow* head shake."

"Huh?"

"As in *wow*, you really love that man."

I blushed. "Is what I just said pathetic? Am I pathetic?"

She laughed. "Pathetic? No? Hopelessly romantic? Yes. Very much in love? Obviously. I'm just really happy for you."

It took a while, but full drinks eventually appeared in front of us again. I picked up my glass and gave her a sheepish look. "So you don't think it's weird that I don't want to do the whole traditional wedding thing again? I'm afraid people might think it's weird. Especially Jake's parents."

She shook her head. "Definitely not. And who cares what they think, anyway? It's your wedding, not theirs."

I leaned toward her, probably speaking way louder than I thought I was. "Because I was thinking it would be cool to do something small—I mean, *really* small." I sat back, a bit unsteadily, and tapped two fingers against my temple. "That's as far as I've gotten, though." I could feel myself transitioning from tipsy to very tipsy.

She laughed and put a hand over mine. "I hate to break it to you, *honey*, but that isn't much of a plan. It sounds like an amazing start to me, though."

I smiled. "Thanks. I'm glad you don't think I'm a bad bride."

"A bad bride? Please. As far as I'm concerned, not having bridesmaids makes you the most awesome bride in the history of time."

I let out a little hiccup and reached for my purse. "Should I text Jake to tell him how much I love him?"

She laughed at me. "Good lord, girl, you are *whipped*." She picked up a cocktail menu. "Now let's order some fancy Wall

Street drinks. Maybe a little something with *whipped* cream on top."

"So, what about you and Nick? Are things still…good?"

She shook her head. "Not tonight, dearie. Tonight we're celebrating *you*."

She was clearly deflecting my questions; there was no use in pretending otherwise. But even after multiple glasses of wine, I knew better than to press the issue with her. So instead I sent Jake a flurry of texts while she ordered us more drinks:

First text: *Hi hndsom*

Second text: *Have I tolf you latly how hansome u are?*

Third text: *Here a limtle somthing to get u in the trabel mood for tomroow*

Fourth text: *Wht did Geronimo yell whn he jumpd out of the plane?*

Fifth text: *Okay, waait for it….*

Sixth text: *MEEEEEEEEEEEEE!*

Seventh text: *Ha ha ha I loooooooooooove u lots, xoxo*

chapter seven

"I can't believe we have to meet your parents for dinner in an hour." I leaned across the hotel sink to study the unsightly dark circles under my eyes. "They're totally going to know I was out late drinking last night. Can I wear dark sunglasses in the restaurant?"

Jake laughed from the bedroom. "I *knew* you two were going to get into trouble. Don't pretend like I didn't call this one."

I frowned at the mirror. "I forgot how powerful that girl is. For such a tiny person, she's like a Jedi Knight the way she can get me to do anything. It's not fair."

"Oh yes, it's entirely *Andie's* fault that you have a hangover."

I poked my head out of the bathroom and pointed at him. "Hey now, we're getting married. You have to support me in everything I do now."

He laughed. "Where exactly does it say in the marriage handbook that I have to support your decision to get hammered the night before we have dinner with my parents?"

"I wasn't hammered. I was…mildly intoxicated."

He pulled his phone out of his pocket. "Do you want me to show you the text messages?"

I cringed and held my hands up in a cross in front of my face. "No, thank you, I don't need to see the evidence."

"Come on now, they were cute."

I shook my head and walked from the bathroom to the closet in my bra and underwear. "You are way too nice. We both know I was trashed and acting like an idiot." I pulled out two dresses and held them up in front of me. "So, which one should I wear to dinner, black or red?"

He looked up at me. "Can you just wear what you have on now?"

"Your parents would love that. So which one?"

"Which one are you wearing to the party tomorrow?"

"Neither."

"Then I'd go for the black. My mom might make a comment about the red being flashy or something."

I tossed both dresses on the bed and put my hands on my waist. "Maybe I should just wear a flannel turtleneck dress. Would *that* make her happy?"

He stood up and put his arms around me. "Don't worry so much about my mom. Besides, it's like eighty degrees out. Flannel makes no one happy when it's eighty degrees out."

I hugged him tight. "I just want her to like me, Jake. Why doesn't she like me?"

"She likes you fine."

"Not as much as she likes Holly." Holly was Jake's pretty ex-girlfriend. I gathered Jake's mom thought she was the embodiment of perfection, but Jake was too polite to go into any detail about it.

"That's not true."

"You're such a bad liar."

He smoothed my hair with his hand. "She'll learn to love you. I know she will. She's just...tough."

I looked up at him and smiled. "Can you believe we're really getting married?"

He put his chin on my head. "Yes, and I can't wait."

I took a step back. "Speaking of which, I guess we should probably pick a date at some point."

"You tell me when and where to show up, and I'll be there."

"Hold it, mister, just because I'm the bride, that doesn't mean I want to do all the planning. Maybe you should do it."

"Maybe *I* should do it?"

I shrugged. "Why not?"

"You mean *all* of it?"

I shrugged again. "If you'd like. I've sort of got a lot on my plate right now, in case you hadn't noticed."

He laughed. "I've noticed. And I'm more than happy to plan the wedding *with* you. *With* being the operative word."

"It would be nice just to enjoy being engaged for a while, don't you think? I mean, what's the rush to jump into the crazy planning phase? Even for just a simple wedding, it's going to take work."

He put his arms around me again. "You know what I think?"

"What?"

"I think that as long as you're with me, I don't care about anything else. That's what I think."

I buried my face in his chest. "It is impossible to stay annoyed with you."

• • •

"If she brings up Holly, I'm going to lose it."

Jake held the door open for me. "I'd say the odds are sixty-forty."

I stopped walking and looked up at him. "Sixty-forty which way?"

He laughed and took my hand. "I don't think you want to know the answer to that question."

"I can still call it off, you know. Just watch me."

"I dare you."

We were meeting Jake's parents at a restaurant called Café Boulud at the Brazilian Court Hotel in Palm Beach. The maître d' said they'd already arrived and led us to a table outside to join them. I took in my surroundings as we walked. The place was undeniably posh, with a chic, expensive vibe that made me feel decidedly not chic. I hoped my discount dress was fancy enough.

As we approached the table, Jake's dad smiled and stood up.

"Well, hello there!" He and Jake shook hands, and then he surprised me with a bear hug.

"Welcome to Florida, Waverly! Welcome to the McIntyre family! We're just delighted about this, absolutely delighted." He squeezed me with genuine affection.

I smiled at him. "Thanks, Mr. McIntyre. I'm pretty delighted too."

"Please, call me Walt."

"Okay," I said, suddenly shy.

"Hi, Mom." Jake leaned down and kissed her on the cheek. She smiled politely at both of us but remained seated.

"Hello, Jake. Hello, Waverly. It's lovely to see you both." The difference in tone between her greeting and her husband's was impossible to ignore.

I mustered all the fake confidence I could, then forced a smile. "Hi, Mrs. McIntyre." We both knew there was no way I'd be calling her *Ava*. "Thank you so much for sending me the gifts. I really appreciate it."

"You're welcome. I thought you might find them helpful."

"First things first, let's see that ring, young lady," Jake's dad said.

I kept smiling as I held up my hand.

He nodded and looked at Jake. "Nice work, son."

"Thanks, Dad," Jake said.

"It's lovely," Jake's mom said.

"Please, have a seat." Jake's dad pulled out my chair for me. "How was the flight down?"

I was briefly tempted to tell him I felt ill the whole trip because I was so hungover, but I rapidly came to my senses when I saw the delicate strand of pearls draped around Mrs. McIntyre's neck.

"Uneventful." I squeezed Jake's thigh under the table. He chuckled, understanding that the contact was a stern warning not to blab about my condition.

The waiter appeared out of nowhere with an open bottle of wine.

"Would you like a glass of pinot noir?" he asked us. Jake looked at me, and I kicked his foot under the table.

I covered my wineglass with my hand. "I think I'm good with water tonight, thanks."

"I'd love some, thanks," Jake said, kicking me back.

Mrs. McIntyre looked at me and smiled formally. "How do you like the Jupiter Beach Resort? Isn't it charming?"

I hesitated, unsure how to respond. Call it the thrill of being on a mini-vacation, but Jake and I had pretty much beelined from the rental car place...right to our hotel room bed. I could feel myself blush and hoped what we'd just been doing wasn't written all over my face.

I glanced at Jake, who was clearly trying not to laugh. Then I nodded enthusiastically at both his mom and his dad. "Oh yes, it's gorgeous. I can't wait to check out the pool tomorrow."

"You and Holly stayed there after Tom and Susan Henderson's wedding, didn't you?" she said to Jake. "That was such a lovely reception."

He ignored her. "Dad, do you think I should get the salmon or the snapper?"

I blinked. *Did she really say that?*

After an awkward silence, Jake's mom appeared to get the message. She looked at me and smiled again. "Has Jake taken you out to Worth Avenue to see the shops yet?"

Jake answered for me. "Not yet, but maybe sometime over the weekend."

I looked at him. "Worth Avenue?"

He shrugged. "It's sort of like the Rodeo Drive of Florida. Not really my thing."

"Oh." I smoothed my hand over my hair and wondered if I looked all right. *Is she trying to tell me something?*

Jake's dad chimed in, his eyes curious and kind. "So, Waverly, how goes the big TV show? From what Jake tells us, you're quite the celebrity."

I smiled, relieved at the change in subject. "A celebrity? Hardly. But the show is a lot of fun, and people really seem to enjoy it. I feel lucky to have the job."

Jake took a sip of his wine. "Do your friends still watch it, Mom?"

"Oh yes, especially the ones from church. They're big fans of Wendy Davenport. She seems like a lovely person."

I squeezed my napkin. "Mmm-hmm."

"She's just so talented, and pretty too. A natural beauty, don't you think?"

I nodded, wondering how many greenhouse gases Wendy's aerosol hairspray habit contributed to *nature* each day. I struggled to glob the delicate liver pâté spread onto a fancy tabletop cracker and winced when I noticed that Mrs. McIntyre was watching me. Thank God the waiter returned to redirect the conversation.

After we ordered, Mr. McIntyre picked up his wineglass and gestured to Jake. "What about you, son? How do the Nets compare to the Hawks?" Jake had left his job at the Hawks in Atlanta for the Nets position in Brooklyn.

"So far, so good. I guess we'll see how the season goes."

"Is it a well-run organization?"

Jake shrugged. "To be honest, the whole mood of any professional sports organization depends on how the team's playing any given week, sometimes any given *day*, so it's hard to say. So far it's been fine, but the season hasn't started yet, which means we haven't lost any games yet."

Jake's mom spoke as I reached for another cracker. "Los Angeles certainly would have been nice, with all that sunshine."

I looked up.

Los Angeles?

Jake had turned down an offer from the Lakers to move to Brooklyn to be with me.

"Mom, please don't go there." I could tell he was getting annoyed, and I loved him for it.

She smiled. "It was just an observation. That's all."

I cringed as I chewed my cracker. I was all for making observations, but not ones that made everyone at the table feel uncomfortable. I tended to observe random yet harmless things, like the fact that America would probably be a lot skinnier if restaurants served carrots sticks instead of…huge baskets of carbohydrates.

"You know we don't get to see Constance and Pierce as much as we'd like to. That's all I meant, Jake," she said.

Who and who?

"Ava's sister and brother-in-law live in LA," Jake's dad explained to me.

Oh.

Jake's mom put her hand on her husband's shoulder. "In Beverly Hills. You know Constance doesn't like it when people say she lives in LA." Then she returned her attention to Jake. "So, you're liking Brooklyn?" The juxtaposition of *Beverly Hills* and *Brooklyn* was hard to miss. This woman was anything but subtle.

He nodded. "I'm still getting used to city living and not having a car, but being able to walk to work is great, I must admit."

She ran her fingers over her pearls. "I love parts of Manhattan, but I could never live in such a big city. Too much commotion, traffic, crime. It's all a bit uncivilized, if you ask me."

I tried not to laugh, and I could tell Jake's dad noticed. *Oops.*

He winked at me. "Waverly, do you have any new jokes for us?"

"You want to hear one of my jokes?"

"Of course. I loved the ones you told at Christmas last year. Got any new ones?"

I looked at Jake and tilted my head to one side. "Did you hear that? Your dad loved my jokes." I slowly crossed my arms in front of me.

Jake shook his head. "Please don't encourage her, Dad."

I pushed his shoulder. "You be nice."

"Let's hear what you've got." Mr. McIntyre rubbed his hands together.

Jake waved his napkin in surrender. "For the record, I'm not responsible for this."

I laughed. "Actually, Mr. McIntyre—"

He held a hand up. "Walt. Please, call me Walt."

"Actually, um…"

I swallowed awkwardly, then finally spoke.

"Um, I feel really uncomfortable calling you by your first name. Can I please call you Mr. McIntyre? At least for now?"

He laughed. "It really makes you uncomfortable?"

I bit my lip. "Um, yes?"

He held his palms up. "Okay, sure, call me Mr. McIntyre… for now. But I can't have any daughter of mine calling me *Mr. McIntyre*, so once you two make it official, I'll have to put a stop to that, okay, Waverly?" He smiled.

I smiled back. "Okay, that sounds reasonable."

"Well, have you got any jokes for us?" he asked again.

I shifted in my chair. "Actually, I do. You ready?"

"Yes, ma'am."

"Okay, here goes." I looked at both him and Mrs. McIntyre, then took a deep breath.

"What do you call a deer with no eyes?"

My eyes darted around the table.

"Anyone?"

"I'll bite," Jake's dad said. "What *do* you call a deer with no eyes?"

I held both my palms up. "No-eye deer."

He laughed. "Not bad."

"God help us all." Jake shook his head and chuckled.

I poked his arm. "I said be nice." Then I turned back to Jake's dad.

"What do you call a deer with no eyes and no legs?"

He picked up his wineglass. "I don't know. What *do* you call a deer with no eyes and no legs?"

I held both my palms up again. "*Still* no-eye deer."

He laughed. "Not bad. A bit stupid yet somehow funny."

"Exactly." I looked at Jake. "Stupid yet *funny.* Did you hear that?"

Jake covered his hands with his face, and I elbowed him. "You're totally going to break off our engagement now, aren't you?"

Before he could say anything, his mom cleared her throat. "Jake, Waverly, speaking of the wedding, I have some exciting news for you."

We both looked at her, and she smiled.

"I called in a few favors, and I was able to book the Breakers for the Saturday of Presidents' Day weekend. Isn't that wonderful?"

The what?

For when?

Say what?

I glanced at Jake. I wasn't sure what to do, so I took a huge sip of my water. There was no way I was going to speak first.

"Isn't that wonderful?" she said again, her smile big and bright. "The weather will be just gorgeous that time of year." She looked at me. "Presidents' Day weekend is the ideal time to get married in Florida, because by the time Memorial Day rolls around, it might be too hot."

I continued to look at Jake, my face still buried in my water glass. *Say something!*

After an awkward silence, Jake manned up and took over. He leaned across the table and gently put both hands on top of his mother's.

"Mom, that was really nice of you, and we appreciate it, but we haven't even picked a date, much less a state, for the wedding."

She smiled and held a palm in the air. "Well, now you don't *have* to. It's all taken care of. The eighteenth of February, a four o'clock reception. It will be lovely. Father McMillan has already agreed to perform the ceremony at the church right next door."

My jaw dropped into my glass.

A church?

The only time I ever entered a church was for other people's weddings, and even that was rare, because most of my friends didn't get married in churches.

I looked at Jake again, my eyes filled with panic.

Again, he stepped up.

"Mom, we appreciate that too, we really do, but we don't want to get married in a church."

She put a hand over her heart. "You don't want Father McMillan to marry you?" Her face looked a bit ashen.

Who is Father McMillan?

As though reading my mind, Jake looked at me. "He baptized me."

I stared back at him. *Are we really having this conversation?*

Mrs. McIntyre began to play with her napkin, a sight that horrified me given my proclivity to do the very same thing under duress. "Jake, you know Father McMillan would be quite upset if he didn't perform your wedding ceremony. You know that, right?"

Jake's dad put an arm around her, then gave me a knowing nod. "Ava, love, they just got engaged. No need to rush things. Give them a little time to enjoy themselves, will you?"

I looked at him, grateful for the intervention. *You are a very nice man,* I wanted to say. *No wonder your son is such a sweetheart.*

After an awkward pause, Jake's mom smiled. "Why don't you two think about it?" she asked in a pleasant voice. "There's no need to make any rash decisions now. Let's enjoy this delightful meal. The food here is delicious, you'll see."

I took another sip of water and resisted the urge to tell her I'd already made up my mind. I wished I weren't still a bit hungover, because I suddenly wanted to order a stiff drink.

"Can we join you?" The sound of a male voice made us all turn our heads.

Jake's brother Brett was walking toward our table with his wife, Michele.

"Hey, bro, what are you doing here?" Jake stood up and shook Brett's hand, then followed it up with the ubiquitous one-armed man hug. "Michele, it's good to see you." He hugged her the regular way and gave her a kiss on the cheek.

"We felt so bad about having to miss the party tomorrow night that we wrangled a last-minute babysitter and thought we'd crash the end of your dinner and join you for dessert," Michele said. A waiter appeared with two chairs, and she and Brett squeezed in on the ends of the table.

Brett sat on the other side of Jake. "We would have told you earlier, but we've come to accept the sad fact that since spawning double offspring, we are rarely able to follow through on any plans beyond five minutes in the future."

Michele looked at me. "We have a horribly boring event for Brett's firm tomorrow that we absolutely can't miss. Otherwise, we would have done our best to try to maybe make it to your party."

Jake laughed. "You would have done your best to try to maybe make it? I love the semantics. How are the girls?" Their twins were nearly two years old.

Brett wiggled his fingers in the direction of the wine. "Sleeping, I hope. Now hand over that bottle." I laughed and remembered how much I liked both him and Michele. I'd met the whole family just once, at Jake's sister's house in Boston last year at Christmas.

As Brett poured her a glass of wine, Michele put her hand on my arm. "It's so nice to see you again, Waverly. We were thrilled to hear the big news."

I smiled, so relieved to have them there. "Thanks. I'm pretty happy too."

"Not as happy as I am." Jake put his hand on the back of my neck and let it linger there just long enough to make my cheeks flush. Then he turned to Brett and pointed at his pants, which I'd noticed were blue-and-green plaid.

"What's going on here? Did you just fly in from Scotland?"

Brett laughed. "*Style*, my dear brother, it's called *style*. Preppy is timeless."

"Can I see the ring?" Michele reached for my hand.

"I'd like to see it too." Brett craned his neck.

"Wow, it's gorgeous! Well done, Jake." Michele smiled at him.

"Thanks," Jake said. "I had a little help."

I looked at him. "You did? From whom?"

"Just a little bird."

I looked back at Brett. "Was it you?"

Brett laughed. "Definitely not. I know men's clothes, not women's jewelry."

"I picked out my own engagement ring," Michele said. "Knowing Brett, he would have ordered one from J. Crew."

"Timeless," Brett said. "Preppy is *time-less*."

Michele rolled her eyes. "*Mas-ters*. You look like you just played in the *Mas-ters*."

"Why, thank you," Brett nodded in gratitude and touched a pretend visor, Phil Mickelson–style. We all laughed, and I noticed that even Jake's mom joined in.

As we dug into our entrées, I looked sideways at Jake, my eyes narrowing a bit. *Hmm*. Who had talked to him? As far as I knew, none of my friends had a clue he was going to propose to me.

I wonder who it was.

"It really is a lovely ring, Waverly," Jake's mom said.

I looked up from my salmon. "Um, thanks, Mrs. McIntyre." I managed an awkward smile.

"Jake's always had great taste," Mrs. McIntyre said. "Clothes, friends, girlfriends, rarely a misstep."

I stiffened at the word *girlfriends*.

Please, let's not go there.

Jake, once again reading my mind, changed the subject. He must have been a little rattled too, because he changed it to one I *know* he didn't want to bring up.

"Brett, you just missed Waverly's new material."

Brett raised his eyebrows and looked at me. "Material as in a joke? Let's hear it."

I looked briefly at Jake and spoke with my eyes.

I love you so much.

• • •

"What did you think? They're not *that* bad, right?" It was a few hours later, and Jake and I were lying on the bed in our hotel room watching TV.

I looked over at him. "Your dad? He's a teddy bear. Brett and Michele? I love them. Your mom? I'm taking the Fifth."

He laughed and squeezed my knee. "She's warming up to you. I can tell."

"Please. She hates me. She didn't even laugh at my jokes."

"You can't hold *that* against her. Besides, I think she cracked a smile somewhere in there."

I laughed weakly. "Okay, true. I guess that's a good sign, right?"

"That's definitely a good sign."

I sighed. "I wish I could make her like me."

He pulled me toward him and put his arms around me. "I have the utmost confidence that in the near future she won't just *like* you, she will fall madly in *love* with you, just like I did."

I leaned my forehead against his chest. "I wouldn't bet on that. You promise you won't ditch me if she never warms up to me?"

He laughed. "I'm not going anywhere."

I untangled myself from him and sat up on the bed. "That reminds me. I have another joke for you."

"Oh no. Do you really?"

"Shut up. So are you ready?"

"Do I have a choice?"

"Of course not. You might not remember this, but when we were flying home from my dad's wedding in February, you warned me not to tell any more jokes about animals with no legs."

He scratched his eyebrow. "So I'm guessing I'm about to hear a joke about an animal with no legs?"

"You are."

He laughed. "Okay, let's hear it. Which animal?"

"You choose."

"Okay, let's go with…platypus."

"*What?*"

"You said I could choose."

I laughed. "Okay, fine. Where do you find him?"

"A platypus with no legs?"

"Yes. Where do you find him?"

"I have no idea. Where *do* I find a platypus with no legs?"

I leaned over and kissed him on the forehead.

"Right where you left him."

• • •

Later, as we were falling asleep, I lay on my back and stared up at the ceiling. The dinner conversation kept replaying itself in my head...as well as the memories it had stirred up. I could hear Jake's steady breathing and wondered if he was already out.

After a few minutes I finally spoke, though it was more of a whisper.

"I don't want to get married in a church," I said softy.

He stroked my hair. "We don't have to get married in a church."

"I don't even think I want to get married in Florida."

He kept stroking my hair. "We don't have to get married in Florida."

I sighed. "Your mom would *love* that."

He shrugged. "It isn't her wedding, Waverly."

"And I'm not getting married on a holiday weekend." I'd had enough long weekends ruined by having to attend someone else's wedding. I wasn't about to be *that* bride.

"No holiday weekends..." He was almost asleep.

"Plus McKenna couldn't even make it in February. That's right when her baby is due."

"Mmm."

Finally I sat up. I knew what was *really* bothering me.

I took a deep breath, then looked at him. "I don't want a big wedding, Jake. I don't want...I don't want to do that again." I hated to go there, but it was true.

He kept petting my hair but kept his eyes closed and didn't say anything. I wondered what he was thinking. Despite her chilly demeanor, I knew how much he loved his mom. This had to be prickly for him.

After an uncomfortable silence, I got up and walked toward the bathroom. "I just don't want this to be stressful, Jake."

"I don't want it to be either."

I stood by the door. "I'd love to do something small, something small and intimate with just our closest friends, you know?"

He didn't reply, so I disappeared into the bathroom. I washed my face and brushed my teeth, and when I came back to the bed a few minutes later, Jake looked asleep.

I laid my head against his shoulder and sighed. "I just want it all to be...fun," I whispered. Planning my first wedding had been a long, nerve-racking process that had proved to be about as enjoyable as trying on swimsuits under fluorescent lights, even *before* the wedding got called off. One of the reasons it had been such a nightmare was the overinvolvement of Aaron's mother.

"You know my take on it, Waverly," he said.

I looked up at him, surprised that he'd heard me. "Your take on it?"

He gave me a sleepy smile. "As long as I get to be your husband, I'm good."

I felt the tension in my shoulders melt away at his words.

"Really?"

He nodded, his eyes closed now. "If you're happy, I'm happy."

I smiled at him and felt a little teary eyed. "I love you. Have I told you that enough today?"

"I could never hear that enough."

We turned out the light and climbed under the covers, and he wrapped his arms around me spoon-style. I loved being the little spoon.

"So, hey, who was the little bird?" I whispered over my shoulder.

"The little bird?"

"You said you talked to a little bird about what kind of ring to buy. Who was it?"

"Actually, it was your dad."

"My dad?"

"We talked about it when I called him to ask permission to propose."

I smiled into the darkness. "I love that you did that. Have I ever told you how much I love that you did that?"

"Of course I'd ask his permission to marry you. How could I not?"

"I still love it. So he really helped with the ring?"

"Yes. During our conversation, he mentioned that your mom had a cushion cut with pavé for her engagement ring, and we both thought it would be nice for me to get the same style for you."

I turned around to face him. "My dad knew the cut of my mom's ring?"

"Mmm."

"But he doesn't know the difference between a tank top and a tube top. How would he know anything about the cut of a diamond?"

He nodded and touched my cheek. "I suspect he's a little more sophisticated than you think he is." My ex–baseball player dad was undeniably bright, but he lacked a college degree, had

a sketchy employment history, and was far from what I'd call...
refined.

He never forgot my birthday, though.

Ah, Dad.

I smiled and was about to speak again when I realized that
I'd never seen my mom's ring. I wondered where it was. My dad
was remarried now, but he clearly kept his first wife's ring in a
special place, physically and emotionally.

I reached under the covers to touch my own ring, which suddenly took on a new meaning.

chapter eight

"Hey I have good news. I—whoa—what happened to your face?"
Jake opened our hotel room door and froze mid-sentence when
he saw me.

I touched my cheek. "I fell asleep by the pool. Am I totally
fried?"

"Define *fried*."

"Do I look like John Boehner?"

"That super tan guy in Congress who cries a lot?"

I nodded.

"A little. You're more on the red side, though. He's sort of
orange."

"Oh, frick." I pushed by him and ran into the bathroom to
inspect the damage.

Total tomato.

A fried red tomato.

Lovely.

Jake followed me into the bathroom.

"So, as I was saying, little red one, I have good news."

I looked at him. "Good news? Do tell."

"I got us courtside seats to the Heat game tomorrow afternoon. They're playing the Lakers."

"Courtside seats? Nice!" I wasn't much of a basketball fan,
but there was no denying the allure of courtside seats to a Heat-
Lakers game. Although now any mention of the Lakers made

me think of how Jake's mom wished he had chosen LA over Brooklyn...and me.

Blech.

She clearly thought he was out of my league. What made it worse was that part of me secretly thought the same thing.

Jake nodded. "My buddy on the medical staff there hooked us up. It'll be fun."

I put my hands over my cheeks. "You think your buddy can hook me up with some ointment?"

He put his hands over mine. "I'm sure it will calm down by the party. You'll just have a healthy Florida glow."

I looked up him. "You mean like from a nuclear reactor?"

• • •

A few hours later we left the hotel and turned off US 1, after traveling north toward Jupiter Island, where Jake's parents lived. Soon we came to a small bridge. As we slowed to cross it, I noticed a tall lighthouse to one side.

"What's that?"

"That's the Jupiter Inlet Lighthouse. It's sort of *the* landmark down here."

I looked out at the structure, which was the color of the Golden Gate Bridge. "It's beautiful, Jake, so serene and elegant, don't you think?" I loved being so far away from the chaos of New York City.

He reached over and interlaced my hand with his. "Yep."

After crossing the bridge, we passed a marina and soon were on a one-lane road. "Now we're on the island," he said. "It's pretty tiny."

"How tiny?"

"Tiny as in this is the only road."

I raised my eyebrows. "For real?"

He nodded. "They don't even have a post office. The population is less than seven hundred."

"*What?* I've eaten at restaurants in New York with more people than that." No wonder Jake's mom was uncomfortable in a big city.

We drove by several high-rise condos, which were soon replaced by progressively larger—and more beautiful—properties. The narrow street was lined with banyan trees, low shrubbery, and flowers of every color—each leaf and petal perfectly manicured, trimmed, and landscaped.

Soon we passed a golf cart cruising down the street just like a regular car. The man inside waved to Jake, who waved back.

"What was that?" I asked.

Jake shrugged. "That's what people on the island do."

"They drive golf carts down the street?"

He nodded.

"Do you know that guy?"

He shook his head. "People also wave at strangers here."

I laughed. "We are *definitely* not in New York."

As the island narrowed, the houses grew bigger and more lavish. Eventually the street became so tapered that the staggered estates on either side had views of both the Atlantic Ocean *and* Hobe Sound, on the other side.

Jake finally pulled up to the entrance of a secluded driveway and turned off the car.

I looked at him.

"Why are we stopping?"

He gave me a strange look. "Because we're here."

"We're here?"

He nodded.

"Your parents live *here*?"

He nodded again.

"*This* is your parents' house?"

He laughed and unbuckled his seat belt. "Yes."

I'd enjoyed the scenery but had assumed we were just passing through the chic part of town and would eventually arrive in a regular neighborhood. I peered down the driveway at the enormous Mediterranean-style "house" at the end. I'm not sure that's even the right word, because it looked more like a hotel.

"You grew *up* here?"

He took my hand. "I grew up in Miami. My parents moved here when my dad retired." He looked a bit uncomfortable. I'd never seen Jake look uncomfortable.

As we walked up the driveway, which was already lined with cars, I slowly took in my surroundings, still in a state of wide-eyed disbelief.

His parents live *here?*

What?

Suddenly his mother's comment from last night about Beverly Hills made sense.

Jake's family is wealthy?

In nearly three years of knowing him, I had somehow never learned that. Had he deliberately hidden that detail because I'd told him how my ex-fiancé's parents had made me feel?

Aaron Vaughn III was an attorney whose parents were regular fixtures in the San Francisco social circuit, and while they had generally been pretty nice to me, I'd always felt a bit like a fish out of water, as though I were faking a level of sophistication that would forever be beyond my grasp. I almost felt as if...as if they knew something I didn't...and never would.

"Waverly, you still there?" I blinked as Jake snapped his fingers in front of my eyes. We were standing in front of the house. Before I could respond, his mom opened the door.

"Jake, Waverly, thank you so much for arriving on time." She waved and looked genuinely pleased to see us. "Waverly, you look just lovely. Your dress is beautiful."

I awkwardly put my hand on the waist of my sleeveless blue dress, glad I'd chosen to wear something on the conservative side. Plus the high neckline hid the tiny blisters beginning to bubble up on my chest. My face still felt hot, but Jake had been right. The violent redness had calmed down a bit, and I didn't look like I was actually *on fire* anymore.

"Thanks, Mrs. McIntyre, so do you." She was wearing a tailored lavender silk jacket over an eggshell-colored silk blouse and matching pants. She smiled again and gestured to us to enter.

We followed her inside, and I tried not to gape as I glanced around the house. Everything looked ridiculously expensive. Plush beige leather couches. Matching dark mahogany armoires filled with leather-bound books. A massive built-in bookshelf took up an entire wall, flanked by intricate fluted columns. A crystal chandelier sparkled in the foyer. I'd never seen a crystal chandelier in someone's *house* before.

Jake kissed his mother on the cheek. "Where's Dad?"

She gestured to the backyard. "Last I saw he was chatting with Larry, our tax attorney. I think they're at the pool bar."

I raised my eyebrows. *The* pool *bar? As in, there's more than one bar?* We made our way from the foyer, which was about the size of my living room, to the living room, which was about the size of my elementary school. Trying not to gawk, I looked out the floor-to-ceiling windows facing the sprawling backyard. Next to a large swimming pool was a white tent filled with tables and buzzing with beautifully dressed people who appeared to be waitstaff.

Waitstaff? Hadn't Jake said this would be a small party?

A fair number of guests were already mingling outside.

I glanced at Jake. My eyes tried to relay the question, *Are we late? Or are people in Florida just super punctual? What is going on?*

He took my hand and gave it a reassuring squeeze as a man in a white dress shirt and black pants appeared out of nowhere.

"Champagne?" He held up a tray of flutes.

I was speechless.

Just then Jake's dad, sporting a navy blue blazer and khakis, strolled into the room. He carried a cigar in one hand and wore a big smile on his face. "There's the happy couple!" He embraced us each in a bear hug as Jake's mom excused herself to go check on something in the kitchen.

"Hi, Dad," Jake said.

"Hi, um, Mr. McIntyre," I eked out. *Ugh, why am I so awkward?*

He gave me a sympathetic smile. "I'll have you calling me Walt, or maybe even *Dad*, soon enough."

"We'll see," I said, returning the smile.

"Looks like you got yourself a bit of a sunburn there, young lady."

I winced and placed my hands lightly on my cheeks. "Is it that noticeable?"

"She fell asleep at the pool," Jake said.

His dad looked concerned. "You've got to be careful down here, you know. The Florida sun's nothing to mess around with. Skin cancer doctors make a fortune down here. Even more than golf instructors and divorce attorneys."

I laughed. "Believe me, I've learned my lesson."

He gestured upstairs. "Want a quick tour before the party gets rolling?"

"Sure." I looked at Jake, hoping he'd come with me. He nodded and took my hand.

As the three of us walked upstairs with our champagne, I wondered what "quick tour" could possibly mean in a house like this.

• • •

When Jake and I entered the backyard about fifteen minutes later, the tent was filled with guests. Dozens of people, all of whom had come here for the express purpose of meeting me.

Suddenly I forgot about the huge house. Now I could think of nothing but the huge crowd in front of me.

And I was nervous.

Excruciatingly nervous.

Oh, sweet sugar, I'm nervous.

Jake's mom approached us and gestured to the tent. "Waverly, come let me introduce you around. Everyone is *so* excited to meet you." She smiled and looked elated that we were there.

I looked out at the sea of unfamiliar faces and forced a smile of my own. I felt myself flush on top of my already-hot sunburn.

"Um, sure, Mrs. McIntyre."

Before I even took a step, a short, top-heavy woman dressed in an outfit similar to Mrs. McIntyre's appeared out of nowhere.

"Why, *there* you are. It's such a pleasure to meet you." She smiled and held out her hand. "I'm Bee." Then she stood on her tiptoes to give Jake a big hug.

"Bee's my dearest friend in the whole world," Jake's mom said. "We practically raised our kids together."

"I've seen you on *Love, Wendy*," Bee said. "You're adorable."

I smiled and felt myself relax a bit. "You've seen the show?"

She nodded. "I never miss it. That Wendy Davenport is something else, isn't she?"

I gritted my teeth and forced a smile. "Absolutely." Wendy was extremely charming and popular with her fans, but off-camera she could be quite a storm cloud. I knew she was seeing a woman, but she was still very heterosexual publicly, and it was hard watching her suffer through the charade of pretending she was a traditional Southern beauty queen. I kept hoping she'd just rip off the Band-Aid, but it wasn't my call to make. So I sucked it up, kept my mouth shut, and kept my distance. It didn't help that Paige's fiancé, Gary, was Wendy's ex-husband.

"Bee drove up from Miami just to be here tonight," Mrs. McIntyre explained.

I raised my eyebrows. "Wow, that was so nice of you. I'm guessing that's quite a ways? I'm not very familiar with Florida geography." I looked at Jake.

"It's about an hour-and-a-half drive," Bee said. "But I wouldn't have missed it for the world. Jake's like a son to me, even if he's not going to be my *son-in-law*."

Jake laughed awkwardly. "Thanks, Bee."

I looked at him. *What did she just say?*

"Besides, we Worthingtons never miss a good party," Bee said.

As the name echoed in my head and finally clicked, I felt like I'd been punched in the gut.

Worthington?

Jake's ex-girlfriend was named Holly Worthington.

Mrs. McIntyre's best friend is Jake's ex-girlfriend's mom?

No wonder I was second fiddle in her eyes.

I stood there, at a loss for words. Jake could clearly tell I was rattled and put his hand on my arm.

"You ready?" he asked.

I blinked. "I'm sorry, what?"

"You ready?"

"Ready for what?"

Jake's mom gave me a strange look. "To meet our friends, dear."

I swallowed. "Oh yes, of course, I'm sorry." I tried to forget what had just happened and looked out at the crowded tent. I remembered the first time I'd gone on camera for *Love, Wendy*. It had gone well enough, despite my jangled nerves. But charming a bunch of faceless strangers through a camera lens was one thing. Doing it in real life was another matter altogether.

Get a grip, Waverly. You can do this.

I smiled out at the faces.

Do they all know Holly too?

Do they all wish she were the one marrying Jake?

I was just about to walk outside when Jake's mom put a hand on my shoulder.

"Waverly, dear, your bra strap is showing."

Ugh.

• • •

Two hours later my face hurt from smiling. So far the evening had been a blur of interchangeable well-wishers in expensive pastel clothing. Almost every woman there appeared to be wearing a variation on Mrs. McIntyre's pants outfit, with the occasional linen hat, silk scarf, or matching clutch bag sprinkled in. Gold jewelry—brooches in particular—gleamed from tanned necks and wrists. I was no expert on Botox, but I suspected it played a role in many of the perfectly smooth foreheads wandering about. As for the men, I'd never seen so many tropical-colored blazers and Tommy Bahama shirts in one place; boat shoes and leather loafers were also part of the uniform. I saw very few ties but did spot a few sweaters tied polo-style around several necks, which brought me straight back to seventh grade.

It was like a summer party in *The Great Gatsby*, only a hundred years later and about a thousand miles south.

"How are you holding up?" Jake emerged from the crowd and handed me a glass of sparkling water. I'd cut myself off after one flute of champagne, determined to avoid any alcohol-induced Waverly moments on such an important occasion.

"I'm hanging in. How about you?" We'd been tag-teamed by inquisitive guests most of the evening, leaving us little time to actually hang out together.

He shrugged. "I know how much this means to my mom, so I'm trying to turn on the charm for her sake."

"You're *always* charming," I whispered. "But you could have warned me about Holly's mother."

He put a hand on my back. "I know, I'm sorry about that. I wasn't sure she would be here, so I didn't want to open that can of worms for no reason. I had no idea the party would be this big."

"It's just a little awkward for me, you know?" I hoped the strain didn't show on my face. God knew how many people were watching us right now.

"I know it is." He reached for my free hand and squeezed it. "It's awkward for me too. I'm sorry."

I smiled. "It's okay. I'm upset with the situation, not you. Plus even if I *were* upset with you, it's impossible to stay mad at you anyway, damn you."

He laughed and took a sip of his champagne. "Bee is actually a really cool lady, you'll see. And she gets that Holly and I are over."

"You sure about that?"

He nodded. "I'm sure. That's why she can joke about it. Plus she means the world to my mom, so I'm glad she's here, even though it's a little...unusual."

"A little?"

He laughed again. "Okay, more than a little. But if something makes my mom happy, I'm usually for it, even if it's a little bumpy."

I leaned closer to him and lowered my voice even further. "You're clearly a good son, but no matter *what* your mom says, we're not getting married in a church in front of all these people. Or in Florida. Or on a holiday weekend."

Before he could reply, the unmistakable sound of a fork clinking against a champagne glass hushed the crowd. Everyone looked over at Jake's parents, who were standing together at the far end of the tent.

Jake's dad spoke first.

"We'd just like to take a moment to thank all of you for celebrating this wonderful occasion with us tonight, especially on such short notice. We've waited a long time for Jake to find a woman who deserved him *and* could put up with him."

Laughter from the crowd.

"But in all seriousness, we're just falling in love with Waverly..."

My ears perked up.

What?

They're falling in love with me?

I found myself getting emotional as he spoke, bits and pieces of his speech poking at my heart in a way I didn't expect.

"...we're thrilled that she's going to be a part of our family..."
They're thrilled that I'm going to be part of their family?
"...can't wait for the big day..."
They can't wait for the big day?
"...she's just a lovely young woman..."
They think I'm a lovely young woman?

I could feel eyes on me from all sides of the tent and did my best to act normal. Sensing my anxiety, Jake put his arm around me and gave me a squeeze.

"...so here's to Jake and Waverly, for the love they share now and for all the love that awaits them as a married couple. We couldn't be happier for you."

Mr. McIntyre raised his glass, and everyone followed.

Jake turned and lightly tapped his glass against mine.

"You getting cold feet yet?"

I shook my head and grinned at him. "Not if you stuck me barefoot into a bucket of ice."

We both looked back at his parents. I was waiting for his mom to say something, and I think Jake was too.

But she didn't.

• • •

After the toast, Jake went inside to use the bathroom, and I took the opportunity to take a little walk. I was feeling drained and wanted a few moments to myself. I set my empty water glass on a table, and when I didn't think anyone would notice, I quietly headed toward the tent exit.

I was nearly there when I felt a hand on my arm.

"Waverly, it's so lovely to meet you."

Damn.

I turned to find an older woman standing next to me. She was wearing yet another pastel pantsuit, decorated with yet another gold brooch. She was carrying a small dog in her purse, an animal so tiny that for a brief moment I thought it might be a hamster.

"It's lovely to be met." I smiled and held out my hand.

"I'm Doris Baker. My husband and I live just down the street. This little darling is Olive."

I saluted the miniature dog. "It's nice to meet you, Olive."

Doris smiled. "I can't tell you how excited our little community is about your wedding."

"I can't say there's much of a wedding in the works just yet, but I'm certainly excited about the engagement, that's for sure. Isn't this a lovely party?"

"You're going to be just a vision in white, that's for sure. And with a hunk like Jake on your arm? The two of you are quite the beautiful couple." She winked.

"Thank you." I could feel my eyes brighten at the thought of Jake on my arm.

"Have you been out to see the Breakers yet?" she asked.

"The Breakers?"

She nodded. "Ava told me she was able to book it for Presidents' Day weekend. That's quite a coup."

My jaw dropped.

"I'm sorry?"

"The Breakers Hotel, hon. Have you been to see it yet? If not, you're in for a treat."

Her voice trailed off, or at least I stopped listening.

What?

His mom has been telling people the date and *location of our wedding?*

I put my hand on her arm. "I hate to be rude, Doris, but I really must visit the ladies' room. I'm so sorry."

She shooed me away. "You go on now, hon. I look forward to seeing you again soon."

"It was so nice to meet you." I gave her a polite hug and hoped she couldn't discern the confusion on my face. I exited the tent, but instead of turning toward the house, I walked across the lawn, toward the water.

Now I really needed some time alone.

I didn't want to be, but I was…angry.

How could she do that?

This is my *wedding, not hers.*

Suddenly I missed having a mother of my own.

I walked across what felt like a football field, until I finally reached the far edge of the backyard, the water rippling gently against the shore. To the left was a picturesque white gazebo, to the right a wooden dock extending over the rocks. A small speedboat was tethered to the end of it.

"Wow," I whispered. The scene was tranquil, peaceful, beautiful.

I was struck by how different this view was from that of Andie's living room. It couldn't have been more different, but it was just as stunning in its own way.

I lost track of time as I stood there, trying to stay calm, trying to believe that Jake's mom's wasn't intentionally trying to hijack our wedding.

Don't be upset.

You don't have to do things her way.

Jake will stand up for you.

The sound of a man's voice startled me.

"Why, hello there. What are you doing down here all by yourself?"

I turned around and saw Jake's dad standing about ten feet away, a cigar in one hand.

"Oh, hi, Mr. McIntyre. I was just, um, taking a little breather." *Please don't ask me what's wrong.*

If he knew I was upset, he didn't let on. "I don't blame you one bit, young lady. That's a lot of people to handle at once. Why do you think I came down here myself? You stole my idea."

I laughed and looked out over the water.

"Quite a view, isn't it?" he said.

"Mesmerizing." I gave a slight nod toward the end of the dock. "Is that your boat?"

"Sure is. Would you like to see it?"

"I'd love to." *Anything to keep me away from the party a few more minutes.*

When we reached the end of the dock, he smiled and held out his arm game-show style.

"Waverly, meet my pride and joy." The boat had a mahogany finish and pristine white leather seats. The back of it said THE MCMILLAN.

The McMillan?

Why does that name sound familiar?

"What does the name mean?" I squinted at it as I tried to remember where I'd heard it before.

He took a puff of his cigar. "It stands for Father McMillan."

I stiffened. Something Jake's mom had said the night before came rushing back: *Father McMillan has already agreed to perform the ceremony.*

Before I could speak, Jake's dad continued. "He officiated our wedding nearly forty years ago…and later…he helped us through a difficult time."

I couldn't think of anything to say, so all I said was, "Oh."

Jake's dad picked up a rock from the deck and skipped it out into the water. "Father McMillan married me and Ava back when we were barely out of college." He gave me a knowing smile. "Of course, that seems way too young to get married *now*, but it was a different time then…"

I nodded.

He tossed another rock into the water. "Before Ava had Jake, she became extremely ill. Did Jake ever tell you that?"

The hair on my neck stood up. *Jake's mom nearly died?* He had never told me that. I wanted to know more but knew it wasn't my place to ask, at least right now, so I just shook my head. "No," I whispered.

"It was touch and go for a while there, and Father McMillan, well, I guess you could say he helped us…keep it together. We were practically babies ourselves back then, you know. And we already had Brett and Natalie, who were both just toddlers. It was a rough time, and we leaned on him a lot."

I didn't reply, knowing he had more to say.

Jake's dad bent down to pick up another rock from the deck. "Granted, I'm far from what you'd call religious, unlike Ava, who grew up very Catholic, but I'll always be grateful to that man."

I offered a weak smile.

"He officiated Brett and Natalie's weddings, and he baptized all three of our kids, and now their kids. That's why Ava is so devoted to him. He's a good man. He would have been here tonight, but he's a bit under the weather. He's nearly eighty now."

He tossed the rock into the water and nodded toward the house. "Should we get back? The belle of the ball can't be gone for too long before people start asking questions."

I smiled, suddenly feeling like I was going to cry. "Good point. Let's go, then."

"Waverly?"

I froze. *Please don't ask me what's wrong.* "Yes?"

"Last night, when Ava talked about your wedding, about having it here in Florida…"

I nodded.

He cleared his throat. "I just want to make it clear that we would never want to push you into anything you're not comfortable with. I know Ava can be a bit much sometimes, but her heart is in the right place, I promise you that. And at the end of the day, it's *your* wedding, not ours. Okay?"

I glanced at the boat. What had he called it? His pride and joy? And he'd named it after the aging, ailing pastor who had baptized his three children and officiated two of their weddings?

I looked back at him, sincerity written all over his kind face, and thought of everything mean I'd said to Jake about his mom.

I suddenly felt like a huge bitch.

• • •

When we were finally alone in the rental car a couple hours later, I turned to face Jake.

"Hey Mr. Secretive, were you ever planning to tell me that your family is loaded?"

He laughed and turned the key in the ignition. "*Loaded* is a relative term."

I gently slapped his arm. "Spare me. I've never seen so much gold in one place. It was like the *Pirates of the Caribbean* ride in there."

"You were great. Everyone loved you."

"You think so?"

He nodded. "I know so."

"They're all sort of blending together in a huge pastel memory right now, but overall I think your parents' friends are pretty nice. Actually, I was sort of surprised at how nice they all were."

"They're good people. Some of them are a little over-the-top, but underneath the glitz, they're good people. My parents are pretty selective when it comes to their friends."

I bit my lip. I wanted to talk to him about my conversation with his dad down by the dock, but I wasn't sure how to bring it up.

Jake looked over at me. "I had no idea so many of them watched *Love, Wendy.* They were quite taken by you."

I smoothed my hair with my hand. "I know! Can you believe that one lady asked me for my autograph? That was nutty."

"Irma from down the street? *She's* nutty. I think she has like a hundred finches in her house."

"Hey now, don't be dissing my fans. It's the Irmas out there who pay my rent."

"What did it feel like to be recognized by complete strangers?"

I looked out the window at the shadowy scenery passing by. I thought for a moment, then turned to him.

"It's hard to explain. On the one hand it's fun because they seem to like me and are so friendly, but then I realize they don't really know me—the *real* me—at all, and then the whole interaction feels sort of fake. Does that make sense?"

He nodded. "A little. NBA players say similar things."

"I'm not complaining...I mean, it's nice to be recognized and appreciated for what I do, but at the same time it's just...*odd*. I don't know how else to describe it. I'm sorry."

He reached over and interlaced his hand with mine. "It's okay, you don't have to describe it. Not everything has to have a perfect answer."

You're my perfect answer, I thought.

I squeezed his hand. "Thanks for tonight."

"Thanks? Why are you thanking *me*?"

"You knew I was nervous, like really nervous, especially at the beginning, but you didn't tease me about it."

"I like to think I know where to draw the line on teasing."

I nodded and pretended to paint a line in the air. "You definitely know where to draw that line. I wish I had your intuition."

"My mom was pretty great tonight, wasn't she?"

I put down my imaginary paintbrush and smiled. "Actually, *yes*. That was the nicest she's ever been to me. I wonder what happened?"

He laughed. "I told you she's not that bad."

A vision of Jake's mom in the hospital years ago, close to death, his dad and Father McMillan at her side, flitted across my brain. I pulled my hand away from Jake's and looked out the window, suddenly afraid I was going to cry.

"Hey, is everything okay?"

"I'm fine." I nodded but didn't look at him. I could feel a few tears run down my cheeks.

"Waverly, what's wrong?"

I didn't reply.

He reached over and squeezed my shoulder. "Waverly?"

I wiped a tear from my cheek, then turned to face him. I cleared my throat.

"What time do we have to leave for the Heat game tomorrow?"

He shrugged. "I don't know, maybe around one?"

I took a deep breath.

"Do you think…do you think we could go see the Breakers Hotel on the way?"

chapter nine

Jake's mom was over the moon when he called her the next morning.

"No promises, but we'd like to have a look," he said into the phone.

Brief pause.

"That should work. Okay, we'll be there at eleven thirty. Bye, Mom."

He hung up the phone and looked at me. "They have brunch plans so can't meet us, but my mom's going to make a few calls and get us a private tour."

I bit my lip. "She knows we're not committing to anything, right? That I just want to take a look at it?"

He nodded. "She knows."

• • •

A couple hours later we pulled up in front of the Breakers.

"Are you kidding me?" I whispered under my breath. When Jake's mom had first mentioned the name *Breakers* at dinner on Friday, I had thought *quaint surfside inn*. I clearly should have changed my expectations after seeing her house last night, but for some reason I hadn't done so.

This was no "quaint seaside inn."

Think more like "sprawling oceanside resort."

"You ready?" Jake asked me as we got out of the car.

I saluted, then reached for his hand. "Let's do it."

I soon learned that the Breakers is widely considered to be the poshest hotel in Southern Florida. It looks straight out over the Atlantic Ocean—and straight out of a movie. After strolling through countless gardens and courtyards, a Mediterranean-style beach club, and multiple oceanfront pools, followed by visits to multiple fitness centers, a deluxe spa, several boutiques, restaurants, and bars, then topped off by tours of a couple tennis courts and an *enormous* golf course, I was wiped out. Talk about luxury.

An hour or so later we said good-bye to our guide in the ornate lobby, which was adjacent to an open-air courtyard. The tour leader had mentioned that many couples hold their wedding ceremonies in the courtyard instead of the church on the adjacent property. When he was gone, I tilted my head back and admired the Italian Renaissance architecture.

"So, what do you think?" Jake said, now that we were finally alone.

I looked at him. "Honestly?"

"Honestly. If it's too much, you can tell me."

I sighed and tilted my head backward again. "I think I want to live here," I whispered to a painting on the ceiling.

He laughed. "But can you see us getting married here?"

I sighed. "I don't even want to *know* what that would cost."

He shook his head. "My parents would take care of it."

I looked at him. "What?"

"My parents want to pay for the wedding."

I opened my mouth to speak, but I didn't know what to say. We both knew my father couldn't afford to help.

Jake put his hands on my shoulders and turned me so that I was facing him. "The only question you need to answer is, 'Do you *want* to get married here?'"

"Don't you mean, 'Do I want you to become my husband here?'"

He laughed. "So noted."

I sighed and looked back up at the ceiling. "I really wanted a small wedding this time...but..." My voice trailed off.

"But what?"

I took his hand and led him over to a plush couch. When we sat down, I told him about my conversation with his dad at the dock.

After I'd finished, I put my hand on his arm. "Why didn't you tell me that your mom almost died before you were born?" Jake knew I'd lost my mom before I ever got to know her. Why hadn't he told me that he nearly had too? It didn't make any sense.

He didn't reply.

I kept my hand on his arm. "Why didn't you tell me, Jake?"

Finally he looked at me. He brushed a loose piece of hair out of my eyes and hesitated before speaking.

"Because she lived."

"What?"

"Because she *lived*, Waverly. Your mom died, and mine lived."

I felt tears welling up in my eyes.

Oh.

He scratched the back of his head. "I just didn't see the point of telling you...when it would only remind you of what you lost. I didn't want to do that to you."

"*That's* why you didn't tell me?" I felt a few tears slide down my cheeks.

He nodded and wiped them away. "I would never want to do anything that would bring you pain."

I didn't know what to say.

"Plus it happened before I was born, so it's not like I was traumatized or anything. I thought it would be extremely selfish of me to compare my situation to yours."

I felt more tears on their way as I was overcome by what I felt for this wonderful person sitting next to me.

I gazed over at the open courtyard, so sunny and airy and bright that it looked...alive.

I turned to face Jake.

"Your dad really named his boat after Father McMillan?"

He nodded. "He's a good man."

"He's that important to your family? Like really important?"

"To my parents, yes. To me and Brett and Nat, he's like...a favorite uncle."

I pressed my palms against my eyes. *Uncle. Brother. Sister. Mother.* They were all things I'd never had. Growing up I'd had my dad, and I didn't doubt that he'd done the best he could to raise me on his own, but sometimes trying to understand what it was like to be part of a traditional family was like trying to imagine having a third arm.

I closed my eyes for a moment, then opened them and took Jake's hands in mine.

"Let's do it. Let's get married here. By Father McMillan."

He raised his eyebrows. "Are you sure?"

"Yes."

"Waverly, are you absolutely sure that's what *you* want? I don't want you to do this for me."

I looked at the courtyard again. "If we can have the ceremony here and not at the church, then yes, that's what I want."

He gave me a brief look that indicated he wasn't entirely convinced, but then he smiled. "My mom is going to flip out."

I smiled back. "I know."

"Okay, then, let's do it."

I stood up to leave, but he caught me on the way. He leaned over and whispered into my ear. "And you wonder why I'm so in love with you."

I blushed and reached for my purse, unsure what to say.

As we walked hand in hand back to the car, I tried to ignore the churning I felt in my stomach.

• • •

"You want something to eat?" Jake gestured toward the crowded food court.

I grinned and nodded like a bobblehead doll. "Given the ladylike weekend I've just had, I'd *kill* for some fries, extra ketchup, and a beer—large, please."

"How about I get the beers and you get the fries, and I'll meet you at our seats?" He handed me a ticket.

I saluted. "Sounds like a plan."

We split up, and soon I had a large carton of fries in my hand. I looked up at the signs as I made my way through the arena, trying to locate the correct entrance to our section.

I made my way down the stairs to our seats, which were practically on the court. Jake was already there and handed me an enormous beer as I sat down. The players were being introduced in the middle of the court, surrounded by cheerleaders who were dancing to extremely loud music. I leaned over to Jake and shouted. "These seats are amazing! If a fight breaks out, there's a good chance one of us is getting a broken schnoz!"

He laughed and took a sip of his beer. "I think we'll be fine."

"I'm serious Jake, maybe we should have brought rain jackets."

"Rain jackets? Why?"

"Because once these guys start running up and down the court, we're totally going to get sprayed with sweat."

• • •

I did my best to watch the game, but eventually I lost interest and pulled out my phone to text Andie. I'd long ago given up texting McKenna, whose inbox was basically a black hole.

Wedding date set. Feb 18, Palm Beach. Probably fancy.

A return text popped up a few minutes later.

WHAT. THE. EFF?

I laughed and typed a quick reply.

CHANGE. OF. HEART.

She pinged me right back:

WHO. ARE. YOU? WHERE. IS. WAVERLY?

A flurried exchange of messages followed. I did my best to convince her—and myself—that I was thrilled about the plan. In the most decorative language I could think of, I also told her about the ritzy engagement party, the ritzy Breakers Hotel, the general ritziness of Palm Beach.

I was about to press SEND on my latest message when a new one popped up on my screen.

It was from Scotty Ryan.

Sweetheart, you're on national television, on the network that employs you. Will you please get your pretty nose out of your phone and at least PRETEND to watch the game?

I dropped my phone into my lap and hoped my jaw didn't drop noticeably too.

Oh, frick.

I looked up and around me.

I'm on TV?

This game is on NBC?

I smiled and started to clap, but then I noticed that the court was empty for a time-out. I looked up at the clock.

The game was almost over, and the score was tied.

Oops.

chapter ten

When I arrived at the staff meeting at *Love, Wendy* the next morning, my head was still a thousand miles away. I'd only been out of town for three days, but given how much had happened in those seventy-two hours, it felt more like three years.

I walked into the empty conference room carrying a latte and bagel from the breakfast cart right outside our building. I was early, so I sat down and pulled out my phone to scroll through my messages, trying to catch up on everything. Despite the chaos inherent in juggling two nontraditional jobs, I enjoyed having an unconventional schedule. I don't know if it was attention deficit disorder or just an allergy to boredom, but I couldn't tolerate the idea of doing the same thing day in and day out. I was scattered and often exhausted, but I loved my life.

I was reading an e-mail from Paige when Justin Wagner, our new producer, walked in. A few months earlier, NBC had brought him on to replace Scotty Ryan, our original producer (and good friend of mine), who was taking on an expanded role at the *Today* show and was now focusing full-time on that. Justin was a Brit who had spent most of his career in London. While Scotty had embraced a democratic approach to planning, Justin was proving to be the complete opposite. In other words, our "planning" meetings amounted to his updating us on what he had already planned. I was beginning to wonder why we didn't just call them "briefing" meetings. Not that I was complaining.

The meetings were short and painless, and he was extremely friendly and professional.

"Good morning, Waverly." Even the way he walked seemed straight out of the Academy of Efficiency. I wondered if he ever just kicked back and took a nap on the couch.

I set my phone down on the table. "Hi, Justin. How are you?"

He took a seat across from me and interlaced his hands. "I'm well, thanks for asking." He glanced at the door, then lowered his voice. "Listen, I'm glad you're here early. I need to run a few changes by you."

I stiffened.

A few changes?

I nodded, trying to appear calm. "Sure, what kind of changes?"

Before he could reply, Wendy walked in.

"Good morning, Justin, Waverly." She gave us each a polite nod.

"Hi, Wendy," we both said. I wondered what kind of mood she was going to be in today.

She smiled and put a hand on Justin's arm. "Justin, my dear, I need to talk to you about something before the meeting, in private."

"Do you want me to leave?" I began to stand up.

She shook her head. "No, no, of course not." Then she looked at Justin. "Could we just pop into my office for a moment? It won't take long."

"Sure, no problem." As they left the room, he caught my eye and mouthed the words, *We'll talk soon.*

I nodded, burning with curiosity about what he had to say to me—*in private.*

I also wondered what he and Wendy would be talking about—*in private.*

Ugh, drama.

No matter how hard I tried to avoid it, there was always a lot of drama that went along with working with Wendy Davenport. Because we produced my segment of the show separately, I did my best to stay on the periphery of it. And so far Justin had been rubber-stamping the topics I wanted to cover in *Honey on Your Mind*, which was just fine by me.

I wondered if that was about to change.

• • •

When Wendy returned several minutes later, I looked up and smiled, determined to be nice to her. "Did you have a good weekend?"

She patted her hair and nodded. "It was fabulous, thanks. I heard *you* were on TV yesterday…several times."

I balled up my fists under the table. "You did?" *Several times?*

She clasped her hands together. "I heard commentators were having a field day. Apparently they recognized you and thought it was a hoot that every time the camera panned to you, you had your face in your phone."

I winced. "Was it bad? I mean, for the network?" *Am I busted?*

She didn't reply right away, and I braced myself for her reaction. With Wendy, you just never knew.

She shrugged. "Hon, I don't think there's much crossover in our demographics, so to be honest I'm not too worried about it."

I exhaled and put my head down. *Thank God.*

"You look quite pretty today, by the way."

I looked up. *What?* Wendy hardly ever threw me a compliment.

"I do?"

"Yes, dear, it looks like you finally got some desperately needed sun."

And there you go.

She stood and hooked her purse over her arm. "I'm just going to run to the powder room before the meeting. Be right back."

As she strolled out the door, Justin returned.

"So, Waverly, can you please drop by after we're done here?" He nodded toward his office.

"Okay, sure."

Had he heard about my unfortunate solo performance on national television? *Way to act like a bored teenager, Waverly.*

Several staff members walked in, followed a few minutes later by Wendy, and the standard premeeting chatter began to float through the room. I pulled out my notebook and pretended to pay attention, but for the next hour I barely heard a word anyone said.

I felt like a high school student asked to meet with the principal after school.

I hope I'm not in trouble.

• • •

After the staff meeting, I stopped by the kitchen to refill my coffee mug before reluctantly heading down the hall to see Justin. I knew from personal experience that it was rarely good news when you were called unexpectedly into a higher-up's office.

When I reached his open door, he was sitting at his desk and on the phone. He motioned for me to come in, so I took a seat across from him and quietly sipped my coffee.

"Yes, she just walked in," he said.

I froze midsip.

"Yep, I'm just about to tell her."

Tell me what?

I fidgeted in my seat while he finished up the call. When he hung up, I did my best to smile.

"Waverly, thanks for stopping by."

"No problem." I kept on smiling, even though I was pretty sure he knew it was forced.

He cut right to the chase.

"Did you have a nice trip to Florida?"

I stopped smiling.

Uh-oh.

I nodded and shifted in my seat. "I did, thanks."

"I heard you made quite the impression at the Heat-Lakers game yesterday."

Oh, sweet sugar.

I laughed nervously. "So I've heard. Was it…um…that bad?" I figured I might as well cut to the chase too.

"That bad?"

I swallowed. "I mean…um…was anyone at the network upset?"

"Upset?" He looked surprised.

"Yes, um, you know, because I wasn't really paying attention to the game?"

He waved a hand in front of him. "Oh, please. If anything, they were pleased the camera guy recognized you from *Love, Wendy*. The show got a good plug out of it."

I felt my shoulders drop.

Thank God.

"I'm glad to hear that. To be honest, I was a little worried. I didn't realize the game was on NBC."

He shook his head. "Waverly, if there's anything I've learned since I joined *Love, Wendy*, it's that most of our viewers don't care a lick about sports. You think Wendy knows the difference between a zone defense and a criminal defense? Please."

I laughed and smiled, this time for real. "You have no idea how glad I am to hear that. So, um, what did you want to see me about?" I winced as I realized how many times I'd uttered *um* in the last three minutes. I hated that it infected my speech when I got nervous. I was usually able to keep the *um*s at bay while on camera, but in person they managed to creep into uncomfortable conversations.

Like this one.

He gestured to a thick manila folder on his desk. "Actually, speaking of our viewers, that's a perfect segue into why I wanted to talk to you."

I raised my eyebrows.

He opened the folder. "Well, as you know, I like to run a tight ship around here, and I don't see the value in wasting our valuable budget on programming that people aren't responding to."

I swallowed.

"Shortly after I came on board, I hired an outside research firm to conduct a number of focus groups on the show," he said.

"Okay."

He tapped a finger on top of the stack of papers inside the folder. "I was very curious to see what the research had to say. I wanted some real insight into what people like about it, what they don't like, what they'd like to see more of, that sort of thing."

I nodded but was having a hard time processing his words.

Is this good news or bad news?

"I got the final report last week, and I found it quite interesting. It wasn't what I expected, to tell you the truth."

"Okay," I said again. I'm sure I had a strange look on my face. *Am I about to get fired?*

He tapped the stack of papers again. "*Honey on Your Mind* tested well, Waverly. In fact, it was very strong."

"It was?"

He nodded. "I was surprised, to be honest. Personally I find your segment quite entertaining, but I thought your sense of humor might be a bit too...how should I put this...*sophisticated* for our viewers."

"Sophisticated?" *He thinks I'm sophisticated?*

He nodded. "I *am* a Brit, you know. We love our wit."

I laughed. "I'm honored that you think I'm witty."

"I do, but I'm not the target audience, which, to be frank, concerned me a bit when I took this job. However, the research shows that people who *are* the target audience really like your segment too."

"They like my segment too?"

He nodded. "They *relate* to it. That was the word that kept coming up in the report. *Relate.*"

"They relate to it?"

"They do."

"They do?" I balled up my hands into fists again. *Why do I keep repeating everything he says? What the hell is wrong with me?*

"Yes. Viewers identify with the situations you report on, and they love the self-deprecating way you present it. They relate to *you*, Waverly."

I exhaled and took a peek down at my clenched, sweaty hands. I could also feel perspiration prickling the back of my neck. *You have no idea how much you just rattled me.*

"So I want to give the viewers what they want."

I looked up. "Excuse me?"

"I want to give the viewers more *Honey on Your Mind.* Starting the first of November, I want you to do a segment on every show."

I coughed. "Five pieces a week?" I was currently doing two or three a week. And drowning.

"Yes. Wendy will be announcing it on the show late next month."

"Wendy knows about it?"

"Of course."

"And she's cool with it?"

"Of course."

"Are you sure about that?"

"Yes. Why do you ask?" He gave me a strange look.

Do you really not know she doesn't like me?

I swallowed and tried to look casual. "No reason. So, um, if I do more segments, what's going to get cut? Or are you going to make the show longer?" God knows what Wendy would do to me if one of her favorite spots got the axe because of me.

He made scissors with his fingers. "I'm cutting viewer pet and baby videos. People get enough of that on YouTube."

I stiffened. Wendy loved those stupid pet and baby videos.

Justin tapped his fingers on the folder again. "I'll also need your proposed topics for all of November on my desk by the first of the month, okay? From now on I want to have the entire month planned a month in advance."

A month in advance? Do you not realize how much I've been flying by the seat of my pants here?

I didn't reply.

He raised his eyebrows. "Is there a problem?"

I didn't want him to know what I was thinking, which was that I couldn't do it.

I can't do it.

"I thought you'd be thrilled by the news. We'll adjust your pay accordingly, obviously."

I hesitated for a moment, then spoke. "Well, it's just that I—"

Just then his phone rang, and he held his hand up to interrupt me. "I'm sorry, Waverly, I've got to take this call. We'll work out the details later, okay?" His demeanor indicated that it was time for me to go.

I guess it was settled.

I'd just gotten a promotion.

A big promotion.

I should have been celebrating my good fortune, but that's not how I saw it.

Double the work?

I'm gonna die.

• • •

I ran into Scotty Ryan on my way out of the building after the meeting. I never ran into him anymore and had even resorted to leaving him a voice mail about my engagement so he wouldn't hear the news from someone else.

"Waverly, love! How are you?" He kissed me on the cheek.

"I'm good, Scotty, how are you? How is life in the executive suite?"

He gave me a weary smile, and I could see the crow's-feet around his eyes. "Exhausting, but I can't complain. So, how goes the wedding planning? When can I expect my save-the-date?"

I laughed. "Not everyone is as organized as you and Tad." Scotty and his husband Tad had gotten engaged on New Year's Day and had already tied the knot in early June at an art gallery in SoHo. "I'm still getting used to being engaged."

"Let me see the ring." He reached for my hand. "Ah yes, that man has good taste in women *and* in jewelry."

"Such a charmer. So, how is married life treating you anyway? I haven't seen you in ages. Why did you have to abandon our show?"

He laughed. "Abandon? Kitten, you were hardly abandoned. If you haven't noticed, Justin Wagner may be the most talented producer at this network."

I nodded, still a bit stunned at the news Justin had just given me. "It's hard not to notice someone *that* organized. He's like a human spreadsheet. He's great, but I just miss you, that's all."

"I miss you too. Life does get in the way, and this new job has me scrambling like never before. I've been keeping tabs on you from afar, though."

I raised my eyebrows. "You have? Do I want to know what you've been tabbing?"

"Probably not."

"What?"

"I'm kidding, princess. Listen, I really must run. We'll have you and Jake over for a drink soon, okay?"

"Promise?"

He nodded. "My schedule is nuts right now, but we'll make it happen."

And with that, he was off.

Life does indeed get in the way, I thought.

• • •

A few hours later I was back in Dumbo at the Waverly's Honey Shop office. Tasha and Beth walked in the door just a few minutes after me, a bag of cookies in tow. As soon as I saw them, I stretched my arms in a *gimme* motion. After the nerve-racking day I'd had so far, I could definitely use some sugar.

"So, how was the engagement party?" Tasha set the bag on the table and began to divvy up the goods. "Any good stories? Any crazy action on the dance floor?"

I took a sip of my coffee. "Well, given that the average age was about sixty-five, I'd have to say…*no*. A lot of flower-print shirts, though."

She nodded. "Of course. Flower-print shirts are where it's *at* in Florida."

"Was it fun?" Beth asked. "I've never been to Florida."

I picked up a cookie. "It was. I wasn't sure what to expect, but it ended up being quite eye-opening." I filled them in on the highlights of the weekend, trying to downplay the opulence of it all. I planned to tell Andie about that part, but I didn't feel right broadcasting it here.

"Wow, sounds like a fairy-tale evening," Beth said.

I nodded. The memory of the night was still a bit surreal. "It was…it was very beautiful."

"I love engagement parties," Paige said. "If the drinks are free, I don't care *how* old the men are."

"Careful, pregnant lady," Tasha said. "People might get the wrong impression with talk like that."

We all laughed, and I decided to share the biggest news of the weekend. "Jake and I, um, we sort of set a date when we were down there." I felt the little pit in my stomach stir and nibbled on a cookie to smother it.

Paige's eyes suddenly turned a bit serious. "Really?" She knew I'd been in no hurry to set a date.

I swallowed the cookie and nodded. "We decided on Presidents' Day weekend."

I could see the *a-wedding-on-a-three-day-weekend?* look flash across her face. Paige was in her midthirties; she knew from her own experience how much those weddings sucked for everyone but the bride and groom. Tasha and Beth were still too young to resent weddings that took away precious holidays.

"That soon?" Paige asked casually, ever the diplomat.

I shifted nervously in my seat, my body language mirroring my awkward attempt at convincing her I was delighted. "Um, well, Jake's mom was able to book a really pretty venue down there for that weekend, and it's important to her to have the wedding down there, so I decided to just go with it." As soon as the words were out of my mouth I realized how forced they sounded, and that I was clearly not delighted. I wasn't *upset.* I just couldn't muster any…enthusiasm.

"You're really getting married in Florida?" Paige asked quietly. Her eyes said everything her voice didn't.

I smiled as convincingly as I could. "Looks like it."

Beth nibbled on a cookie. "I'm sure it will be lovely." Beth never said anything that wasn't nice.

"Why would you want to get married in Florida? You hardly know the place," Tasha said.

"Tasha!" Paige was clearly appalled by her candor.

Tasha shrugged. "It's an honest question. Waverly's from San Francisco, and she lives in New York." She looked at me. "Do you even know anyone in Florida?"

I bit my lip. "I know Jake's parents."

They all nodded.

"And his brother," I added quickly. "His brother and his wife live down there too."

They all nodded again.

"They're super nice," I threw in. It was sort of sad, actually. Like a full-court shot at the buzzer—when your team is down by forty.

They all nodded again.

"It would just…mean a lot to his parents if we got married there," I said quietly. "It's…complicated."

With that, they got it.

Even Beth.

"That's big of you, Waverly," she said softly.

Tasha looked embarrassed. "I'm sorry for questioning your decision. If you hadn't noticed, I can be sort of a bitch sometimes."

I smiled and put my hand on her arm. "It's okay. If you hadn't noticed, that's why we keep you around."

Paige held up her cup. "Well, girls, Waverly is officially tying the knot. Let's celebrate."

"Thanks, Paige." I shot her a grateful look.

We toasted with our coffees, then turned our attention to the cookies. After a minute or so, Tasha cleared her throat. "While we're on the topic of relationships, I have a good story to share."

We all looked up, and I pointed a cookie at her. "Do tell."

She wiped a few crumbs from her mouth. "Actually, it's on the topic of *looking* for a relationship. Beth and I went speed dating last night."

Beth turned beet red. "Tasha!"

Tasha shrugged. "Please. Who are they going to tell? Your boyfriend? Oh, wait, that's right, you don't have one."

Paige laughed. "You were right. You *are* a little bitchy sometimes."

"But don't you adore her for it?" I said to Paige.

Paige nodded. "Definitely."

I turned to Beth. "Not that we don't adore you too."

Paige nodded in agreement.

Beth gave us each a grateful smile. "Thanks."

I focused on Tasha, happy that the focus of conversation was no longer on me. "So? You went speed dating...and..."

She stood up as if she were giving a presentation. "We signed up online, and we expected to meet, I don't know, a dozen, maybe fifteen guys, all young professionals from the city. Right, Beth?"

Beth nodded quickly, clearly still embarrassed.

"So we walk into the back room of this bar to check in and pick up our name tags, and after a quick look around, I turn to Beth and am like, 'So, where are all the guys?'"

"How many guys were there?" Paige asked.

Tasha tapped her index finger against her chin. "That would be...five. For ten women. "

I covered my mouth with my hand. "I don't think I like where this is going."

"Believe me, you don't," Beth said.

Tasha took a sip of her coffee. "So the first guy I met was literally pushing sixty."

Paige coughed. "Sixty?"

Tasha nodded. "*Sixty.* For real. And that wasn't the worst of it. I swear to God, he was wearing a tan linen jacket with the words HATE THE SINNER, NOT THE SIN painted on the back."

"What?" I said.

Tasha looked at Beth. "It was painted, right? In bright red?"

Beth nodded, herself still a bit red.

"There's no way that's true," Paige said.

Tasha set her cup down and held up both hands. "Why would I lie about something this embarrassing? Tell me that."

"Okay, you're right," Paige said. "So that guy was a bit... religious?"

Tasha nodded. "A minister."

I coughed. "At a speed-dating event?"

She nodded. "You heard me. He said he'd befriended the organizer in *church*...in *Vegas*."

"What?"

Beth put her hand on my arm. "It's true. I met him too."

I made a face. "Yikes."

Tasha nodded at me. "Exactly. *So* scary. God knows what sort of perv cult situation *that* was. At one point he even used the word *prophet* to describe himself."

By then, Beth was laughing as well, finally loosening up. "It's true," she said. "When I talked to him, he told me the same story. And actually, I think he might have been even older than sixty. He kind of reminded me of my grandfather."

Paige and I stole a glance at each other, sharing an unspoken understanding of how grateful we were to be done with this phase of our lives.

"How much did you pay to go to this thing?" I asked.

Tasha waved a finger at me. "Don't even get me started on that. So after Father Grandpa leaves, we all do the musical chairs thing, and then PowerPoint Paul sits down."

I raised my eyebrows. "PowerPoint Paul?"

Beth let out a little squeak and put her head down on the table. Paige chuckled and began smoothing the back of Beth's head. "I can't *wait* to hear this one."

Tasha tapped her palms crisply on the table. "PowerPoint Paul, who, by the way, lives like fifty miles out in New Jersey, was quite direct about the qualities he's looking for in a relationship." She held up a hand and began counting them off with fingers. "Chemistry. Conversation. Compatibility." She looked at Beth, who was still facedown on the table. "What was the last one again? He gave you the same spiel."

"Communication," came the mumbled reply.

"Ah yes, thanks. I keep forgetting that one." Tasha listed them on her fingers again. "The four C's. Chemistry. Conversation. Compatibility. Communication. There you have it from Paul, corporate robot, of BFE, New Jersey."

I laughed. "He really laid it out like that?"

Tasha nodded. "Oh yes. And he was quite serious about it. *No sense of humor for PowerPoint Paul.*"

"I think I've probably dated him," Paige said.

Beth finally sat back up and groaned. "I'll never find love."

Tasha tossed another chunk of cookie in her mouth. "You won't find it at speed dating, that's sure as hell the truth."

I smiled and realized how much I enjoyed the camaraderie of our little office. Who says you can't mix business with pleasure?

I also realized the pit in my stomach wasn't bothering me anymore.

Paige put her hand on my arm. "Want to grab a coffee? I can catch you up on the latest."

I raised my eyebrows. Unless we were discussing something sensitive, we had our meetings in the open. *Grab a coffee* was our code for *We need to talk in private.*

"Sure." I think my eyebrows were still raised in alarm.

Paige looked at Tasha and Beth. "Can you two finish the inventory report while we're gone?"

"We're on it." Tasha put her arm around Beth and led her to the conference table. "Come on, farm girl. Let's go crunch some numbers."

Paige and I headed downstairs. As soon as we were out of the building, I looked sideways at her.

"Is everything okay?"

She nodded but didn't make eye contact. "Yes...and no."

"I'm not sure I like the sound of that."

Once inside Almondine Bakery across the street, we ordered our lattes. A double for me, a decaf for her.

"Man, how I miss caffeine." She stared longingly at my cup as we settled ourselves in at a table.

I gave her a look. "More than alcohol?"

"Are you kidding? I'm *pregnant*. I'm not dead."

I smiled. "Just checking. So are you getting excited for the baby? Or are you nervous?"

"Both, but way more excited than nervous."

I took a sip of my latte. "That's exactly how I feel about getting married."

"My three-year-old nephew is *super* pumped to meet his new cousin. I saw him a couple weeks ago, and he asked me if there's a toilet inside my belly for the baby to go potty."

I nearly spat out my drink. "That is so gross, yet so funny."

She laughed too, but she looked a little distracted.

"So what's up? You have me worried." I reached over and gave her arm a squeeze.

She interlaced her hands tightly on the table but didn't say anything for a moment. She just stared at her hands.

"Paige?"

I was about to take another sip of my latte when she finally looked up and spoke.

"I'm moving to Nashville."

I froze.

What?

I set my cup down and tried to mask the anxiety that suddenly appeared out of nowhere and seized my entire body.

"I thought the plan was for Gary to move here once his son left for college." Gary and Paige had been dating long-distance ever since they'd met.

She squeezed her cup. "It was, but now his son wants to go to junior college and live at home, which has sort of thrown a wrench into everything."

I didn't reply.

"And the cost of living is so much cheaper there..."

I still didn't reply.

"And his job is based there..."

"And?" I knew what she was really getting at.

She sighed again. "And while I love New York City, I've reluctantly come to terms with the fact that raising a kid here is just... not...ideal."

Bingo.

Ugh.

Why did *everyone* bolt for the burbs once they had a kid? My friends Kristina and Shane, who were also expecting their first child, had already moved back to a town outside Chicago to be closer to both their parents. And I vividly recalled when a pregnant McKenna—who had once proudly vowed to stay in San Francisco until the day of her funeral—quietly broke the news that she and Hunter were moving to Mill Valley. I'd reluctantly watched all of them leave, all the while feeling selfish for not wanting them to go.

Sitting across from Paige now, I knew I shouldn't complain.

Or meddle.

Or try to guilt her into changing her mind.

But I couldn't help myself.

"But what am I going to do without you?" I blurted a bit too loudly. An elderly couple at the adjacent table looked at me askance, then returned to their quiet conversation.

I stared at Paige, who wouldn't look me in the eye.

The fact was, we both knew I couldn't run Waverly's Honey Shop by myself. Sure, I'd started it, but Paige had helped me turn it into a *real company*. She'd practically single-handedly turned it from a tiny online store operating out of my apartment into a growing brick-and-mortar business with several national accounts. My products were now available in boutiques and department stores across the country. While I'd been along for the ride, we both knew that Paige had been the one steering the ship. The business was now operating at a whole new level, far beyond my management abilities—and availability. Though we were equal partners on paper, she kept things running like a Swiss watch. Because of the incessant demands of *Love, Wendy*, I only made it to the Waverly's Honey Shop office two or three times a week—on a good week.

And after the news I'd just heard from Justin, my time was soon going to become even more stretched.

I stared across the table at her, pregnant, happy, and about to start a brand-new life with her fiancé. I knew I should be supportive of her decision, but I couldn't get past one thought.

I'm so screwed.

We sat in silence for a few moments before she finally looked at me and spoke.

"I'm really sorry, Waverly. I'll do my best to help find my replacement before the baby comes."

I smiled weakly but said nothing.

She did her best to fill the silence. "Now, instead of finding someone to cover my maternity leave, we'll just make it a permanent position."

I nodded.

"And it's not like it's happening tomorrow. We still have a few weeks," she added. "I've already put some feelers out."

I was still at a loss for words.

"It will work out," she practically whispered.

She was clearly doing her best to reassure me, but it wasn't working. I could already feel the stress bearing down on my shoulders like a vise. I'd already been worried about how we'd manage while she was out for a few weeks on maternity leave.

But leaving for good?

Good...God.

Finally I answered her. "What about working remotely from Nashville?" I could practically see my hands grasping for the straws.

She frowned. "I thought about that, I really did, but I just don't see how we could do it. With the office here and all the face-to-face meetings we have to keep you in the loop on everything, it would just be too hard. Plus Beth and Tasha are great, but they still need someone *here* to tell them what to do, you know what I mean?"

My face fell.

I knew.

I pointed nostalgically out the window toward our office across the street. "None of that would have happened without you. You know that, right?"

She reached over the table and put her hands over mine. "We can find someone to fill my shoes, I know we can."

"You really think so?"

"I know so. Remember, this company was *your* idea, Waverly. It was a great idea when I met you, and it's still great now. I just helped you take it to the next level, that's all."

I frowned. I knew I'd figure things out, but I wished I didn't have to. "Damn that Gary Davenport. He certainly took *you* to the next level." I jutted my chin toward her stomach.

She laughed. "True, but he's more than just a sperm donor, you know."

I finally took a sip of my latte, which was now lukewarm. "I'll give you that," I said with a shrug. "Even though he's taking you away from me, I do like him."

She smiled. "I like him too."

We sat in silence for a minute, and then she held her cup up to mine. "Talk about a year of life-changing news for both of us, huh?"

I tapped my cup against hers in a bittersweet toast. "You got that right. So, are you going to name the baby Waverly to make up for the fact that you're abandoning me?"

"I'd love to, but it's a boy."

"No way! I didn't know that."

"Actually, we haven't told anyone. But I figure I owe you, so consider yourself the first to know."

"Wow, a boy. You have a *penis* growing inside of you."

She laughed. "I hadn't thought of it that way, but I guess you're right. So while I *am* extremely fond of you, my friend, I can't name my son Waverly. I'm sorry."

I shrugged again. "I understand. Believe me, it's unusual enough for a girl."

"I'm really going to miss you, Waverly—inside *and* outside of the office." She reached across the table and squeezed my arm.

I set my cup down and put my hand over hers.

"I'm going to miss you too."

chapter eleven

The next afternoon I'd just finished up interviewing some tourists in Times Square for *Honey on Your Mind* and was walking back to NBC when my phone rang. I didn't recognize the number but answered anyway.

"Hello?"

"Waverly? Is that you?" The voice was familiar.

"Yes?"

"It's Ava McIntyre."

I stopped walking.

Jake's mom had never called me before. Ever.

"Oh, Mrs. McIntyre, hi."

"How are you, dear?"

"I'm good." *Why is she calling me?* "Um, how are things?" I slowly started walking again.

"I was wondering if you're around this weekend. I'd love to fly up to do some dress shopping."

"Dress shopping?" She would fly all the way to New York to go shopping? Don't they have enough stores in Florida?

"Not for *me*, dear. For *you*."

Oh lordy. She means wedding dress *shopping.*

"Oh," I said. "I'm sorry, that didn't compute right away."

"Should I book a flight? I haven't been able to reach Jake today, so I don't even know if you'll be in town."

I didn't know how to respond.

Before this call, I'd never even spoken to her on my own.

Now she wanted to spend an entire day shopping with me?

I wasn't sure my nerves could handle an entire day of Ava McIntyre.

"Waverly, are you still there?"

I suddenly realized that I hadn't said anything.

Tell her you're busy with work.

Tell her you'll be out of town.

Just say something, anything, *Waverly!*

"Um...sure," I heard myself say.

No!

"Wonderful. I'll book a room at the Plaza and will arrive Friday night. I'll make some appointments for us, so plan to meet me Saturday at eight for breakfast at the hotel. And please tell Jake I'll get us tickets to a show that night and will make dinner reservations. It will be lovely."

"Jake? I, um, I don't think he'll be in town this weekend," I squeaked out the words, praying to the NBA heavens that I had his schedule wrong. Breakfast at eight on a Saturday? Who in New York is even *awake* at eight on a Saturday?

"Well, if it's just the two of us, then it's just the two of us. I'll be in touch."

"Okay. Bye, Mrs. McIntyre."

I hung up the phone and stared at it.

This is going to be brutal.

• • •

That night I went over to Andie's palace for some ice cream.

"So you'll come with me? I don't think I can do this alone."

She shrugged as she scooped us each a bowl of reduced-fat chocolate chip. "Sure. Although I'm *not* meeting you at eight in the morning, that's for sure. I'm going out with some work people on Friday night, and I have a feeling it could get ugly."

"That's okay, you can catch up with us if you have to. I'll take you for every minute you can spare. I'll need the moral support."

She handed me a black ceramic bowl. "I wonder why his mom wants to go dress shopping with you anyway. I mean, she's not *your* mother. Isn't that the sort of thing you do with your own mother?"

I shook my head and slogged my way toward the couch. "I have no idea. Maybe it's because she knows I never really had a mother of my own. That would make it a really kind gesture, actually. Right?"

"Maybe…or maybe she just wants to make sure you pick a dress that meets her standards."

I stopped midstride and turned around. "No way. You really think so?"

She shrugged. "I don't know, I've never met her. I'm just saying it's possible, given how particular you say she is."

I plopped onto the couch. "But that would be so…*awful*."

She put the carton in the freezer and joined me in the living room. "Some women don't see it that way. I can totally picture my mom doing something like that and not having a clue that it could possibly offend anyone."

"But you hate your mom. I don't want to hate Jake's mom."

She lifted a spoon to her mouth. "Well…maybe that's not her intention at all. Maybe it's exactly what you said, that she just wants to get to know you better, be a mother figure, that sort of thing."

I stared at my ice cream, which I'd noticed blended perfectly with the checkerboard décor of her apartment. "Shopping for a wedding dress is a...huge thing." I wanted to say *once-in-a-life-time thing*, but for me, that just wasn't true.

"For some people, yes, it is. Personally, I could take it or leave it."

I looked up at her. "I should be excited about it, right?"

"Perhaps."

"I *want* to be excited about it."

"Then be excited about it."

I sighed.

I just...wasn't.

"You know you're going to end up with something crazy-expensive," Andie said. "Is she paying for it?"

"I would think so. Jake said they wanted to pay for the wedding. Does the wedding include the dress?"

She nodded. "I think it does. That would make sense, right?"

I sighed again. "This is all getting so complicated. I don't want to be indebted to them."

"Don't worry so much. Sounds like they can easily afford it."

"It's not just that. It's that I don't want to be *indebted* to them. Financially, emotionally, in any way. I want to start this relationship off with a clean slate."

She gave me a weird look. "You do realize this is a family you're joining and not a company, right? This isn't a bank merger, Waverly."

I laughed and scooped up some more ice cream. "You're right. I'm totally losing it. I think everything that's going on with Waverly's Honey Shop is clouding my judgment."

"What do you mean?"

I felt my shoulders tense.

"Paige is leaving."

"What?"

"She's moving to Nashville after she has the baby. She just told me yesterday. "

"Who's going to take over for her?"

I lifted the spoon and made an *I-have-no-idea* face. "You want a job?"

Just then, we heard a knock on the door.

"Are you expecting someone?" I asked. "Did someone slip by the Secret Service team downstairs?"

She shook her head and went to open the door. A young, sandy-haired guy with broad shoulders was standing there. He was wearing a gray hooded sweatshirt that said USA HOCKEY.

He was also holding a bottle of red wine.

He was also very cute.

"Hey, neighbor, thought you might be up for a drink." He held up the bottle.

"Hi, Morgan, thanks, but I have company." Andie looked over her shoulder at me. "Waverly, this is Morgan. He lives down the hall."

I waved from the couch. "It's nice to meet you." *She has an amazing boyfriend!* I suddenly wanted to add.

"Waverly's my best friend from home, but she lives here now," Andie said.

"Cool." Morgan nodded and stood there for a minute. When it became obvious that Andie wasn't going to invite him in to join us, he looked disappointed. "Okay, well, then I guess I'll see you Friday? We're still on for drinks, right?"

Huh? Hadn't Andie just said she was going out with work people on Friday?

"Sounds good. Bye, Morgan." She shut the door and walked back to the couch.

When she sat down next to me, I narrowed my eyes.

"What was that?"

She shrugged. "I met him the day after I moved in. He's nice."

"He also clearly has a crush on you. Stopping by with a bottle of wine? Who does that?"

She rolled her eyes. "Please. He's twenty-three."

"So?" Andie had always had a thing for younger guys, sort of like I'd always had a thing for eighties music. And stupid jokes.

She shook her head. "It's nothing. He's cute, but he's basically a trust-fund baby. Not my type."

"Did you tell him you have a boyfriend?"

"Can you give the third degree a rest, *Mom*?" She looked annoyed.

I held my hands up. "Okay, I'm sorry. I just didn't like the way he was looking at you. And you know how much I love Nick." Nick and I had been coworkers before I'd introduced him to Andie; he'd always watched out for me like a big brother, so I felt a bit protective of him in return.

"Yes, I know how much you love Nick." She picked up our empty bowls and walked into the kitchen, stomping a bit too hard on the linoleum.

An awkward silence followed while she washed the dishes. Andie and I never had awkward silences.

I flipped through a magazine until she finished up in the kitchen, the sound of the running water soothing the tension between us. Something was clearly up, but it was pointless to push before she was ready to talk about it. I just didn't know how much longer I could wait to find out.

When she returned to the living room a few minutes later, things seemed back to normal. She clapped her hands together. "Hey, I have something for you."

I looked up and grinned. "Something for me? As in a present?"

She nodded and walked toward her bedroom. "It's from Nick. I forgot to give it to you the last time you were here."

"I love him!" I yelled after her.

"I guess the feeling is mutual!" she yelled back.

She came back into the living room and tossed a small plastic bag at me.

"Ah, I just adore the wrapping paper." I reached inside and pulled out a green T-shirt that said THE HOTTEST GUYS LIVE IN SAN FRANCISCO.

I laughed. "I love it! I won't be able to wear it outside of this apartment, but I love it."

"I'll tell him you plan to sleep in it. He'll be thrilled. So, listen, I've got some work to do before I hit the hay, so I'm going to have to kick you out. I guess I'll see you on Saturday?"

I nodded. "Sure. I'll let you know where to meet me as soon I hear from Mrs. McIntyre."

"You're really calling her *Mrs. McIntyre*?"

I sighed. "You'll see."

As I rode the fancy elevator back down to Earth, I could only hope Andie was really doing work up on the forty-eighth floor.

chapter twelve

By Thursday afternoon, I was beginning to worry. Paige had already put up the job announcement for a temporary replacement, so we started interviewing right away in hopes of finding a permanent candidate. The bulk of applicants were more or less qualified for the position, but no one seemed quite right. And while I admitted to being a bit picky, I wasn't the only one holding us back from pulling the trigger. Paige agreed we had yet to find the perfect match. Everyone we met was either too corporate, or too artsy, or too inexperienced, or too weird, or too bland. It was like interviewing people in the Three Bears' house.

"We're *never* going to find someone," I groaned after yet another failed interview. The woman we'd just met, a Portland transplant with several years of retail experience, had seemed like a good fit until the end of the meeting. As we were winding things down, the conversation had turned personal, and the candidate let it slip that she had several snakes in her apartment... as *pets*. Yikes. This was on the heels of another applicant who had seemed pretty normal, until she adjusted her hair to reveal a small tattoo on her neck...a small tattoo of the Budweiser logo.

"Don't give up, Waverly. We haven't quite interviewed *everyone* in New York yet." Paige handed me my purse as I turned out the office lights.

I locked the door, and we stood waiting for the elevator. "This is like dating, you know that? I thought I was done with dating."

She laughed. "You're right. It totally *is* like dating. Can I tell you again how glad I am to be done with that for good?"

"Amen to that," I said.

We exited the building, and as we walked toward her subway stop, I interlocked my arm with hers and intentionally slowed down. She followed my lead and also relaxed her pace. We strolled in silence for a bit, both of us aware that our moments together like this were numbered. *I'm going to miss this.*

I removed my arm and held up a finger. "The thing I hate about dating is that you never know what's lurking even *one layer* below the surface. I remember making out with a guy I'd met over an entire day of drinking beers and watching college football at a sports bar. So, granted, my judgment was a little impaired, but at the time he seemed like a nice, normal guy."

She tilted her head to one side. "Don't they all seem nice and normal before we hook up with them?"

"Good point."

"So what happened?"

"So the next morning, as I was getting ready to embark on the walk of shame, I noticed that he had only one framed picture in his apartment."

"Just one?"

"Just one."

She shrugged. "That's not so weird. A lot of single guys don't put pictures up."

"Yeah, but this picture was...of *him*."

She looked over at me. "Of *him*?"

I nodded.

"You mean of *just* him?"

I nodded. "Just of him, standing on a random street or something."

"Okay, that's a little strange."

"I guess I wasn't the only one who thought he was a great guy. Apparently he did too."

Paige laughed. "I love it."

"I'd totally forgotten about him until right now. What an ass. He never even called me."

"He was probably too busy Googling himself."

"Why are guys so *weird*, Paige?"

She shrugged. "God knows. When I lived in Baltimore, I once met a guy in line for pizza after a night of drinking and dancing with my girlfriends. He was cute, so I gave him my number when he asked."

I looked at her. "I can already tell this is going to be a good story."

She smiled. "Oh yes. He called me a couple of days later and asked me out to dinner. I was drunk when I met him, so I thought it best to meet at the restaurant."

I nodded. "Usually a good call."

"Well he parked about four blocks from the restaurant, and it was on my walk there, so I met him at his car and we walked the rest of the way together."

She paused.

"And?" I said.

"And halfway there—in other words, *two* blocks from his car—he announced that he forgot his wallet in the car but that it was okay because he just wouldn't eat."

"What?"

"Yep."

"Oh my God."

"It gets better. So we got to the restaurant, and we—in other words *me*, because he would only eat the free chips and salsa—were halfway through the dinner I was paying for when he grabbed my foot and pulled it into his lap."

I covered my eyes with my free hand. "Stop."

She laughed. "I was wearing flip-flops, and he said my foot was just so sexy that he needed to suck on my toes right then."

My jaw dropped. "That might be the best dating story I've ever heard."

She took a little bow. "I knew I could one day top you."

Just as we reached her subway stop, my cell phone rang. I pulled it out of my purse and looked at the caller ID.

"It's Jake. I'll see you tomorrow?"

She adjusted her purse strap over her shoulder. "You bet. And on a more serious note, don't worry about the position, Waverly. We'll find her…or him."

I nodded and tried to look more confident than I felt. "I know."

Paige descended into the subway as I answered the phone. "Well, hello there, fiancé. How's it going in Dallas?"

"It's Dallas. It's going. Any luck with the interviews?"

I stuck my tongue out. "Unfortunately, no, and it's beginning to stress me out. I've always known Paige is amazing, Jake, but I didn't realize how hard it would be to find *other* people who are amazing. What if I can't find someone to replace her?"

"It's only been a few days, Waverly. Try not to worry so much. It will work out eventually."

I immediately felt myself relax. I knew he was right—things *would* work themselves out one way or another. Jake's calming influence on me was undeniable. After years of tearing my hair out over things I couldn't control, I was finally learning to get a grip and just go with it. A younger version of myself would have been completely freaking out about Paige's leaving. The new, mature me was only...*sort of* freaking out.

• • •

That evening I went for a run. With a wedding looming, not to mention a day of dress shopping in just a few days, I knew I had to step up my workout routine beyond walking to the coffee shop for lattes and sticky buns. I'd found a hill near the Brooklyn Bridge and hauled myself up and down it several times, wondering how much longer I could withstand this self-inflicted torture. Working out just wasn't as easy as it had been in my twenties.

In a few weeks I'll be thirty-two.

That's closing in on midthirties.

Wow.

I wasn't a kid anymore.

So much had changed.

And I'd never been so happy.

Then I thought of the dilemma I was facing with Paige and Waverly's Honey Shop, not to mention my expanded workload at *Love, Wendy.*

Ugh.

Being a grown-up certainly had its fun moments, but I was also realizing it wasn't always a bowl of ice cream.

When I was done with the final trek up the hill, I clasped my hands behind my neck to catch my breath. I walked over to the promenade and lifted one leg onto the railing to stretch my hamstring. I gazed out across the East River and smiled. I never got tired of the view. To my left was the Statue of Liberty, to the right the Brooklyn Bridge. As I switched legs, I surveyed the buildings in lower Manhattan straight across the river and wondered which one was Andie's ivory tower.

When I got back to my building, I didn't feel like going inside yet. It was a gorgeous evening, and I just wanted to enjoy the weather and the endorphins I'd whipped up during my run. Despite everything I had coming down the pike—professionally and personally—right then I truly believed I could manage it. I'd forgotten how exercise can make you feel like Superwoman.

I've got this!

I can *handle it all!*

Or maybe I was just in denial.

At that moment, I didn't care.

Instead of calling it a night, I bypassed my brownstone and continued on toward Atlantic Avenue. I admired the scenery as I strolled along the quiet streets. When I reached Atlantic, I turned around and wandered through Brooklyn Heights for a while with no real plan or destination, feeling lighthearted and free.

The sun was setting when I finally opened my apartment door nearly two hours after I'd left. I stripped off my sweaty clothes and tossed them into the hamper, then poured myself a huge glass of water and was halfway to the shower when I glanced at my left hand.

There was no ring on it.

Oh my God.

I freaked out. I bolted into the kitchen and set the glass down, threw on some clothes, and grabbed a flashlight and my keys. I had to retrace my steps before it got too dark out.

OhmyGodohmyGodohmyGodohmyGod.

I was sure I'd been wearing the ring when I left for my run. How could I have lost it?

I ran down the steps out the building door. Which way should I go? Forward or backward? I decided to start from the beginning. I set out, scanning the sidewalk at every step, trying not to cry.

• • •

An hour later I returned, empty-handed and distraught. It was dark outside now, and I was cold.

And shaking.

And crying.

And furious at myself.

How could I have done this?

What am I going to tell Jake?

I paced around the apartment. Was my memory failing me? Maybe I hadn't worn it running? I looked in my bedroom, in my jewelry box, in my nightstand, all through my dresser drawer. Under the bed.

Nothing.

Had it come loose when I took off my workout clothes? I pulled everything out of my hamper and went through it all on the floor.

Nothing.

Then I scoured the living room. Couch cushions, phone stand drawer, desk drawer, bookcase, even my mom's wooden box.

Empty.

I moved to the kitchen and checked every nook and cranny. Nothing. A search of the bathroom yielded the same result.

When there was nowhere left to look, I stood in the living room and wiped the remaining tears from my cheeks.

Once again, I stripped off my clothes and tossed them into the hamper, then took a long, hot shower, hoping to wash away the sick feeling that was engulfing me.

It didn't work.

Wrapped in my bathrobe with my hair up in a towel, I grabbed my phone. I had to call McKenna or Andie. I saw that I had two new voice mails and frowned as I sat down on the couch to listen. I knew they were probably from Jake and was crushed about what I had to tell him.

7:13 p.m.: Hi, Waverly, it's Dave. I'm at Bayard's Ale House, but don't see you. I'll order you a Blue Moon with an orange slice. I hope that's still your favorite.

7:46 p.m.: Waverly, it's Dave again. I guess we got our wires crossed, either that or I overestimated how much you appreciated all those years I paid your salary—ha, just kidding. I'm leaving now, hope to connect soon.

Oh my God.

I'd totally forgotten my plans with Davey.

I hadn't seen him in, what, three years, and I stood him up?

I leaned back into the couch and sighed. I wasn't a flake. I *hated* flakes.

First my ring, now this?

What was going on?

I tossed my phone onto the wicker chest. What had I been thinking earlier about having things under control?

I'd convinced myself I was juggling everything okay, but it was increasingly clear that I wasn't.

• • •

I barely slept that night. When my alarm went off at seven, all I wanted to do was pull my duvet over my head and spend the day in bed, feeling sorry for myself. But that wasn't going to happen. I had a taping for *Honey on Your Mind* and several interviews scheduled at Waverly's Honey Shop, so I got dressed and did my best to put the horror of the day before behind me.

Without saying exactly why I was calling, I'd left voice mails the night before for Jake, Andie, and McKenna. I didn't have it in me to face Davey on the phone, so I'd sent him an apologetic text message asking to reschedule for Monday.

I dug around in my purse before I left my apartment, hoping for a miracle. But instead of my ring, all I found was seventy-three cents in change and an empty chocolate bar wrapper.

Nice.

When I got to the set of *Honey on Your Mind*, which was at the Seaport downtown for this segment, I saw an unexpected face.

"Scotty!"

He smiled and held open his arms. "Well, hello there, kitten. How are you?" He was as attractive as ever, but he looked exhausted. I'd never seen him this way.

I hugged him a bit too tight. "What are you doing here? It's so good to see you."

"I was in the neighborhood for a meeting and thought I'd stop by to see how my favorite up-and-coming features reporter is doing."

"You really came by to see me?" I murmured into his shoulder.

"Yes, why so surprised?"

When I didn't stop hugging him after a normal amount of time, he put his hands on my shoulders and held me away from him. "Is everything okay? The last time you hugged me like that, tears were involved."

I sighed and held up my bare left hand.

"No! What happened?" He looked shocked.

I shook my head. *Waverly, you're an idiot.* "Oh gosh, no, I'm sorry. It's not *that*. I'm still engaged. I just…lost the ring." My shoulders slumped.

He made a sad face. "Oh, princess."

"I know. I suck. Who loses her engagement ring?"

"Do you know when you last had it?"

I nodded. "Right before I went running. I retraced my steps for like an hour last night. I also ransacked my entire apartment looking for it."

He touched a hand to my cheek. "I'm so sorry. I don't know what to say."

"It's okay. There's nothing *to* say. I'm a loser, and I know it."

He smiled and shook his head. "I guess you're a loser in the technical sense of the word since you lost your ring, but you're not a loser in the *true* sense. You're a loveable and adorable woman with a stand-up man who loves and adores you, and everything is going to be fine, ring or no ring. I promise."

I laughed. "Once again, you make me feel better when I'm swimming in the toilet. How do you do that?"

He lightly pinched my nose. "It's a gift."

"Can we please get together soon, Scotty? I never see you anymore. I miss you."

He smiled. "I miss you too. I'm always either on a plane or in a meeting these days. I'm sorry, kitten. I'll call you when things settle down, okay?"

"Okay." I knew he meant it, but I also knew it would probably be a long time before I heard from him. Ever since his promotion, trying to get on his calendar was harder than not eating tortilla chips at a Mexican restaurant. *Is that what happens when you make it big? You have to give up a normal life?*

I wasn't sure that was something I would ever want.

As he hustled away, I couldn't help but feel like I'd lost more than just my ring.

• • •

After Scotty zoomed off, I turned my attention to the *Honey on Your Mind* segment we were there to film. Today's topic was job interviews. Now that I was on the hunt to find a replacement for Paige, I thought it would be fun—not to mention therapeutic—to ask others about their own experiences.

Camera crew in tow, I wandered around the Seaport in search of interesting subjects. Nine out of every ten people I approached were tourists who didn't speak English, and almost everyone who did either flat-out ignored me or—without stopping—said they were too busy to stop and talk. But my persistence paid off, and eventually I got some entertaining answers to the question: *What's the strangest thing that's ever been on your mind during either side of a job interview?*

Blonde woman in crisp navy dress: "*Years ago I was being interviewed by three people at the same time for an investment banking job, and all I kept wondering was if any of them could tell I wasn't wearing any underwear.*"

Thick bald man in disheveled suit: "*I interviewed this eager beaver for a sales position once, and what kept running through my head was, If this clueless clown had any idea what a bleep* place this is to work, he'd hightail it out of here faster than the royal family can embarrass the queen."

Tall thin man, receding hairline: "*I once had to interview a partner's nephew for a junior finance position, which he was going to get no matter what I thought of him. The privileged little* bleep *listed his private* country club *on his résumé. What a spoiled* bleeping bleep."

Male hipster with ponytail, flannel shirt, skinny jeans: "*Dude, a couple weeks ago I interviewed for a designer position at a digital agency, and all I could think was,* Dude, I'm so hungover right now, I honestly may yak right here in this dude's fancy office."

Older brunette woman in stylish black pantsuit: "*I remember interviewing a college student for an entry-level accounting position and being completely distracted by the bow in her hair. Who wears a bow in her hair to an interview? What is this, a cheerleading camp? Or Kansas?*"

And this was by far my favorite:

Short perky blonde woman: "*Oh my God! Once I was interviewing for a paralegal job, and all I could think was,* Oh, *bleep.* I totally forgot the name of this *bleeping* law firm. I'm so *bleeped.*"

The crew and I agreed that I should have the editing team play Donna Summer's "She Works Hard for the Money" in the background of the final cut. After we finished, I didn't feel so bad about the difficulty I was having finding someone to run the Honey Shop. As Paige and I had surmised, the torture of job interviewing in New York City seemed to be right on a par with dating—for both interviewer *and* interviewee.

The subway was just a short walk from the Seaport, so I said good-bye to the crew and ducked into a deli to pick up lunch before heading back to Brooklyn—and real interviews. *Ugh.* The man behind the counter had just handed me my turkey and Swiss when I heard a familiar voice laughing behind me.

"Oh no you don't. Be careful, dearie," the female voice said.

I turned around and saw Andie standing there.

At her side was her cute neighbor.

"Andie?"

"Waverly! What are you doing downtown?" She gave me a hug.

I pointed out the window. "I, um, I just finished a taping at the Seaport and was grabbing a late lunch before heading back to Dumbo for some interviews."

She put her hand on the neighbor's arm. "You remember Morgan?"

I nodded at him. "Yes, of course, how are you?" *What is he doing here?*

He smiled. "Good, thanks."

Yep, he was cute. There was no denying it.

Damn.

"Waverly's a celebrity," Andie said to him. "She's on the show *Love, Wendy*. Have you ever seen it?"

Morgan shook his head. "Can you stream it to your phone?"

Andie laughed. "*TV,* Morgan. It's a *TV* show."

He nodded. "Oh, got it."

Wow, he's young, I thought.

As Morgan stepped up to the counter to order their sandwiches, Andie turned to me. "I got your message late last night. What's up? You sounded a little stressed."

I grimaced and held up my left hand.

"No!" she practically yelled. "What happened?"

I quickly shook my head. *You suck, Waverly.* You'd think I'd learn.

"No, it's not that. I…I lost my ring last night."

"What? How?"

I sighed. "I don't know. I went for a run, and when I came back, it was gone."

"Oh, Waverly, I'm so sorry." I managed a weak smile. "Thanks."

"Better to lose the ring than the guy, right?"

"I guess so."

"Is it insured?"

"I don't know, I'll have to ask Jake. I haven't told him yet."

Morgan appeared with their sandwiches, and the three of us exited the deli together. If they were having drinks tonight I wanted to ask Andie why they were already together so early in the afternoon, but there was no way to do it without coming across like a snoop, even though that's precisely what I was, of course. Besides, I had other things on my mind.

"So I'll see you tomorrow?" Andie said.

I nodded.

"I'm sorry about the ring. That really sucks."

I shrugged. "Thanks. I'll live. If Jake's mom doesn't kill me, that is." I was hit by another wave of anxiety at the prospect of facing her with my bare left hand. How would I explain myself? What kind of bride loses her engagement ring?

Andie laughed. "Okay, then, see ya soon."

"Bye, Waverly," Morgan said. "It was good to see you again."

The two of them turned in the direction of the water, and I slowly trudged toward the subway.

Before I descended into the station, I turned around and watched them walk down the street until they disappeared around a corner. It looked innocent enough, but I couldn't help but wonder if something was going on between them. Given how straightforward Andie usually was about everything, it was rattled me that she'd been giving such mixed signals about Nick.

I turned back toward stairwell and forced myself to take a step.

Let her be.

chapter thirteen

Later that afternoon we interviewed a candidate who left me wondering why I'd spent a single minute worrying about finding a replacement for Paige.

She was perfect.

Her name was Courtney, and I liked her immediately. In addition to having stellar professional qualifications, she would clearly be lots of fun to have around. I could already picture us grabbing a drink after work and talking about everything *but* work—something Paige and I had done countless times, and which I enjoyed as much if not more than the business itself.

During the interview I kept waiting for some red flag to pop up, and I could tell Paige was waiting for it too. Our brief search experience had led us to expect the worst.

But it never happened.

She was lovely.

"So, Courtney, do you have any questions for *us*?" I finally asked, thinking that might do the trick and unleash her inner craziness.

She nodded. "Yes, actually. I was wondering if you'd thought about adding a line of cocktail napkins to your product line."

"Cocktail napkins?" I said.

She nodded. "I think people would love them for parties. Can't you just picture a Honey Napkin that says something like IF I'M NOT WRAPPED AROUND A STIFF DRINK RIGHT NOW, SOMETHING IS WRONG?"

Paige and I both laughed, then exchanged a quick glance. I wanted to mouth the words *I love her*, but I thought that might be a little much.

So I waited until she left.

"I love her," I said as soon as I shut the door.

"Me too," Paige said. "I think I want to marry her."

"There *has* to be something wrong with her. You think she's bipolar? Schizophrenic?"

Paige laughed. "Don't be so cynical. Interviewing is often a numbers game, and we've certainly seen a lot of numbers. Maybe it's finally time for things to tip in our favor."

"I sure hope so. How do you think she'd get along with Tasha and Beth?"

"I bet they'd love her too. She'd probably have them babysitting her kids before the end of her first week."

As if on cue, Tasha and Beth strolled in the door. They were holding coffees and a paper bag from the bakery across the street.

"Bonjour!" Tasha announced in a French accent.

I waved them over. "You're going to make us fat with all these goodies, but let's see what's you've got."

"I'm already fat, what do I care?" Paige pulled out a chocolate croissant.

"I need fat *and* sugar today." Tasha sat down with a *thud*.

I looked up from the loot. "Oh no, what happened?"

Beth reached for a croissant. "She had a bad date last night."

I winced. "Another one?"

Tasha sighed. "I should write a book."

"Get in line," Beth said. "I might have to move back to Indiana soon."

"What happened?" Paige asked.

Tasha looked at Beth. "What do you think? Too awful to tell them?"

Beth looked at us. "It *is* sort of awful."

I smiled, then pointed to myself and to Paige. "Honey, you're talking to us. Nothing shocks us anymore."

Tasha let out a weak laugh. "This is the best place to work. *Ever.*"

"So what happened?" I asked.

She fished a croissant out of the bag. "Okay, I hung out with this guy last night, a guy I *like*, you know? And he knows it."

"He knows you like him?" I said.

She nodded.

"I hate when they know," I said.

"Me too," Beth said.

"First date?" Paige asked.

Tasha shook her head. "It's complicated. We've been friends for a while, and sometimes we hook up, but other times we just hang out as friends."

I raised my hand. "Been there."

Paige raised her hand. "Done that."

Tasha sighed. "I hate it. I never know how it's going to go when we're together. It's like he has all the control." She tore off a piece of her croissant. "So I *know* I shouldn't hook up with him, or that I shouldn't have any expectations when we do, but I can't help myself. It's like he has a spell over me."

We all nodded but didn't speak, knowing she wasn't done.

"So anyway, we ended up hooking up last night, and afterward it was sort of late, like one o'clock, so I assumed I'd just spend the night."

Paige looked at Beth. "I'm afraid to hear where this is going," she whispered.

"I hate him," Beth whispered back. She looked...angry.

Tasha sighed. "So I was literally naked in his bed, *at one o'clock in the morning*, and he got up to get a glass of water. I could hear him moving around the kitchen a bit, and then he came back into the bedroom."

She paused for a moment, and we stared at her.

"And you know what he said?" Her voice cracked a little.

I made a pained face. "I don't think I want to know."

Beth put her hand on Tasha's arm. "He's horrible, Tash."

Tasha smiled at her. "Thanks." Then she looked at me and Paige and took a deep breath. "When he came back into the bedroom, he said...'I'm going to go meet a friend for a drink.'"

"At one o'clock in the morning?" I said.

Tasha nodded.

"That might be the meanest thing I've ever heard," Paige said.

"I think I might have to agree," I said.

Tasha set her croissant down and put her hands in her face. "I'm so embarrassed."

"*He's* the one who should be embarrassed," Paige said. "What an asshole."

For a moment I thought Tasha might start crying, but she composed herself and continued the story. "I couldn't even say anything, because I knew if I did, he'd make me out to be the crazy girl, you know?"

We all nodded.

We all knew.

She sighed. "So I kept my mouth shut and got dressed, and then we left his building together. He put me in a cab, gave me a kiss, and walked away, and that was that. I couldn't believe it."

Beth shook her head. "It's his loss, Tash."

"I'm an idiot," Tasha said.

I put my hand on her shoulder. "Honey, *he's* the idiot. You know what? This has just given me an idea for a new Honey Tee."

She looked at me. "Really? What would it say?"

I stood up and walked over to our whiteboard, then picked up a big purple marker. On the board I wrote one sentence.

REAL MEN STAY THE NIGHT.

They gave me a standing ovation.

• • •

That evening I finally connected with Jake on the phone. I knew there was no sense in hiding the bad news about my ring, so I told him the whole story. When I finished, I sighed and flopped backward on my bed, relieved to have it out there yet bracing myself for his reaction.

"I'm so sorry, Jake. I can't believe this happened."

"It's okay, we can get you another ring. I insured it."

"You're not upset?"

"It's just a ring. Why would I get upset?"

I sat up and squinted into the phone. "Do you really work for the NBA? Are you sure the reason you're away so much isn't because you have a wife and like five kids stashed away somewhere? There must be *something* wrong with you."

"Sorry to disappoint. So are you excited for the big shopping trip with Ava?"

I coughed. "*Excited* would not be high up on my list of adjectives to describe how I'm feeling about it."

"What time are you meeting her?"

"Eight. It may still be dark out."

"I'm sorry I can't be there."

"It's okay, it's not like you could come dress shopping with us anyway. Andie's going to tag along to provide emotional support."

"That's nice of her. How's she liking New York so far?"

"She loves it. She's out every night like the moon. Unlike some of us less fortunate individuals, she doesn't need a lot of sleep, so she can do happy hour, dinner, drinks, and God knows what else every day of the week and not suffer for it like a normal person. I hate her for that."

"I want to see that apartment of hers. Maybe we can go over there for a drink next week? I have Thursday and Friday off."

"Sure, I'll talk to her. You'll love it. Blanco and Whitey are such nice pups."

"She brought dogs with her?"

"Not exactly. So, hey, I told you the lost part of my day, but I didn't tell you the found part."

"English, please?"

"I mean I *lost* my ring, but I *found* something else."

"And that would be…"

"A replacement for Paige!"

"Really? That's great news. Who is it?"

"Her name is Courtney, and she's amazing. Smart, experienced, friendly, potential friend material, the whole package."

"No outstanding arrest warrants?"

"Nope. I had the interns call her references *and* do their Internet magic, and nothing shady turned up. Glowing reviews all around. Can you believe it?"

"When does she start?"

I shook my head. "I haven't offered her the job yet. We're going to bring her back in for one more round so she can meet Beth and Tasha, just to make sure the chemistry is good. If they don't feel comfortable enough with her to share their dating woes, we'll have a problem. But it's more of a formality than anything, because I know they'll love her."

"Are you running a business over there or a sorority house?"

I laughed. "Hey now, Waverly's Honey Shop is a special kind of operation. It's not *all* about profits. So you get home on Sunday?"

"Yep, should be back in Brooklyn by six."

"Date night sound good? Maybe dinner at Armando's?"

"I'm counting down the hours."

"Me too."

chapter fourteen

Early the next morning I rode the R train to the corner of Central Park South and Fifth Avenue, where the über-deluxe Plaza Hotel was located. As I approached the grandiose building to meet Jake's mom for breakfast, I was flooded with memories of the one time I'd stayed there as a guest. It had been three years ago, when I'd been a contestant—albeit a reluctant one—in a charity singles auction. For reasons I will never understand, but for which I will always be grateful, Jake decided to keep bidding on a date with me until he won.

Thank God.

I'd met him at a trade show in Atlanta nearly a year earlier, but we'd never been in the same city long enough to share more than an awkward conversation. Or rather, awkward on *my* end. Jake, damn him, didn't seem to have an awkward bone in his body.

I gazed at the hotel entrance and wondered what my life would be like now had I not agreed to participate in the auction. Would we not have started dating? Or would we have found another way to share that first kiss? Was it destiny? Or just luck?

I wasn't sure if I believed in luck *or* destiny. But if Jake was my destiny, I was certainly lucky.

I nodded in greeting to the immaculately dressed doorman in top hat and tails outside the front doors. A horse and hansom cab idled off to one side of the entrance. I wondered what time the first carriage ride into Central Park would happen. In New York City, it was never too late, and never too early, for anything.

At 7:58, I walked through the foyer into the timeless Palm Court restaurant, which I'd first been introduced to back in high school on the pages of *The Great Gatsby*. The thought of Fitzgerald's book reminded me of how I'd felt at the engagement party at Jake's parents' house—completely out of my element. I hoped I wouldn't always feel this way around his parents, but I wasn't too optimistic.

"May I help you, miss?" A friendly hostess smiled at me.

I smoothed my hands over my plain black dress and smiled at her. "I'm supposed to meet someone here."

"Are you a guest at the hotel?"

"No, but she is. The name's McIntyre."

She looked at her list. "Ah yes, we have it right here, a table for three. Would you like me to show you to your table?"

A table for three?

"Um, sure."

I followed her through the restaurant, wondering who could possibly be joining us. Maybe Mr. McIntyre? That would be a welcome surprise.

I took a seat and had just unfolded my napkin across my lap when I heard Mrs. McIntyre.

"Waverly, hello." Though her voice was pleasant and warm, she still made me nervous.

I placed the napkin on the table and stood up a bit too fast. "Hi, Mrs. McIntyre." Without thinking, I gave her a hug, which she didn't quite return.

Well done, Waverly.

After completing our awkward, one-sided embrace, she gestured to the woman standing next to her.

"Waverly, you remember my best friend, Bee Worthington?"

I tried to mask the look of shock that suddenly appeared on my face.

Holly's mother?

Inviting her to our engagement party was one thing. But to shop for my wedding dress?

How awkward is this?

I swallowed. "Oh yes, of course. It's nice to see you again, Mrs. Worthington. How are you?"

She smiled and put her hand on my arm. "*Please*, call me Bee. And I'm wonderful. I just love New York in the fall, don't you? It's so crisp and clear this time of year. I'm so glad I decided to join Ava for this fun weekend."

As we sat down, a waiter appeared with a sterling silver carafe. He poured us each a steaming cup of coffee, then disappeared to let us peruse the menu. I stirred cream and sugar into my coffee and tried to act normal. Did Holly know her mom was in New York, *with Jake's fiancée*, to look at wedding dresses?

"Um, how was your flight?" I asked.

"Nothing special. No turbulence, thank God for that." Jake's mom put a hand over her heart.

"You hate turbulence?" I asked.

Her eyes got big. "Oh yes, scares me to death."

I smiled and relaxed a little bit. "Me too." Fear of turbulence was an odd thing to bond over, but I was grateful for anything we had in common other than her son.

Mrs. Worthington picked up her coffee cup. "We had dinner with a friend of mine at the Metropolitan Club last night. It was wonderful."

"The Metropolitan Club?" I'd never heard of it.

"Yes, you don't know it?" Jake's mom looked surprised. "It's right across the street from here."

I shook my head. "What type of food do they serve?"

They both laughed and exchanged a knowing look. "It's not just a restaurant, my dear, it's a *club*," Mrs. McIntyre said.

"Oh, you mean like a country club?"

"Something like that," Mrs. Worthington said.

I tried to nod knowingly, but I had no idea what she meant. The only time I'd ever been to a real "country club" was for other people's weddings, McKenna's included. *Oh, how I wish Mackie were here to help me navigate these awkward waters.*

How was it that I was the one who lived and worked in New York, but they were making *me* feel like a country bumpkin?

Mercifully the waiter appeared to take our order, which temporarily stopped the bleeding. I opted for the Belgian waffle, hoping a mound of sweet whipped cream might soothe my anxiety.

After he left, Mrs. McIntyre turned to me with a look of concern.

"Waverly, what happened to your engagement ring?"

I froze. How had she already noticed that? My hand was currently in my lap.

"Um..." I struggled to reply.

I wanted to tell the truth. I really, really did.

They both raised their eyebrows, waiting for an answer.

Tell the truth, Waverly!

You can do it!

"Um...it's getting sized," I said quietly.

Jake's mom put her hands together. "Oh, thank goodness, you had me scared for a moment there."

"Me too," Mrs. Worthington said. "It's never a good story when a woman stops wearing her ring *before* the wedding. After? Well that's another story." She laughed, and I wondered what that meant. She wore an enormous ring on her left hand, but I couldn't tell if it was a wedding ring or just a big chunk of gold.

I had no idea what to say next, so I took a huge sip of my water and forced a smile. "Would you excuse me for a moment? I just want to run to the ladies' room." I stood up and gently placed my napkin on my seat, hoping that was the proper etiquette.

On the way to the restroom, I pulled out my phone and sent Andie a quick text.

Wake up! I need you.

• • •

"I need to get out of here," Andie whispered.

"You can't leave me," I whispered back.

"She's exactly like my mom."

"Really?"

"*Yes.* And if you hadn't noticed, I'm finally living three thousand miles away from my mom, yet it's like she's right here with me."

"How do you think *I* feel? Do you *see* what I'm wearing right now? I look like a swan." I held my arms out.

Andie and I were huddled in an enormous dressing room at a place called Mark Ingram Atelier on Fifty-fifth and Park. An *atelier*, for God's sake. I had no business being in an *atelier*. Jake's mom and Mrs. Worthington were waiting for me to try on yet another ornate dress they'd selected. Each one seemed more elaborate (and expensive) than the one before, and further away from the simple design I'd imagined wearing. In my head I'd pictured something similar to a silky nightgown with spaghetti straps—only a bit more graceful.

These dresses were hardly that.

Epaulettes with bows.

Buttons wrapped in lace.

Embroidered butterflies.

Poufy hoopskirts covered in tulle and taffeta.

Miles of trains.

The entire store was like a Disney wardrobe chest, with everything probably sewn by tiny fairies.

"I should have brought a flask in my purse," Andie said.

I laughed. "Shhh, they'll hear you."

She shrugged. "Maybe they need to. They suck."

"Andie!" I whispered.

"What? I'm just speaking the truth. Who picks out wedding dresses without first asking the bride what *she* wants? It's just rude."

I sighed. "I know. But it's Jake's mom, and this is clearly important to her, so I'm sort of walking a tightrope here. And to be fair, she did ask. I just told her I'd be up for anything because I thought it would be easier that way."

"And bringing along his ex-girlfriend's mother? That's crazy-inappropriate."

I bit my lip. "I know, but they're best friends. And Jake swears she harbors no hope of their getting back together. He really likes her, actually."

She crossed her hands in front of her chest. "You're a better person than I am. If I were you, I'd be giving someone a piece of my mind about now."

"I just don't want to rock the boat. In a few months she's going to be my mother-in-law, and I really want to begin our relationship on the right foot. *You're* the one who told me this wasn't a business merger, remember?"

"I know, I know." She nodded toward the dressing room door. "Let's just get this over with so we can get out of here. I'm starving and cranky."

"You're still coming to the show tonight, right? And dinner?" I made a hopeful face.

She sighed. "Yes, yes, I'm still coming. But I need a snack soon, or I'm not going to make it."

"You know how eternally grateful I am, right?"

"I know. You totally owe me for this."

I nodded. "Big-time."

I poked my head outside the dressing room. "Mrs. McIntyre?"

"Yes, dear?"

"Um, do you think we could get something to eat?"

She jumped up. "Of course! I'll run out and get us some snacks. What would you like? Sandwiches? Cookies? Chips? Fruit? I'm happy to get anything you like." Her eyes shone with enthusiasm.

I looked at Andie and raised my eyebrows. "You heard that? What do you want?"

"Food," she said.

I laughed and looked back at Jake's mom. "Anything will do, thanks so much."

She reached for her purse. "I'll be right back. Bee, you'll hold down the fort here?"

Bee gave the thumbs-up sign. "Will do."

Mrs. McIntyre trotted away. Just as I was about to shut the dressing room door, Bee stood up and walked over to me.

"Waverly, dear?"

"Yes?"

She smiled. "I just want you to know how much I appreciate how truly gracious you've been to me since we met. I know it must be awkward, given my daughter's history with Jake."

I opened my mouth to reply, but I was so stunned that what came out was...nothing.

She put her hand on my shoulder. "You're a class act, and Jake is lucky to have you."

I smiled. "Thanks, Mrs. Worthington."

She winked. "Please, *please*, call me Bee. All my friends call me Bee. Now, if you'll excuse me, I'm going to pee out some of the coffee I've been drinking before it's too late and I cause a scene."

I laughed as she darted out of the room. When she was gone I shut the dressing room door and looked at Andie.

"You get what I'm dealing with here?"

She shrugged. "Okay, maybe I was wrong about her."

"Which one?"

She shrugged again. "Both."

• • •

Several fancy bridal boutiques, an expensive dinner, and one Broadway show later, I was finally alone in my apartment. I felt like I'd put in two full days at *Love, Wendy*, plus a couple at Waverly's Honey Shop, maybe with a red-eye flight in between—all while feeling slightly on edge.

I was exhausted.

Thank God the day was over.

Jake's mom and Bee were flying back to Florida early the next afternoon. They were meeting up with Bee's friend for brunch the next morning, and then getting their nails done at some expensive salon I'd never heard of, so I was off the hook as hostess.

I opened the hamper and pulled off my dress, the only one I'd worn all day that cost less than a small car. I'd lost track of how many wedding gowns I'd tried on, but at some point in the late afternoon Mrs. McIntyre and Bee had both squealed with delight at one of them. Andie and I both knew it wasn't my style, but they were clearly thrilled, and it was pretty enough. I simply couldn't face the idea of trying on another embroidered taffeta-lace-tulle powder-puff of a dress, so I decided to go with it. I didn't even look at the price tag before Mrs. McIntyre rushed off to pay for it. To be honest, I was afraid to know.

I changed into a tank top and shorts, then shuffled into the bathroom. I looked at my reflection in the bathroom mirror and could see the strain of the day on my face.

First the wedding venue.

Now the dress.

How had I let this happen?

I thought about what Jake's dad had said at the engagement party.

I know Ava can be a bit much sometimes, but her heart is in the right place.

I closed my eyes and focused on that.

She means well, Waverly. You know she does.

There was no getting around it—she was now a part of my life. I wanted to impress her. I wanted her to like me. I wanted our relationship to be a good one, even if I wasn't her first choice for her son, even though I would never be...Holly.

I just wished I knew how to make all that happen without letting her take over our lives.

I wanted to try to sort it all out in my mind, but exhaustion trumped thought, and I had barely finished brushing my teeth before I fell asleep.

chapter fifteen

Courtney came back Monday for a second interview. The plan was for her to go over the technical details of the job with Paige, then have a casual lunch with Tasha and Beth. I had morning meetings at NBC, but I dropped by the office in the afternoon to see how everything had gone.

I walked through the door with a hopeful expression on my face. "Well?"

Beth and Tasha were sitting at the conference room table, and Paige was in her office. When they saw me, all three of them dropped what they were doing and converged in the reception area.

"Love her," Tasha said.

Beth nodded. "Me too. She's just like you guys."

Paige waddled over. "Just like what guys?"

Beth pointed to me and then to Paige. "*You* guys."

I looked at her. "In what way?"

"I mean, she's older, but you wouldn't know it. She's like the kind of person we could hang out with after work, you know?"

Paige and I looked at each other. "I will try to take that as a compliment," I said with a laugh.

Tasha nodded. "Oh, it definitely is."

"Plus she's super smart. You can just tell," Beth said.

Paige interlaced her fingers over her belly. "She was even more impressive today than when we first met her. She really knows her stuff. I could learn a few things from her."

I was beyond relieved. "So I should offer her the job?"

"Yes!" Tasha and Beth said at the same time.

I looked at Paige. "Yes?"

She nodded and smiled. "Without question."

I exhaled. "Great. I'll call her tonight."

• • •

A couple hours later my phone rang as I was leaving my apartment. I felt tempted to answer it, but I was about to go for a run, and I'd learned from experience that if I stalled my momentum before I'd even *started* my workout, there was a good chance it would never get going again. So I shut the door behind me, then trotted down the stairs and jogged toward the hill. Jake was coming over later, so as I passed by Grimaldi's famous pizzeria, I decided we should have dinner there after I called Courtney. It was definitely an evening to celebrate.

I got home around seven thirty, which gave me a half hour before Jake came over. I hopped in the shower. As the hot water ran over me, I closed my eyes and made a mental list of all the things I had to accomplish over the next few days. The burden of finding a replacement for Paige was gone, thank God, but the list was still pretty long. One looming item was to come up with a list of topics for future *Honey on Your Mind* segments.

A list within a list, great.

After I was done showering, I wrapped my hair in a towel and sat down on the couch to call Courtney. I had one voice mail, from just before I left for my run.

6:41 p.m.: *Bryson, it's Dave. Are we still on for a drink tonight? Say seven thirty? I don't want to get stood up again, so I thought I'd call to confirm this time…ha. Let me know.*

I pressed my free palm over my eyes.
Oh no.
I hadn't stood Davey up again, had I? I knew I'd asked to reschedule for Monday, but he'd never replied, so I figured that meant he couldn't make it. It had seemed like a logical conclusion—until now.

We had our wires completely crossed.

I called him back right away but got his voice mail.

"Davey, hi, I just heard your message and am soooo sorry. I didn't think we had plans for tonight because I didn't get a return text from you. Or maybe I just didn't see it? Who knows, because apparently I'm losing my mind. Please call me back so we can try again. Again, I'm so sorry. By the way, um, this is Waverly. Thanks, bye."

I set the phone down and shook my head.
You are pathetic.
I decided to get dressed and dry my hair before calling Courtney. That would give me time to compose myself and put on a professional face, or voice. How could I have screwed up meeting with Davey *twice*?

It was almost eight when I finally sat down to make the call. I'd just dialed her number when the sound of a knock on my door startled me. It had to be Jake. With the sound of Courtney's phone ringing in my ear, I trotted to the front door and opened it.

Jake was standing there, holding a bouquet of flowers.

I wanted to hug him, but instead I pointed to my phone and put a finger over my lips. Then I mouthed the words *I'm sorry.*

He smiled and gestured to the kitchen, then mouthed the word *vase*? I nodded and hurried to the couch just as Courtney answered the phone.

"Hello?"

"Hi, Courtney, is that you?"

"Yes."

"Hi, it's Waverly Bryson, um, from Waverly's Honey Shop?" I pressed my hand against my forehead. *Get it together.*

"Waverly, hi. How are you?" Her voice was soothing and kind, which helped me relax a little. I could hear Jake turn on the faucet in the kitchen.

"I'm good, thanks. I heard you met the rest of our little team today."

"Yes, Tasha and Beth. They were lovely."

"Well they loved *you*, that's for sure."

"Really? I'm glad to hear it."

"Paige too. Actually all of us. We all loved you, um, *love* you." For a moment I wondered if professing your love to a prospective employee was wildly inappropriate, but I quickly moved on. "So, um, well, we've all discussed it, and we'd love to offer you the position."

"Really?"

"Yes, if you'd like to take it. We think you'd be perfect." I sat up straighter in an effort to project more authority into my voice.

She didn't reply for a moment, so I kept talking.

"I know Paige is going to be hard to replace, but she and I are both convinced that if anyone can do it, you can."

"Thanks, Waverly. I can tell Paige is great, so I appreciate that."

"So…what do you think?" I bit my lip.

She hesitated for a moment, and I held my breath.

"I'm sorry, Waverly, but I accepted another offer this afternoon."

My heart sank.

No!

"Oh," I said, my professional demeanor melting away. From the corner of my eye, I could see Jake lingering in the kitchen, giving me space. "Did I wait too long to call you?"

"No, it's not that at all. I think you guys are great, but the other position is with a larger company that can offer me better benefits, more vacation, on-site child care, things that I just couldn't turn down."

"Oh," I said softly.

"I'm sorry, Waverly."

"It's okay, I understand." I felt like I'd just been turned down by a boy I'd asked to the Sadie Hawkins dance. In all the time that we'd been searching for the right person, it had never occurred to me that the candidate I wanted wouldn't want me back.

"I'm sure you'll find someone great," she said.

I smiled weakly into the phone. *If you only knew how hard it was to find you.*

Neither of us spoke for a moment, and then she mercifully pulled the plug.

"Well, thanks again for calling, Waverly. You take care, okay?"

"You too. Bye, Courtney."

I hung up the phone, then looked over at Jake without speaking.

"I'm sorry," he said with a sympathetic smile.

I put my face in my hands, and before I even realized it, I was crying.

• • •

"There has to be someone in New York City who could do what Paige does," Jake said.

I picked up a piece of pizza. "I wish I believed that."

He looked around the restaurant. "Cheer up. You've been talking about this place for months, and now we're finally eating here together. Small victories, right?" We'd finally made it to Grimaldi's.

I half laughed. "I guess so."

"And speaking of small victories, that hill you've been running looks like a great workout."

I took a bite and raised my eyebrows. "For *you*, probably not. For me, definitely."

"Come on, give yourself a little credit."

I sighed and set the pizza down. "I'm sorry, I'm just feeling… sorry for myself. Two hours ago I was on top of the world, and now I'm in the gutter." I picked up a napkin and slowly tore it into little pieces. "Now I know what people mean when they describe something as being an emotional roller coaster."

"A roller coaster would be pretty boring if it never went downhill, right?"

I looked up at him. "What?"

He pointed out the window. "What would be the point of running up that hill if it weren't hard?"

"What are you talking about?"

"I'm talking about *life*, Waverly. This is what happens in life. Sometimes things don't go the way you thought they would, and it's not fun, but you just have to keep going anyway."

I sighed and kept making napkin bits. "I know."

"Do you?"

I raised my gaze again. "Do I?"

"Yes, *do* you know? It's hard watching you beat yourself up for things that you have no control over."

I looked at his beautiful blue eyes, and for a moment I saw myself through them. Whiny, weak, defeated.

It wasn't a pretty sight.

"You're right. I'm sorry, Jake. I need to snap out of it."

"Don't apologize to me, Waverly. But you *do* need to snap out of it." He smiled and reached a hand over mine. "It's just a bump in the road. A very long road."

I interlaced my hand with his. "You're right. You're *always* right, damn you."

"Of course I'm not *always* right, but trust me—this is just a tiny speed bump. You'll be past it in no time."

I pulled my hand away and picked up a piece of pizza. "I haven't even told you everything yet. I also flaked on Davey again tonight."

"Again? Why?"

"Total communication breakdown. He thought we were getting together for a drink because I'd suggested tonight, and I thought we weren't getting together because he hadn't confirmed. But however you slice it, I look like a flake."

"So what's he doing in New York anyway?"

"His wife's in school."

"I remember you mentioned that, but what about him? Where's he working?"

I shrugged and swallowed a bite of pizza. "I have no idea, because I still haven't seen him. I imagine he's looking for a jo—"

The word was halfway out of my mouth before the lightbulb in my head went off.

"Oh my God! I should see if Davey can help me out until I find someone. He'd be amazing!"

Jake tapped a finger to his temple. "There's the girl I love."

I narrowed my eyes. "Wait a minute. How long have you been thinking that?"

"Not long. Longer than *you*, but not long."

I laughed. "Damn you, Jake McIntyre."

"Maybe those casablancas I brought you tonight will be appropriate after all."

"Is that what they were?" I'd been too distracted by the Courtney situation to ask what the flowers were called, much less if they stood for anything.

He nodded. "Casablancas mean celebration."

"I have no idea how you know that, but I like it."

He reached across the table and wiped a bit of pizza sauce off my chin. "Me too. I was thinking we could use them in our wedding, if you like that idea."

"You're declaring a preference for something that has to do with our wedding? What's gotten into you?"

He coughed. "I must be coming down with something."

After dinner, I left Davey a message on the walk home.

"Hey, it's me again, um, Waverly. I'm so sorry for messing up tonight, I'm sort of a bit scattered these days, but what's new, right? Anyhow, um, I'd love to get together with you as soon as possible. And, um, I actually have something important to talk to you about, so please let me know when you're free. Okay, then, well, thanks, okay, bye."

I hung up and looked at Jake. "Do you think I'll ever get better at leaving voice mails?"

He pointed up the hill. "I'm not answering that. Want a piggyback ride?"

I grinned and prepared to jump on his back. "What a perfect way to change the subject."

chapter sixteen

Davey didn't call me back all week.

By Friday I'd left him two more voice mails and sent him a couple of texts. Nothing.

Where is he?

Is he really that annoyed with me?

I was beginning to feel like a stalker.

Paige's baby was inching closer to the oven door, and I was getting desperate.

I'd just finished taping a segment for *Honey on Your Mind* on the steps of the New York Public Library in Midtown when I felt my phone buzz inside my purse. I rushed to answer it, hoping it would be Davey. No luck.

I stiffened, then forced a smile into the phone.

"Hi, Mrs. McIntyre."

"Waverly, hello. How are you today?"

I figured there was no reason to get into my overwhelmed state of mind, so I lied.

"I'm doing well, thanks. Um, what's up?"

"I'm calling because I'd like to throw you a bridal shower."

I stopped walking.

"Really?" *How nice of her.*

"Of course, dear. You're going to be my daughter-in-law soon. The least I can do is throw you a proper shower." I knew that "proper" was a euphemism for "fancy."

You mean in addition to throwing me a fancy wedding, buying me a fancy dress, and paying for a fancy honeymoon?

I was…touched.

"Wow, um, that's really nice of you, Mrs. McIntyre. Thanks."

"My friends have already been asking about it, so I'd like to get it on the calendar soon. I was thinking the second weekend in October. Would that work for you?"

I flinched. That was my birthday weekend.

I hesitated, not sure what to say.

"Waverly?"

Just say no, Waverly.

You can do it!

"Waverly, dear, are you there?"

I swallowed and finally answered. "Um, well, um, that's actually my birthday weekend." I could barely get the words out but was proud that I had. *Why am I so afraid of her?*

"Oh gosh, then, even more reason to celebrate."

Huh?

My subtle approach was clearly not working.

Just tell her you can't do it, Waverly!

Say you already have plans that weekend!

I hesitated.

Just say it!

I bit my lip.

"Um, okay, sure, that weekend should work," I heard myself say.

Caved again.

"Wonderful. We'll do it that Saturday afternoon. Where are you registered?"

As if we had even thought about registering.

I pressed a palm against my forehead. "Um, we haven't done that yet."

"You haven't registered?" She sounded horrified.

"Not yet. I've…I've been really busy…at work."

"Oh…"

I winced. Even though her friends watched *Love, Wendy*, I knew it bothered her that my career was so important to me.

"But we'll do it right away. I promise, Mrs. McIntyre."

"Yes, yes, please do so I can include it in the invitation. And please let me know when you've booked your flight. I'll pick you up at the airport, of course."

"Okay, thanks."

"It will be lovely, just lovely. While you're down here, we can also pick out the dresses for the attendants. Have you decided how many you plan to have yet?"

"You mean bridesmaids?"

"Yes, dear, have you chosen them?"

"Um, I, um, sort of." I already knew McKenna couldn't be there. That left Andie, who was going to kill me when I told her I'd changed my mind about that too.

"Well, you should do it quite soon. When your attendants don't live in the same city, coordinating fittings and alterations can take much longer than you might think. I imagine you'll be having some friends from San Francisco in the bridal party?"

"Um, yes, of course." *Friend, singular.*

"If any of them would like to come to the shower, they're more than welcome. It would be so nice to meet them." She sounded so sincere, and I hated myself for all the evil thoughts running through my head. Given how I clammed up every time I was around her, how could she know that all I *really* wanted was an intimate wedding with no attendants, no shower, no fuss?

"Okay, thanks, Mrs. McIntyre, I'll be sure to ask them." *Her.*

"I'm happy to pay for their hotel. And yours too, of course. Just give me a number when you know how many will be coming. I'll book you rooms at the Jupiter Beach Resort."

"Thanks, Mrs. McIntyre. I'll let you know."

"Super. It will be a beautiful weekend."

I hung up the phone and sighed. *What did I just agree to?*

I stared at my phone for a moment, then sent Jake a text.

Yo, husband-to-be. We need to register. Yesterday.

Then I dialed Andie's new work number.

She answered on the second ring. "Andrea Barnett."

"Hey, it's me."

As usual when I called her at the office, *Andrea's* voice rose a few octaves, and she became Andie. "Oh, hey, I'm just about to run into a meeting. What's up?"

"Um, how do you feel about a weekend in Florida?"

"You mean for your glam wedding? You already know how I feel about that. Not a fan."

"Um, no, for my birthday."

"You want to spend your birthday in Florida?"

"Actually, it's not for my birthday. It's for a bridal shower."

"A shower?"

When I didn't reply, she kept talking. "Let me guess. Jake's mom wants to throw you an extravagant shower to impress her rich friends, on your *birthday weekend* no less, and you caved and agreed, and now you want me to go so you won't have to deal with that scene alone. Am I right?"

I could feel my cheeks get hot. "Perhaps."

She sighed. "Do you realize how pathetic that is?"

"Perhaps."

"It's going to be a bitch walking down the aisle in February…
you know, without a *spine*."

I laughed. "Come on, Andie, please? She'll put us up at a nice
hotel. Pretty please?" I made a hopeful face into the phone. "I
can't face it all by myself."

"Okay, fine, whatever. It's beyond lame, but it's your life."

I smiled and exhaled. "You have no idea how much it will
mean to me to have you there."

"I lived with my mother for eighteen years. Believe me, I
know."

I laughed. "Have I told you lately that I love you?"

"That's the name of a song, Waverly."

"Oops. I believe you're right."

"Listen, I've really got to go to this meeting. I'll call you later,
okay?"

"Deal."

When I hung up the phone, I felt a wave of relief wash over
me.

Then I noticed my left hand, which was still empty.

Uh-oh.

I wouldn't have to face the shower by myself, but how was I
going to face it without my engagement ring?

I thought about calling my dad.

Ever since Jake had mentioned their conversation about the
cut and setting of my diamond, I'd been wondering what had
happened to my mom's engagement ring.

Does Dad still have it?

Maybe I could wear it?

The more I thought about it, the more I liked the idea. Not
only would it solve my current problem, but it would connect me
to my mother in a way I'd never been before. A very cool way.

And if her ring was even half as beautiful as the one Jake had given me, I knew I'd love it. Actually, I knew I'd love it no matter *what* it looked like. I imagined it was probably much smaller than the one I'd lost, but I didn't care.

I looked at my hand again.

My dad was remarried now, and Betty had her own ring.

Why not?

I decided to call him.

He and Betty had recently opened a small café out in Sacramento. They'd named it Waverly's Place, partly to thank me for the money I'd sent my dad during the years that he'd been struggling financially, and partly to let me know I'd always have a home out there. Not that I could ever see myself living in Sacramento again, but I was touched by the gesture.

I dialed the phone.

A female voice answered. "Waverly's Place. How may I help you?"

"Betty, is that you?"

"Yes indeed. Waverly?" She sounded thrilled. No matter how busy she was when I called, Betty always sounded thrilled, and I loved her for it.

"Yep it's me. How are you? How are things at the café?"

"I'm doing just fine, and so is Waverly's Place, thanks so much for asking. Knock on wood, but we've been slowly building a solid business out here. Who would have thought?" She laughed.

"*I* would have thought," I said. "I'm glad to hear it's going well."

"Enough about us. February will be here before you know it. Your dad and I are just tickled for the wedding. Neither of us has ever been to Florida. Did you know I've never even been out of California?"

She'd never been out of California? I wondered how she'd get along with Jake's mom, who left the state just to go shopping.

"It will be wonderful to see you there. Um, is my dad around? I need to ask him something."

"Of course, he's in the kitchen. I'll get him. You take care now, hon."

I could hear voices in the background, then footsteps, and then my dad got on the line.

"Well, hello there, baby."

"Hi, Dad." I'd long given up trying to get him to stop calling me that, but I still hated it. "Is this a bad time to talk?"

"Are you okay? Betty said you needed to ask me something."

"I'm fine. But, yes, I wanted…to ask you a question."

"Sure thing."

I swallowed. "Um, I was wondering about Mom's engagement ring."

Silence.

"Dad?"

"Yeah, baby. What about it?"

"I, um…I was wondering if maybe I could wear it?"

"You want to wear your mom's engagement ring?"

"Yes."

"But why? Didn't Jake get you a ring? Did he tell you he and I talked about it?"

I nodded. "Yes, he did buy me one, and yes, he did tell me that. But…"

"But what?"

I sighed. "I lost it, Dad."

"You lost your ring?"

"Yes."

"Oh, baby, I'm so sorry to hear that."

"Thanks. I feel *awful* about it, but it is what it is. Jake said he'd buy me a new one, but I was thinking it would be really neat to wear Mom's. I mean, if you're okay with it. I think it would pretty special, actually." I was getting more and more excited about the idea.

I waited for his reply.

He sighed.

"I'm embarrassed to have to tell you this, Waverly, but I sold the ring years ago."

What?

"You sold it?"

"I had to."

"But why?"

He sighed again. "To pay off a big gambling debt."

I closed my eyes and pressed a palm against my forehead.

Oh.

"I'm sorry to let you down, baby."

"It's okay, Dad."

"You know all that's behind me now, right?"

I slowly opened my eyes. "I know."

"I wish I had a different answer for you."

"It's all right, I understand."

"Listen, I hate to run, but the lunch rush is about to start, and I've really got to go."

"Okay," I said softly.

"You take care, okay, kiddo?"

"Thanks, Dad."

I hung up the phone and tried not to cry.

chapter seventeen

Paige's baby, damn him, arrived a week early.

He was super cute, though.

They named him Graham.

"How bad did it hurt?" Tasha asked Paige. She looked scared out of her mind.

Paige offered a weary smile from her hospital bed. "You look freaked out enough as it is, so I'm not going to answer that." She was cradling her new son, all seven pounds of him, in her arms.

"He's so tiny and helpless." Beth reached for Graham's little fingers. "Aren't you afraid you won't know how to take care of him?"

I laughed and pointed at her. "*That's* why you're too young to get married, Beth."

"I'm never getting married," Tasha said.

I turned my head and looked at her. "Didn't we just have this conversation last week? I feel like we just had this conversation."

Beth rolled her eyes. "We have it every week."

Paige laughed. "I'm going to miss this conversation."

"We're going to miss *you*." I put my hand on her arm. "You have no idea how much."

Tasha and Beth went in search of a vending machine, and when they were out of earshot, Paige reached up from the bed and took my hand, suddenly serious. "I'm so sorry we weren't able to find a replacement for me before the baby came. I was hoping he'd be late, but the little guy had other plans."

I waved a hand in front of me. "It's not your fault. God knows how hard we both worked to find someone. Apparently you are simply irreplaceable."

She smiled. "Any leads since I went into labor?" Paige had been at the office, diligently weeding through résumés, when the first pains struck.

I laughed and put my hand on her forehead. "Given that that was less than twenty-four hours ago, the answer would be…no."

"Darn."

"Let's not talk about that now. Let's talk about this beautiful baby boy of yours. Can you believe you're a mom?"

She smiled at the sleeping bundle in her arms and shook her head. "It's surreal, Waverly. I can't explain it. It's like nothing I've ever felt."

"Where's Gary?"

"At my place, taking a shower. He should be back soon."

"Is he over the moon?"

"Yeah. It's pretty cute, actually. I wasn't sure how he would react, given that he's been through this three times before, but when Graham came out, he was practically giddy."

I squeezed her hand. "I'm so happy for you, Paige. I guess now you can finally start planning your wedding."

She laughed. "Yeah, right. Let's talk when I've lost some of this baby weight. I don't want to look like a marshmallow in my dress. Speaking of weddings, how are the plans going for yours? We haven't talked much about that lately."

I shook my head. "Today is about you, not me."

"Thou doth protest too much, Waverly."

I stiffened a bit. "It's going fine, at least from what Jake's mom tells me. She's basically doing everything for us."

"And you're okay with that?"

"I don't really have a choice."

"Yes, you do."

I shook my head. "You haven't met this woman."

"You always have a choice, Waverly."

I looked at the wall for a moment, then at her. "Then I guess I'm...*choosing* to let her plan the wedding."

"But it's not what you want?"

"Not entirely, but it's important to her, and I just don't want to be selfish."

"You don't want to be selfish?"

I nodded.

"For your own wedding?"

I nodded again.

"You do realize that doesn't make any sense, right?"

I sighed. "It's just really important to her that Jake and I have a big wedding in Florida, and that somehow seems...more important than what I want right now."

"More important than what *you* want for your own wedding?"

I nodded.

"Why exactly?"

"Because...because I want her to like me."

"You can't be serious."

I didn't reply.

"That's ridiculous, Waverly."

I tried to laugh. "Hey, sneaky, you broke the rules. We're talking about *you* today, not me, remember?"

She rolled her eyes. "Okay, fine, fine. But just remember, it's *your* wedding, and it's not wrong to choose what makes *you* happy."

I nodded. "Got it. I guess I'm still trying to figure out what that scenario would look like."

Just then Tasha and Beth walked back into the room.

"No cute doctors here. Darn." Tasha unwrapped a Snickers bar and shook her head. "Such a shame."

Beth sat down on the edge of Paige's bed. "In the movies, the male doctors are always so good-looking. The reality simply doesn't measure up."

I laughed. "Beth, in the movies, everyone is good-looking. Have you not noticed that?"

Tasha lightly tapped Beth in the back of the head with her Snickers. "Yeah, Einstein, that's why they're in the *movies*."

"I hate to break up the party, but if you ladies don't mind, I'm going to steal the mother of my son for a little while." The sound of a deep voice made us all turn our heads.

Gary, his hair still wet, was standing in the doorway. He'd clearly rushed straight from the shower back to the hospital.

"Gary!" I hurried over to give him a hug. "Congratulations!"

"Thanks, Waverly." He was beaming.

Tasha raised her eyebrows. "You're Gary?"

Gary nodded and replied in his sexy Southern drawl. "So they tell me."

Tasha looked at Paige and nodded. "Nice *work*, mama."

"Tasha!" Beth looked mortified.

Tasha held up her palms. "What?"

I picked up my purse and stewarded them both toward the door. "And on that note…"

• • •

A half hour later, I'd just surfaced at the Clark Street subway stop in my neighborhood when my phone rang. I fished it out of my purse.

Davey!

I answered as fast as I could.

"Do you hate me?"

He laughed. "Did you just answer the phone with *Do you hate me?*"

"So it seems. So do you hate me?"

"Why would you think I hate you?"

"Because I flaked on you twice, and then you didn't return my calls or texts. I figured you'd given up on me and deleted me from your life."

He laughed again. "Okay, Bryson, slow down, take a deep breath, and please come back to the land where the sane people live. I don't hate you, and I didn't give up on you, and I certainly didn't delete you from my life. I was in Europe for a couple weeks, so I'm just now digging through a mountain of voice mails and text messages."

"So when can we get together? I'm dying to see you."

"You're dying to see me? Those are words every man loves to hear, but you do realize I'm married, right?"

I laughed. "Shut up. So when are you free?"

"How about tonight? Lindsay has class."

I nodded enthusiastically, even though he couldn't see me. "Tonight would be perfect. Anywhere you want to go. Just let me know where and when, and I'll be there."

"I'm liking all this eagerness. Very good for the ego."

"So where should we meet?"

"I just read about a place in the West Village called Bobo. You know it? Apparently they make a mean jalapeño margarita."

"Nope, but that means nothing. I'm not very hip, Davey."

He laughed. "Please. It's on West Tenth at Seventh Avenue. Meet you there at seven?"

"Perfect. And thanks for not deleting me out of your life."

"Bryson, stop with the crazy talk. See you soon."

• • •

"Holy missing persons agency, it's really you." I stood just inside the entrance to Bobo and put my hands on my hips. Davey was sitting on a barstool to the right, halfway between me and the wall and halfway through a jalapeño margarita.

He stood up and held out his arms. "Bryson! Come give a guy a proper hello."

I trotted over to the bar and hugged him tight. "I'm so happy you're here, Davey. I honestly can't remember the last time I saw you in person. Can you?"

He turned and gestured to the bartender. "Hold that thought. You still drink Blue Moon with an orange slice?"

I put my hands over my heart. "You remembered."

He gestured to his margarita. "You sure you don't want to try one of these?"

I shook my head. "Waverly Bryson and mixed drinks do not a happy couple make."

He laughed and ordered me a beer, then sat back down on the barstool. "I think the last time we saw each other was when I told you I'd eloped and was quitting JAG."

"That's right! You left me working for that horrible woman who took over managing our agency. She was awful to me, you know. Basically got me to quit."

He put his palms in the air. "What can I say? I'm irreplaceable."

"*Then* after you ditched me at work, you went traveling and basically fell off the face of the Earth, which finished off my fragile little heart."

"You're killing me." He pretended to stab himself in the chest and die.

I laughed and accepted a cold beer from the bartender. "Clearly your flair for dramatic interpretation hasn't changed."

"Touché. But lots of other things certainly have. *You* went and turned into a bona fide TV star."

I coughed. "TV star? Please. Have you even seen the show?"

"No, but I hear it's quite popular with the Midwestern homemaker crowd, *which*, as everyone who works in marketing knows, is a coveted demographic. Impressive stuff, Bryson. Very impressive."

I patted my lips with a napkin. "Ah, now, there's the Davey Mason I've missed so much. Always has an eye on the analytics."

"So any news on the dating front?"

I nodded. "You always had an eye on my dating life too."

"Of course. Got to live vicariously through my single friends while I still can. So what's the word?"

"Actually, I'm engaged."

"What?"

"You heard me."

"The heartbreaker is finally settling down?"

"Stop it, Davey. You know I was never a heartbreaker." When he was my client, Davey had always liked to tease me, but he knew how insecure I was about my track record with the opposite sex.

"Who's the lucky guy?"

"His name's Jake McIntyre. He's from Florida."

He clinked his glass against mine. "Look at you, Bryson, not a pup anymore. You're all grown-up now."

"Thanks. I'm doing my best." I set my drink down, and then held up my bare hand. "Sometimes I don't feel that grown-up, though."

He gave me a strange look. "Why are you showing me your hand?"

"Because it's where my engagement ring would be if I hadn't lost it."

"You lost your engagement ring?"

I grimaced. "All signs indicate…yes."

"Ouch."

I smiled. "Thanks."

"So when's the wedding? Talk to me, goose."

"Presidents' Day weekend, which is approaching too fast for my comfort. Will you come?"

"Of course. Wouldn't miss it."

"I'm still trying to wrap my head around the fact that I'm engaged…again."

"It'll be a layup this time. I promise." He pretended to shoot a basketball.

"How do you know that, may I ask?"

"Because you're glowing."

I squinted at him. "Did you just say I'm *glowing*?"

He nodded. "I know I just lost some testosterone by saying that, but it's true."

"I forgot how funny you are."

"And smart too." He tapped a finger to his temple. "Don't forget smart."

"And so *modest*."

"But seriously, Bryson, you look happy. When I looked you up online, I could tell you were doing great, but it's awesome to see it's true in person."

The perfect segue.

I cleared my throat. "So, smart guy, tell me something. When you looked me up, did you happen to see anything about my other business, the one with the Honey products?" Davey had been there back when I first came up with a line of greeting cards called Honey Notes, the original idea that eventually led to Waverly's Honey Shop.

"I did."

"What did you think?"

"I think it's fantastic. Seriously, Waverly. I'm beyond impressed with what you've done since we last caught up."

"Thanks. So, um, do you think it's a business that you would find interesting?"

"Waverly's Honey Shop?"

I nodded.

"It seems like a cool business. Cool products, very creative."

I shifted on the barstool and took a deep breath. "Cool enough to want to…run sales and marketing for it?"

He looked surprised. "What?"

I gave him an awkward grin. "Would you like to…come work for me?"

"For real?"

I sighed. "It's sort of a long story, but I need you, and I need you yesterday. Are you interested?" I interlaced my fingers in front of me and pleaded with my eyes.

He took a long sip of his margarita, and then slowly shook his head. "Damn, Waverly, I wish we'd had this conversation a couple weeks ago."

My heart sank. "A couple weeks ago?"

"Before I took a job with Blush and Company."

"What?"

He nodded. "I just accepted it."

Blush and Company was one of the biggest—if not *the* biggest—high-end cosmetics and women's accessories companies in the world.

"Blush and Company, as in *the* Blush and Company?"

"Yep. I started on Thursday. That's why I was in Europe. Lindsay and I had one last hurrah before I jumped back on the corporate treadmill. You're looking at the new VP of global sales and marketing."

"Were you talking to them before you moved here?"

"Not at all. It all happened really fast, actually. I was surprised, given how big they are, but they moved fast, and it was a good fit, so I decided to go with it."

I put my face in my hands. "So I just missed my window?"

He nodded. "Looks like it."

I kept my face in my hands. "And if I hadn't stood you up that first night, you might not have taken it?"

"Do you really want to kick yourself when you're down?"

I sighed and finally removed my hands. "I can't believe this. Do you have to take it, Davey? Can't you turn down your big fancy corporate-glamour job to come work for my little fledgling startup?"

He laughed. "I wish I could help you, but alas, *hell no.*"

I pressed my palm against my forehead. "If I don't find someone to run this company for me soon, it's all going to fall apart before my eyes, and I'm going to lose everything I've worked so hard for."

"How about I score you some free Blush products. Would that make you feel better?"

I raised my eyebrows. "I do love Blush products. The makeup artists on *Love, Wendy* use them, and I always feel like a new person when they're done with me."

"That's what everyone says. That's why the company makes so much freaking money."

I laughed. "I can't believe *you're* working for a cosmetics company."

"That makes two of us."

"Are you the only straight guy there?"

"I suspect so. It's quite a change from the world of sporting goods. I have a serious learning curve ahead of me, that's for sure."

I reached over and touched his face. "Have you been using them? Your skin looks amazing."

He swatted my hand away. "Enough about me. Tell me about this Jake guy who's stolen your heart. What does he do?"

"He's the head of physical therapy for the Brooklyn Nets."

"The Nets? Nice. I'll have to hit you up for some tickets. How did you meet him?"

I took a sip of my beer. "Actually, you were there."

Davey gave me a strange look. "*I* was there? How so?"

"I met him at the Super Show."

"In Atlanta?"

I nodded.

"Which one?" We'd gone to several together.

"The last one before you left JAG."

"The one with Shane Kennedy, when he was still with the Knicks?"

"Yep. Jake went to college with him."

"You met this guy way back then? And you never mentioned him to me? Where's the love, Bryson?"

"Please. You know I love you. Besides, I *met* him then, but we didn't start dating until nearly a year later, after you'd quit to go globetrotting. We did the long-distance thing on and off for a while, and then he moved to Brooklyn early this year."

"So then it was just...*on*."

I smiled. "And then it was just on."

"And now you're engaged."

I nodded. "And now I'm engaged."

"And he's a good guy?"

I got happy just thinking about Jake. "He's a *great* guy, Davey. He's smart and funny, and he even beats me sometimes at Scrabble. That's not easy to do, you know."

Davey put a hand on my arm. "And he treats you well?"

"He treats me very well. Thanks, *Dad*."

He sipped his margarita. "I used to worry about you a little bit, did you know that?"

I tilted my head to one side. "Worry about me? How so?"

"I know I used to give you a hard time about your love life, but to be honest, I always felt like you were too guarded with men."

I rolled my eyes. "I know. You used to tell me that *all the time*, remember? Just what I wanted to hear in a client meeting, by the way."

He laughed. "I was just worried that you wouldn't ever let anyone in, that's all."

"It's okay. You were right to be worried. It took me a long time to get over Aaron and trust that someone would love me for me. But I finally did, and I found a really great guy, so you don't have to worry about me anymore, okay?"

"I'll always worry about you a little bit. You're like the little sister I never had."

"And you're still like the big brother I never had. Always getting in my face about something."

He held up his glass to me. "But in a caring way."

I laughed. "Sometimes. So how's Lindsay? Things are good?"

He nodded. "So far, so good."

"How long have you two been married now?"

"We celebrated two years in August."

"Wow, two years already?"

"Yep. When it's good, it goes fast. You'll see."

I laughed. "And when it's not good?"

"Like watching paint dry. Or so my unhappily married friends say."

"You have unhappily married friends?"

"Sure. Everyone does."

I shook my head. "I don't."

He laughed. "Sure you do."

"No, I really don't."

"You do, but you just don't know it."

I narrowed my eyes. "What are you implying?"

He laughed. "I'm just saying that you never know what's really going on in a relationship unless you're in it."

I opened my mouth to protest, but then I realized he was right. I also thought about Andie and Nick. *What is going on there?*

I blinked, then nodded. "Actually, I know someone I thought was *the* poster girl for a happy marriage, and she turned out to be a lesbian." I didn't want to mention Wendy Davenport by name.

"Point proven." He finished his drink and set it on the bar.

I frowned. Thinking about Wendy made me think about Gary, which made me think about Paige, which made me think about the looming collapse of Waverly's Honey Shop. "This conversation has taken a depressing turn. Can we please change the subject to something a little happier?"

"Sure. Go for it."

"How long is Lindsay going to be in school?"

"Her master's program is two years, but to get licensed for private practice, which is what she wants to do, will take another three years or so after that."

"So what about kids?"

"What about them?"

"Are you going to have them?" Davey and Lindsay were in their late thirties.

"No." His answer was firm.

"No?"

"No."

"Why not? You'd be such a great dad."

He smiled and bowed his head. "Why, thank you, and you are probably correct. But Linds and I have discussed it up and down and all around, and in the end we decided that it's just not for us."

"Why not?"

He shrugged. "There's no one reason in particular. We like to travel. We love quiet weekends. We enjoy being spontaneous. We already have nieces and nephews to spoil. Overall, it's just not something we want to do."

"Oh." I nodded slowly, impressed by his conviction.

"What about you and Jake? Are we going to see any mini Waverlys in the future?"

I smiled. "I'm not sure. I'll give you a definite maybe on that."

"A definite maybe? What kind of answer is that?"

I laughed. "The only honest one I can give you."

"I bet you'd be a great mom."

I coughed. "You're lying, but thanks."

"Come on now, I'm not lying. You're smart and organized and kind as all hell. Those qualities a good mother do make."

"Thanks, Davey." I looked down and interlaced my hands in my lap. *Would I ever know for sure?*

"But if kids aren't for you, that's totally fine too. Just make sure you do what makes *you* happy. You'll get yourself into trouble if you start living your life to make other people happy."

I looked up at him. Paige had said practically the exact same thing to me at the hospital just a few hours earlier. Were all my friends conspiring to tell me something?

About an hour later his phone buzzed with a text message.

"Is your hall pass up?"

He laughed and gestured to the bartender for the bill. "You could say that. Lindsay just got out of class, so we're meeting for a late dinner."

"How romantic." I crossed my hands over my chest.

He nodded. "Yet another perk of not having kids. Hey, speaking of Lindsay, her birthday is coming up. Can I get my hands on one of your canvas Honey Totes? I really like those."

"Sure, which one?"

"How about the one that says JUST SMILE? She'd love it."

I nodded. "Of course. Just tell me where to send it. I'll overnight it, no charge."

He pulled out his wallet and handed me a crisp new business card. "Nice. Send it to my office so she won't see it."

I looked at the card and sighed. "You know, my birthday is coming up too. As a present, can you ditch your new high-paying job and come work entirely on commission for me?"

He shook his head. "You know I'd love to, but alas, I don't want to."

I laughed. "Damn you, Davey Mason."

"I've missed you too, Waverly Bryson."

chapter eighteen

After my hopes of having Davey come work with me were dashed, I cranked the search into high gear. There had to be someone out there who could do the job. There *had* to be. After all, it wasn't like I was hiring someone to run a nuclear reactor. Just a charismatic, smart, organized person with loads of retail experience. How hard could it be?

A week and several more disappointing interviews later, my renewed optimism was struggling to stay alive. Why was finding the perfect candidate so hard? As I waited for the last applicant of the day to arrive one afternoon, I wondered if my standards were simply too high.

Then I met Eunice.

She was about forty, with an impressive background in retail operations spanning nearly fifteen years. She was efficient, organized, and professional.

She was also boring.

So boring.

And even more importantly: humorless.

"So what part of New York do you live in?" I smiled and hoped her personality might shine through if we talked about something other than work.

"Upper East Side." No elaboration.

"What do you like to do for fun?" I tried to picture us going out for drinks.

"I'm very involved in my church."

Church? I couldn't remember the last time I'd been in a church.

"What's your favorite TV show?"

She shook her head. "I don't own a TV."

"Do you ever go to the movies?"

"Not really."

"Do you like to travel abroad?"

"I'm not very adventurous."

It was like pulling out my own eyelashes with pliers.

When it came to business, however, Eunice really knew her stuff. And despite my dream of maintaining the chummy culture of Waverly's Honey Shop, at the end of the day, it was…a business.

Right?

Eunice was certainly all business.

• • •

"To the birthday girl." Andie held up her glass and smiled.

"To the birthday girl." Jake held up his glass and smiled.

"To wishing I'd brought a jacket." I held up my glass and shivered.

That Friday the three of us were sitting at one of the crowded outdoor benches on Stone Street, a quaint cobblestone throwback located in the heart of the financial district. The tiny stretch was lined on both sides with pubs and wine bars, and all summer long it was packed with people and *pitchers*, German beer garden–style, and everyone drinking up a storm.

It was early October, but the day had been so warm that the bar owners brought out the tables, which quickly filled up with revelers. A few opted for wine, but the vast majority looked like poster children for Oktoberfest: attractive, happy, and a little buzzed. Actually, that's how the majority of Manhattanites looked on any given Friday afternoon. Or Saturday afternoon. Or Saturday evening. Or Sunday Funday, as people called it here. I never ceased to be amazed at the amount of alcohol consumed on this relatively small island.

My birthday wasn't until Sunday, but we were celebrating early because Andie and I were headed to Florida the next morning. It seemed like everyone in Manhattan had left work early to soak up the last natural heat of the year. Unfortunately, however, the tall buildings of Lower Manhattan were blocking out the direct sunlight, and as the afternoon wore on, a chill had crept into the air, San Francisco–style.

Jake put his arm around me. "I'll keep you warm."

"Enjoy the breeze, because it's going to be hot as hell in Florida," Andie said.

I thought about the weekend ahead. I still hadn't packed, and I also hadn't come up with a good excuse for why I wasn't going to be wearing my engagement ring. *Ugh.*

"So Waverly, I know you've been interviewing like a madwoman to find someone for the Honey Shop. Have you found anybody good?" Andie asked.

I sighed. "In the past week alone, I think I've interviewed ten people. With one exception, if I saw any of them walking down the street I would probably hide under this table so I wouldn't have to face them. That's how awful they were."

"Ouch."

"Exactly. One of them wasn't bad, though, a woman named Eunice. Her personality didn't make me want to sing in the shower or anything, but her résumé is stellar, and she seemed to have a good head on her shoulders."

"Could be a fair compromise," Jake said.

I nodded. "That's what I figured. Beggars can't be choosers, so I think I'm going to ask her to come back to meet Tasha and Beth."

"The you and me from ten years ago?" Andie said.

I laughed. "Exactly." Then I turned to Jake, who had a confused look on his face. "Our interns remind me of Andie and me when we were younger."

Andie picked up the pitcher and refilled our beers. "She means they are smart, super hot, and amazing. And the sassy one of the two is me, of course."

Just then my phone buzzed with a text. I read it, then set my phone on the table, stood up, and clapped my hands high above my head. I jumped up and down a few times, my arms still in the air.

"What in God's name are you doing?" Andie said.

"That was Davey. He's here but can't find us in the crowd."

"So you're scaring away everyone else to clear his line of vision?"

I pointed to him. "See? He just spotted me from way over there." I waved to Davey, then took a seat and calmly picked up my beer.

"I'm so embarrassed for you," Andie said.

Jake looked at her. "So, Andie, how are you liking New York so far?"

She grinned and raised her cup in the air. "It's amazing, Jake. I love it love it love it. I adore San Francisco, but I could totally live here too."

I looked at her. *But what about Nick?*

Jake nodded in the direction of her building. "That place of yours is off the charts. I'd probably never leave my apartment if I had a view like that."

"I know, isn't it amazing? Totally makes up for the cheesy décor," she said.

He scratched his eyebrow. "I didn't think the décor was that bad, actually. Given the way Waverly described it, I expected at least a waterbed or zebra-print sheets or something."

Andie laughed. "Touché. It's a bit gauche, but it could be worse. You've got to give it up for the porcelain dogs, though. What is *that* all about?"

Jake nodded. "The dogs, I'll give you."

I squeezed Jake's thigh under the table and tried not to laugh. On our way out of Andie's apartment earlier he'd hung back, saying he was going to use the restroom, but what he'd really done was dress Blanco and Whitey in BROOKLYN NETS T-shirts and hats. When he whispered later what he'd done, I was tempted to head straight to city hall and marry him right then and there.

Now, that would be nice, I thought.

"There's the birthday girl."

"Davey!" I stood up and gave him a hug. "Thanks so much for coming." I turned around and gestured to the bench. "This is my good friend Andie, and this is Jake, my, um, my fiancé." I stumbled awkwardly over the introduction.

He shook their hands and laughed. "Let me guess. That's the first time you've used the word *fiancé* to introduce him."

I blushed. "How did you know?"

"Everyone trips over it the first time." He looked at Jake. "Have you introduced Waverly to anyone as your *fiancée* yet?"

Jake shook his head. "I don't think so."

Davey nodded. "It will be awkward, trust me."

I poured him a beer. "Thanks for skipping out of work early to join us. That must have been hard, now that you're *the man* and all."

He shrugged. "Actually, being *the man* made it quite easy. I left, and no one asked where I was going, and now I'm here."

Andie laughed. "I like you. So you used to be Waverly's boss?"

He took a sip of his beer. "Not technically. I was her client."

"So basically, *yes*," I said to Andie. "Don't listen to him."

"Waverly told me about your new job. Congratulations," Jake said to Davey.

Andie reached for the pitcher. "What job?"

"He's running global marketing for Blush and Company," I said.

Her jaw dropped. "No way. I *love* that company."

Davey smirked at Jake. "It hasn't been long, but if I had a dollar for every time some chick said that to me…"

Jake laughed too. "I hear you. Try working for the NBA. It gets a little old."

Andie nodded. "Seriously, *all* my makeup is Blush. Look." She opened her purse and started pulling out an arsenal of pink products with the Blush and Company logo. Mascara, lipstick, powder, and, of course, blush. She lined them all up on the table. "See?"

Davey looked impressed. "What's your favorite? I'll hook you up with some free samples."

Andie's eyes got big. "Really?"

"Sure thing. We have tons at the office."

She looked at me. "Why did you quit your PR job again? Who wouldn't want to work with *this* guy?"

I laughed. "That's not quite how it went down, but yes, Davey is great to work with. I even tried to get him to come run Waverly's Honey Shop, but he shot me down."

Davey gave me a sympathetic look. "Have you found someone yet?"

I nodded. "I think so. She's not *you*, but she'll do."

"You sound far from thrilled."

I shrugged. "I'm just trying to be realistic."

I got the impression that Davey was going to say something, but before he could speak, Andie interjected.

"Hey, babe, want a beer?"

I was about to reply when I realized she wasn't talking to me.

I turned my head to see who she *was* talking to, and there was Morgan.

"I'd love one, thanks, Andie. Happy birthday, Waverly." His nervous smile spoke for him. He definitely had a crush brewing, and not on me.

"Thanks Morgan," I said without much enthusiasm. I knew I wasn't being all that nice, but I just didn't like the way he looked at Andie.

Andie pointed around the table. "Jake and Davey, this is Morgan. Morgan, this is Jake and Davey. Jake is marrying Waverly, and Davey sells awesome makeup."

Davey laughed. "As a heterosexual married man, I'm not quite sure how to take that."

Andie held up a finger. "Trust me, my new friend, it's a compliment."

Morgan sat down next to Andie, and I could feel my body tense up. Jake, perceptive as ever, immediately noticed.

"You doing okay, birthday girl?" He brushed a loose strand of hair out of my eyes and softened his voice. I loved it when he softened his voice.

"Yep." I nodded and forced a smile that didn't fool him for a second, but he was discreet enough not to push it.

I silently thanked him for it.

• • •

"Do you want to talk about it?"

I unbuttoned my jeans and pulled them down over my hips, not making eye contact. "Talk about what?"

Jake laughed as he removed his shirt. "Don't play dumb. What's going on with Andie and Morgan?"

I looked at him and sighed. "I don't know, and to be honest, I'm not sure I want to."

We'd just gotten home from Stone Street. As the group had scattered in various directions, I'd suspiciously watched Andie and Morgan head toward their building.

"He likes her. That much is obvious," Jake said.

"I know."

"Does she like him back?"

"I'm not sure." I pulled on a pair of pajama shorts. "You've met Nick. You see how great he is, right?"

Jake nodded. "But that doesn't mean anything. You know that, right?"

I sighed. "I know."

"Are you going to ask her about it this weekend?"

"You mean in between drinking tea and eating tiny sandwiches?"

"Is that what you do at showers?"

I nodded. "It's *so* painful, Jake. You have no idea."

He scratched his eyebrow. "So no one actually takes a shower?"

"So witty. Now if you'll excuse me, I need to pack." I playfully pushed him out of the way and headed for the hall closet to find my suitcase.

"What time do you need to leave for the airport? I'll call a car service."

I stopped to think. "Eight should do it." Then I remembered something. "Hey, speaking of airports, you have to see the card my dad sent me for my birthday." I walked over to my desk in the living room and picked up a bright-yellow envelope, then fished out the suitcase and rejoined Jake in my bedroom. "Check it out." I pulled the card out and handed it to him.

He laughed as he read it. "Does he think you're turning eight years old?"

The front of the card showed a kitten seated in a small model airplane. The inside said "Hope your birthday's a trip!"

I shrugged and smiled. "I agree it's hardly age-appropriate, but I guess it's better than a corny joke about being over the hill or something." The important thing was that my dad had—as always—remembered my birthday. He and Betty had also serenaded me with a surprisingly good rendition of "Happy Birthday" over the phone earlier.

I opened the suitcase on my bed and thought about what to pack.

"Have you come up with a plan for the ring yet?" Jake asked.

I looked up at him. "You mean what to tell your mom and company about why I'm not wearing one?"

He nodded.

I looked hopefully at him. "I was thinking…maybe I could just not get on the plane?"

He walked over and put his arms around my lower back. "Good luck with that. We should probably go shopping for a new one when you get back. Or do you want me to take care of it because you're so busy with work right now? I've done it before, and to some acclaim, as you may remember."

I smiled and leaned my cheek against his chest. "I'm just not ready to accept that it's really gone. It was so pretty."

He smoothed the back of my head, and I wrapped my arms around him.

We stood like that for a few moments until he finally spoke.

"The ring's gone, Waverly. I'm not," he said softly.

He knew me so well.

He nuzzled my neck. "How about you pack a little later? I'd like to celebrate your birthday…properly."

I smiled into his warm cheek. "It's not really my birthday until Sunday."

He breathed softly into my ear and gently slipped his fingertips down the back of my shorts. "Then I guess we'll have to celebrate twice."

chapter nineteen

"Do you see her?" Andie asked.

I shook my head. "Do you?"

"No. What kind of car does she drive?"

"I have no idea."

Andie and I were standing outside the West Palm Beach airport, waiting for Jake's mom to pick us up. We had a few hours before the bridal shower, which gave us plenty of time to take a literal one and get girlied up for the occasion.

"Is that her?" I squinted at an enormous silver Mercedes approaching the curb.

Andie pushed her sunglasses on top of her head and nodded. "Oh yes it is. I can spot that snobby attitude a mile away."

"Andie!" I tried not to laugh.

She shrugged and put her sunglasses back on. "I'm sorry. It's just who I am. I blame it on my mother."

I put my arm around her and squeezed. "Thanks so much for coming down here with me. I don't think I could have survived this without you."

"I'll find a way for you to pay me back."

Mrs. McIntyre emerged from the car wearing an outfit that was almost identical to the one she'd worn the night of our engagement party. Silk shell, blazer, pants.

I decided to speak first.

"Hi, Mrs. McIntyre. Thanks so much for picking us up." This time I refrained from trying to hug her and instead just stood there awkwardly. She looked happy to see me.

"It's no problem at all. How was your flight?" she asked.

I blushed. "Piece of cake. I slept through most of it." What would she have thought if she knew I'd needed to nap on the plane because I'd been up so late last night hooking up with her son? "You remember my friend Andie?"

She smiled politely at Andie. "Of course. I'm glad you could join us."

We were about to get in the car when Jake's mom put a hand on my arm.

"Waverly, where's your engagement ring?"

I felt my face flush. "Oh, um, I haven't picked it up from the jeweler yet. I've, um, just been so busy at work that I keep forgetting."

She looked a bit distressed. "So you're not going to wear it to the shower?"

Andie, the consummate professional, immediately jumped in to defuse the situation. "I'm excited to visit Florida again, Mrs. McIntyre. I've been here only once before, and that was for the requisite family vacation to Disney World in eighth grade. I'm sure this will be much more fun. Waverly said she had a wonderful time when she came down for the engagement party." She smiled brightly.

Jake's mom looked pleased. "We're happy to have you."

"I hear your house is beautiful too," Andie said.

"Why, thank you."

I gave Andie a grateful look as we climbed into the car, then tried to forgive myself for lying to Mrs. McIntyre about my ring, *again*.

• • •

"I swear to God, if one more of these women asks me what my father does for a living, it's going to get ugly," Andie said under her breath.

I laughed. "Shhh." We'd finished lunch, which was elaborate and delicious—think crab cakes, tuna tartare, and Kobe beef sliders—and gifts, which were elaborate and expensive—think china, crystal, and personal checks. Now the two dozen or so immaculately dressed women—all well past fifty—were sitting around in their designer clothes sipping tea, nibbling on fancy cupcakes and cookies, and chatting. Thankfully no one had brought out any ridiculous shower games. And no one had questioned my story about why I wasn't wearing my ring, though it had certainly raised some eyebrows.

After I'd finished opening the mountain of presents, Andie and I had managed to find a small table in the corner with just two seats.

She leaned toward me and lowered her voice. "Have you noticed the crazy nicknames? *Bee. Candy. Cookie. Bunny.* Everyone's either a small animal or a snack."

I tried not to laugh. "Shhh. Don't be rude."

She looked around the room. "And the clothes? It's like a freaking Easter basket in here. Any one of these women could be my mom or one of her friends."

Andie's mom was named Bitsy. Yes, Bitsy. I'd only met her a few times, but I could easily picture her fitting seamlessly into this crowd. She was always perfectly coiffed and styled and manicured, no matter what time of day it was or what the occasion was. Unlike Andie, who was determined to pave her own way in the world, you could tell Bitsy *came* from money just by looking at her.

Just like Aaron's parents.

And now Jake's.

I decided to change the subject.

I unwrapped a miniature red velvet cupcake. "So, listen, can we please—finally—talk about what's going on with you and Nick? I know you hate it when I pry, but you've been avoiding this conversation since you arrived in New York, and after yesterday I can't take it anymore."

She sighed and broke a chocolate-dipped macaroon in half. "Do we have to?"

"You can't avoid it any longer, Andie. It's obvious something's going on, and I think I've been pretty good about not butting in so far. But the time has come."

She nodded and lifted the cookie to her lips. "You have. I expected you to butt in a long time ago, actually."

I nodded, glad we were finally going to address the situation. "Okay, let's get it over with. What is—"

The sound of a woman's voice interrupted me.

"Waverly! How are you? I haven't had a chance to chat with you yet."

I set my cupcake down and looked up. Bee Worthington was standing there.

I smiled "Hi, Mrs. Worthington. I'm fine, how are you?"

"Oh, please, call me Bee!" She waved a hand in front of her face and laughed a bit louder than necessary. I wondered how much champagne she'd drunk.

I gestured to Andie. "You remember my friend Andie?"

"Of course, Andie! From our shopping day. Wasn't that a hoot?" She slapped her thigh.

Andie nodded, and I could tell she was trying not to laugh. "Oh yes. A scream."

Bee patted her poufy hair, which today actually sort of reminded me of a bee. Or at least a bee*hive*. "I'm just delighted with the dress we chose, aren't you?" she asked me.

I nodded. "It's beautiful."

"And with a figure like yours, it's going to be just stunning." She looked at Andie. "Doesn't Waverly have a great figure?"

Andie nodded several times. "Oh yes, she's hot."

"You've got a nice figure too," Bee said to Andie. "It's just harder for us short and busty girls to pull off the long and lean thing, especially with hips like ours."

I tried not to laugh at the comment. *Short and busty girls? Hips like ours?*

Bee polished off her champagne. "I'm so excited to go dress shopping again with you both tomorrow."

Andie looked confused. "Dress shopping tomorrow? Didn't we find the dress last time?"

Bee set the empty flute down and put a hand on Andie's shoulder. "That was for Waverly, dear. First thing tomorrow we're headed to Worth Avenue to find the perfect gown for *you*."

Andie slowly turned to face me, her eyes narrowing. "Oh, *really*?"

I winced and gave her a sheepish smile. "I might have forgotten to mention that part of the weekend."

"Something tells me you forgot on purpose."

"It will be wonderful," Bee said. "Ava has all sorts of ideas already."

"*Really*." Andie slowly ate another bite of cookie but kept her eyes on me.

I stood up. "Um, I'm going to go talk to Mrs. McIntyre about getting all these gifts shipped back to New York. Will you two excuse me for a minute?"

Andie laughed. "Sure, you go ahead and do that." We both knew I was busted.

"I'll go with you, dear. I need a refill of this delicious champagne." Bee grabbed me a little awkwardly by the arm and led me away from the table. As we walked away, I looked back at Andie and gave her a *Please-don't-kill-me* face.

"You owe me forever," she mouthed.

"I love you," I mouthed back.

Bee and I walked over to the dessert table, where Jake's mom was standing with a few of her friends. As we approached, they turned to us and smiled.

"Waverly, dear, we were just talking about you," Jake's mom said. "Everyone's a bit surprised to hear you're only having one bridesmaid in the wedding."

I could feel myself blush.

"Oh, um, well, I—"

Jake's mom looked at Bee. "Didn't Holly always say she'd have eight bridesmaids when she and Jake got married?"

I froze.

Did she really just say that?

Bee nodded. "At least eight, maybe ten."

Jake's mom laughed. "Holly has always had *so* many friends. That girl is quite the social butterfly."

I was speechless.

The shower was in my honor, but at that moment it certainly didn't feel like it.

I smiled awkwardly and reached for a madeleine cookie.

I was trying my best to stay focused on the big picture, but right at that moment I was having a hard time seeing it.

• • •

"Okay, spill."

"Can we at least order first?"

I sighed and looked at the menu. "Fine."

Andie and I had just sat down at a seafood restaurant called Jetty's. Jake's mom had made us an early dinner reservation and hinted that we should get a good night's sleep before the shopping expedition the following morning.

A man in a suit and tie approached our table, accompanied by what looked to be our waiter.

"Miss Bryson?"

I looked up. "Yes?"

He smiled and extended his hand. "I'm Phillip, the manager here. I just wanted to welcome you to Jetty's."

I smiled a bit awkwardly and shook his hand. "Thanks, Phillip." I hoped my response wasn't too cardboard. You'd think I could at least *pretend* this sort of thing happened to me on a regular basis, as opposed to…never. I wondered why he was talking to us. *Has he seen me on TV?*

He kept smiling. "The McIntyres have been regular customers of ours for quite some time now. Lovely people."

Ah, that's why.

I nodded. "Yes, they are."

"I hear you're marrying their son?"

"Um, yes, in February." I sneaked a look at Andie, who was clearly enjoying this.

"At the Breakers," she said nonchalantly. Then, clearly to embarrass me further, she casually threw in, "over Presidents' Day weekend."

Phillip raised his eyebrows. "The Breakers? Over Presidents' Day weekend? Wow, that's just wonderful. I hope we'll be seeing more of you before then."

"I hope so too." I smiled, hating that he felt the need to suck up to me like this. He seemed like a nice man, but the whole exchange was so painfully...fake.

"By the way, Mrs. McIntyre has already taken care of your bill tonight," he said.

"Our bill?"

He nodded. "It's all taken care of."

I glanced at Andie, then back at him. "But we haven't ordered anything yet."

He smiled and looked amused. "Yes, of course. But whatever you choose to order, the bill is taken care of, including tip. Not to worry."

"Oh. Um, thanks." By the surprised look on my face, he had to know *this* had never happened to me either. I was clearly in uncharted territory.

He clasped his hands together, then gestured to the waiter standing next to him. "Well then, I'll let Jeremy take care of you from here. Enjoy your evening, and if you need anything at all, please let me know."

"Um, okay, thanks, Phillip."

He'd barely stepped away from our table when Jeremy took over, a basket of warm, fresh bread in one hand, a wine list in the other. "Can I start you ladies off with something to drink?"

I looked at Andie. "You want to choose?" I couldn't bear to further display my lack of sophistication by trying to select a suitable vintage.

She gestured for the menu. "Sure."

After perusing the options, she sent Jeremy off to retrieve a bottle of Malbec. As soon as he was out of earshot, she leaned forward. "Now, that was unexpected."

I laughed. "You think? Who does that?"

"Nice people do. *Rich* nice people, that is. I totally get what you mean about the hot and cold thing now. Jake's mom is all over the place."

"See? It's like that Whitney Houston song." I started to sing. "'How will I know...if he...real-ly...loves...me?' Only it's *she*, not *he*, of course."

Andie gave me a look. "Why does everything always come back to eighties music with you?"

I dipped some bread in olive oil. "Because eighties music is the best. Now will you please look at your menu so we can eat? I'm starving."

After we'd ordered and each had a glass of wine in front of us, I spread my palms on the table and looked at her.

"Okay, enough of the chitchat, Ms. Barnett. Time to spill."

She picked up her glass and tried to look casual. "Spill what?"

I rolled my eyes. "Give me a break. *Spill.*"

She took a sip of her wine. "I know what you're thinking."

"You do?"

"Yes."

I raised my eyebrows. "What do I think?" *That you're sleeping with Morgan.*

"That I'm sleeping with Morgan."

I flinched, then went with it.

"*Are* you?"

"No."

I narrowed my eyes. "You wouldn't lie to me, right?"

"I'm insulted that you would even ask me that." The look on her face made me regret the question.

I leaned back in my chair. "I'm sorry, you're right. I…I know you wouldn't lie to me." *But what is going on?*

"Thanks."

"So…what *is* going on, then?" I asked.

"With Morgan?"

I nodded.

"Nothing. I've never even made out with him."

I exhaled. *Thank God.*

She pushed her hair behind her ears and sighed. "But I've definitely flirted with him too much, probably even led him on a bit. I'll admit to that."

"But why, Andie? Why would you do that?"

Jeremy appeared out of nowhere with our entrées. It must have been obvious that we were in the middle of a serious conversation, because he was gone before I could even say thank you.

I picked up right where I'd left off. "Why would you do that, Andie?"

She stared at the ceiling. "Because…because…"

"Because what?" *Please don't say because you don't love Nick.*

She hesitated, then looked straight at me.

"Because Nick asked me to marry him."

My jaw dropped. "*What?*"

She nodded.

"When?"

"Right before I moved to New York."

"What? That was like a month ago!"

"I know."

"And you didn't tell me?"

She shook her head. "I didn't tell anyone. I still haven't. Until just now, that is."

I was floored. "What did you say?"

She made the swirly *crazy* sign with her finger. "I flipped out on him, Waverly."

"Flipped out? How so?"

"I don't know. I just…flipped out. I got mad at him for asking me."

I tilted my head to one side. "You got *mad* at him?"

She nodded.

"You got mad at him for asking you to *marry* him?"

She nodded again.

"But…why?"

She sighed. "Ever since he and I started dating, I've been saying I might freak out on him. You know that. I said I might get scared and run, remember? Remember, I called myself emotional Teflon?"

"Yes, I remember, but I didn't think you really meant it. I thought you were just, you know, being *you*, being tough."

"Well apparently I meant it—and then some, because I freaked out, then got scared, then *ran*." She gestured toward the exit with her fork.

I didn't reply for a moment, and we sat there in silence, picking at our food.

"Do you still love him?" I finally asked.

She nodded.

"Then…what made you get scared? I don't get it."

She pressed her hands against her temples. "I don't get it either. That's why I didn't tell you. I couldn't handle it, Waverly. I couldn't handle it like an adult, so I flipped out on him, told him I needed space, and moved to New York."

"So that's why you've changed the subject every time I asked about him." It wasn't a question.

"Yes."

"And that's why you've been flirting with Morgan."

"Yes."

"But you still love Nick?"

"Yes."

"Have you talked to him?"

"No."

"*No?*"

She nodded. "I'm not kidding, Waverly. I flipped out and left town. I don't know what's…wrong with me." Her voice cracked a little. I'd never heard Andie's voice crack.

"Nothing's wrong with you, Andie. You're just…scared. That's the most natural thing in the world."

She picked up her glass. "*You're* not scared."

I laughed. "You don't think I'm scared about getting married?"

"No, I don't."

"Well, you're wrong."

She cocked her head to the side. "*Are* you scared?"

"Of course I am."

"You sure don't seem like it."

I swallowed a bite of salmon. "Well, that's because…because I guess I don't really think about it like that."

"Like what?"

I set my fork down and started twisting my napkin in my lap. "I mean, I don't really think to myself, *I'm getting married.*

Instead, I think about how much I love being with Jake, and how I don't want to stop being with him, so I'm not going to."

She gave me a weird look. "Say that again?"

I gave her an awkward smile. "I know that's a roundabout way of looking at it, but that's how it makes sense to me. Do you remember what I told you he said to me right before he proposed?"

She took a sip of her wine. "Would you hate me if I said no? Because I have no idea."

I shook my head. "Of course not. He wasn't proposing to *you*. Anyhow, he told me that he'd realized that for him, marriage isn't about being able to imagine living your life *with* a person, it's about *not* being able to imagine living your life *without* that person."

She nodded. "Romantic."

"I know. But it's also makes it a lot easier to wrap your head around the idea of getting married, which is scary. Believe me, Andie, I know it's weird to think about spending your entire life with someone. But when you think about *not* being with that person, and you realize you don't want that, then it makes sense. At least it does for me."

She sighed and picked at her pasta. "Really?"

"Definitely. You know, in a way I'm happy I lost my engagement ring."

She looked up at me. "Have you gone insane?"

"Okay, maybe the word *happy* is a little strong. But it made me realize that while yes, it was beautiful, at the end of the day it was just a piece of jewelry. It doesn't really *mean* anything, Andie. With or without it, Jake is still here, and that's what's important. It's being with Jake that really makes me happy. Everything else is just for show as far as I'm concerned."

She shrugged. "I bet that rock meant a lot to the jeweler, who is probably putting his kids through college with his commission."

I laughed. "Not to mention whoever found it."

"So are you going to get a new one?"

"I don't think so. Jake said he'd buy me one, but I don't know if I want him to. I mean, I'll have a wedding band, so I was thinking that might be enough."

"Really?"

I nodded. "I just don't feel like I need a big diamond, like I need to make some statement about our love to the world. That's what I'm trying to get across here. All that really matters to *me* is that I'm with Jake. Or, to return to the verbal gymnastics of a few minutes ago, all that really matters to me is that I don't stop being with Jake."

She leaned back in her chair. "Wow, you have really grown up."

I smiled. "Thanks. But enough about me. I want to get back to *you*. How does it make you feel when you imagine not being with Nick anymore?"

She paused to think. I slowly picked at my salmon and did my best to wait patiently for her response.

Please don't break his heart.

After a few moments of silence, she finally spoke.

"How does it make me feel to imagine not being with Nick anymore? That's what you want to know?"

I nodded.

"Honestly?"

"Honestly. You can tell me." I had a bad feeling.

Poor Nick.

She leaned forward in her chair.

"Honestly, Waverly…it makes me feel sort of sick."

I let out a little gasp. "It does?"

She nodded. "I miss him more than I ever thought I would."

I smiled. "That's not what I expected you to say."

"It's not?"

"No."

"What did you expect me to say?"

I hesitated.

"You really want to know?"

She took a sip of her wine. "Of course. If I'm opening the kimono, you have to as well."

I laughed. "Fair enough. Okay...to be completely honest...I thought you were going to say something like...you love Nick, but just not the way I love Jake, or the way Mackie loves Hunter. Or something about how you didn't want to let us down because you know how much we like Nick."

She laughed. "You think I've been dating Nick for a year and a half because you and McKenna *like* him?"

I blushed. "Okay, now that I've said that out loud, I realize how self-centered it sounds."

She gave me a look. "Good. Because that was pretty bad."

"Let's just forget I said that. So you've thought about life without Nick, and it makes you sick."

She nodded.

"But the idea of marrying him...is still scary to you."

She nodded. "Crazy scary."

"So essentially, you love him, but you're just not there yet."

Another nod. "Essentially."

"Hmm."

She took a sip of her wine. "Why does everything have to happen so fast?

"Everyone is always trying to get to the next rung in the ladder. Why can't we just enjoy things the way they are once in a while?"

For a moment I felt like I was looking in a mirror. I'd had those exact same thoughts last year when I was trying to figure things out with Jake. At the time, I'd thought Andie and Nick were so far ahead of us because they were living together, while Jake and I weren't even living in the same city.

Clearly I'd been wrong.

I picked up my wineglass. "What you just said makes perfect sense, Andie. Why don't you just tell Nick that?"

"Tell him what, exactly?"

"That you're just not there yet and would like things to stay the way they are."

"Because he wouldn't believe me."

"Why not?"

She rolled her eyes. "Waverly, if you asked Jake to *marry you*, and he told you that he *just wasn't there yet*, what would you think?"

I flinched. "Oh gosh, you're right. I'd think he wasn't into me."

She nodded and lifted a forkful of pasta. "Exactly."

"But then again, guys are different. Maybe he won't react the way a girl would?"

She shrugged. "Maybe not."

"Well you have to tell him *something*. I mean, you can't just never talk to him again, right?"

"I know, I know I do. I've just been using this New York thing as a hiatus from dealing with it."

"And Morgan. You've been using him too."

"Yes, and Morgan."

"He *is* cute, though."

She nodded. "Isn't he? Serious eye candy. Doesn't have half Nick's sense of humor, though. Or his brain."

"So you really never hooked up with him? Like not even a little? He seems like he'd be hard to resist."

She shook her head. "There were a couple times I could have, and part of me was tempted out of some twisted impulse for self-sabotage, but in the end I couldn't bring myself to even kiss him."

"Why not?"

"Because each time it would have been easy to take the flirting one step further, I'd find myself thinking...about Nick." A smile crept onto her face as her mind drifted back to San Francisco. It was the first time I'd seen her smile like that since she'd been in New York.

"It's going to be okay, Andie." I reached across the table and squeezed her hand. "Just be honest with him."

"You really think so?"

I nodded. "If you're completely honest with him, then yes, I really do."

"But what if he won't wait for me?"

"I think he'll wait."

"And if he doesn't?" She looked nervous, which was so unlike her.

"*If* that happens, we'll deal with it then. Just talk to him, okay? Tell him you love him, but that you need to go at your own pace right now." I parroted what Paige and Davey had both recently told me. "If you start living your life to make other people happy, you're not being true to yourself."

She laughed. "You're one to talk."

"What?"

She gestured to our surroundings. "Please. Look at us, Waverly. It's your birthday weekend, and we're in *Florida*, having a dinner at a fancy hotel that probably costs more for a weekend than your rent. You're getting married in front of a bunch of people you don't know, in a dress you didn't pick, all to please a woman who you're pretty sure wishes her son had chosen someone else. Maybe you should take your own advice."

I gasped.

Before I could speak, Andie reached across the table and grabbed my hand. "Oh my God, I'm so sorry, Waverly. That was mean. That was *so* mean. I'm sorry."

I didn't respond.

She squeezed my hand. "Can I take that back? Please, can I take that back?"

Slowly I began to shake my head. "No, it's okay. I deserved it."

"No, you didn't. That was below the belt. I'm so sorry."

"It's okay, really. You're right. I *am* living my life to make her happy right now."

"I know you're just trying to keep the peace, Waverly. I get it."

I smiled weakly. "Thanks."

She leaned back in her chair. "Damn, I really *can* be a huge bitch sometimes, can't I?"

I laughed. "That's why I love you."

"I'm lucky that you love me. I do realize that, you know. I'm well aware that I'm a handful."

I smiled. "You're a handful and a half, but well worth the trouble. Thanks for coming down this weekend to help. You've been a lifesaver."

She held up her wineglass. "Anything for you. And for being such a bitch just now, I'll happily wear whatever monstrosity Jake's mom and her tipsy friend Bee pick out for me tomorrow."

I laughed and clinked my glass against hers. "You noticed that about Bee too? She did seem a little…happy."

"Definitely happy. But not unexpected."

"What do you mean?"

She shrugged. "At pretty much every shower I've ever been to, especially the super swank ones for my cousins up in Marin, someone's mom or aunt or grandma has overindulged a bit, and usually on champagne. It comes with the territory, like how the poor maid of honor has to make that stupid bouquet out of the ribbons from the presents."

I winced at the memory of the awful bouquet from this afternoon. "Thanks for making that, by the way. I know it pained you to do it."

She shrugged. "I pretended I was making a voodoo doll."

I laughed. "A voodoo doll?"

"Yep."

"Of whom?"

"My mom."

I held my glass to hers. "Nick is lucky to have you, Andie."

She clinked her glass against mine. "Thanks. And I'm sure your wedding is going to be beautiful, Waverly."

"I'm sure it will be too." The *It's just not the wedding I wanted* went unspoken, but we both heard it.

An uncomfortable yet somehow unavoidable silence followed, and we both let it pass. Then Andie rubbed her hands together. "Okay, bride, let's have some outrageously priced cheesecake on Mrs. McIntyre, and then I'll go call Nick and ask him to come visit as soon as he can. Sound like a plan?"

I smiled. "Sounds like a *great* plan. I'd love to see him. Have I ever told you how much I love that guy?"

She laughed. "Shut up."

chapter twenty

"You think Bee's going to show up wearing dark sunglasses?"

I coughed a laugh. "Andie!"

She shrugged. "It's a legitimate question. So where are we going anyway?" We were standing outside the hotel the next morning, waiting for Jake's mom to pick us up.

"I have no idea. Somewhere expensive, I suppose."

"Ya think?"

I laughed. "Be nice. Hey, there she is."

Mrs. McIntyre drove up with Bee in the passenger seat.

She was wearing dark sunglasses.

"Well, look at that," Andie said under her breath.

I squeezed her arm. "I'm going to kill you if you make me laugh in front of them."

"Waverly, Andie, good morning." Mrs. McIntyre emerged from the car wearing a bright smile to go with her designer pant-suit. "Happy birthday, Waverly."

"Thanks." *I can't believe this is how I'm spending it, but thanks.*

"How was your evening last night?"

"Delicious," Andie said.

I nodded a bit too enthusiastically as we got in the backseat. "It was wonderful, Mrs. McIntyre. Thanks so much for treating us."

"It's our pleasure. Consider it a birthday gift from Jake's father and me. Isn't that restaurant just lovely? I hope Phillip took care of you."

"Yes, definitely. He was great."

Andie reached over the passenger seat and squeezed Bee's shoulder. "Good morning, Bee, how are you?"

"Hello, ladies. I'm not feeling all that great this morning, to be honest."

Andie and I exchanged glances, and I wondered what excuse she would give. *Husband was snoring all night? Leg cramps kept her up?* She had to be embarrassed.

"That's too bad, Bee," Andie said. "What's wrong?"

I tried not to laugh at Andie's temerity. She and I were clearly thinking the same thing, but I didn't share her nerve.

Bee turned around to face us and pushed her sunglasses on top of her head. "To be quite honest, my dears, I have a touch of the Irish flu."

We both laughed. *The Irish flu?* I hadn't heard that since college.

"Nice, Bee." Andie gave her a proud nod. "Way to own it."

Mrs. McIntyre looked over at Bee. "Why, how about that? And you're not even Irish," she said with a little smirk.

Bee turned to face the front again and put her sunglasses back on. "Hell, if a lady can't have a few drinks to celebrate the marriage of her best friend's son, then…hell."

Andie and I looked at each other and laughed. Who knew Bee had such a good sense of humor?

"Bee, I like your attitude," Andie said.

I smiled and leaned back into the plush leather seat.

Maybe this birthday won't be so painful after all.

Before I knew it we were sitting in the back room of an elegant boutique I'd already forgotten the name of, facing a mountain of elaborate dresses made by designers I'd never heard of.

I didn't have to try anything on this time, so I didn't actually mind all that much. The plush couch was super comfortable, and they even served us coffee and bagels.

Andie, however, was not happy. But true to her word, she put on her game face and became the perfect bridesmaid. I could hardly believe my eyes as I watched her in action. The girl could really turn it on when she wanted to.

She sifted through the enormous rack of gowns. "Wow, they're all so beautiful. How will we ever decide?"

I tried not to laugh.

"Won't this be fun?" Mrs. McIntyre clasped her hands together. "It will be like a fashion show."

I laughed and smiled at her. "Well put." Then I looked at Andie. "Ms. Barnett, looks like you're a runway model today."

Andie put her hands on her hips. "Just what I've always dreamed about."

Bee held up her coffee cup. "Here's to models under five three. Now let's get this show on the road so I can go back to Ava's place and lie down."

• • •

One hundred dresses later, give or take a few, Andie tried on one that Jake's mom loved. It was a navy blue, floor-length, one-shoulder number made out of some wildly extravagant fabric I'd never heard of.

Mrs. McIntyre beamed at us. "Oh, it's gorgeous, just gorgeous, don't you think?"

I did not share her enthusiasm.

I looked up at Andie from the couch. She was doing her best to grin and bear it, even though I knew her patience had worn threadbare about ninety dresses earlier. *What do you think?* I asked with my eyes.

She gave me a look back that said, *I don't care anymore.*

"It's not my favorite, but I think it's quite lovely," Bee said from her chair.

The dress was objectively pretty, but it wasn't anything close to something Andie or I would ever wear of our own free will. Then again, none of the dresses at this shop were. They all screamed, *I am expensive yet forgettable!* which wasn't something Andie or I would ever scream. I realized I was doing just that with my wedding dress, which was hard enough to stomach.

"Waverly, don't you think it's just exquisite?" Mrs. McIntyre turned toward me on the couch. "Just perfect for an elegant evening wedding, don't you think?"

I hesitated.

How am I supposed to answer that?

Yes, it's exquisite, but it's your taste, not mine.

I would never want that for my wedding, but I clearly have no say in this.

Yes, it's perfect for an elegant evening wedding, but I wanted a casual afternoon wedding.

I bit my lip.

Maybe it was finally time to speak my mind?

"Plus that color will look lovely with the freesias," she said.

I gave her a confused look. "What are freesias?"

"They're flowers, dear." She looked slightly embarrassed for me. "For the bridal bouquets and centerpieces."

She's already picked out my flowers?

But what about our casablancas? The casablancas that your son wants?

I glanced at Andie, whose incredulous look now said it all.

Yes, it was time to speak my mind.

This has to stop.

"Um, actually, Mrs. McIntyre…"

She put her hand on my shoulder and smiled. "Please, dear, call me Ava."

I froze, momentarily taken aback.

Then I swallowed and cleared my throat.

"You want me to call you Ava?" I eked out the words in a whisper.

"Don't you think it's about time?" She smiled again and gave my shoulder a gentle squeeze. "After all, you're going to be my daughter soon."

Did she just call me her daughter?

I felt a lump forming in my throat.

I stole another look at Andie, whose face softened. She gave me a sympathetic nod.

She understood.

I turned back at Mrs. McIntyre and smiled a bit awkwardly. "Okay, um, then Ava it is."

"Wonderful. That reminds me, I have something for you." She opened her purse and pulled out a small rectangular box wrapped in silver paper with a tiny blue bow.

I smiled in genuine surprise. "For me?"

"Happy birthday, Waverly. It's from Walter and me."

I carefully unwrapped the box, then slowly removed the lid.

Inside lay a delicate strand of pearls.

I put my hand over my mouth.

"Oh my gosh, it's gorgeous." I wasn't even lying. It was.

She smiled. "I thought you might like it. Pearls will look lovely on you because of your nice jawline and neck." She looked at Bee. "Doesn't Waverly have a beautiful jawline and neck?"

Bee stood up to stretch. "Waverly's a looker, that's for sure. I think I may have mentioned that yesterday after my fourth glass of champagne. That bubbly certainly did a lot of talking for me."

Andie laughed and put her arm around Bee. "I like you more every time I see you."

Ava gestured toward the necklace. "Would you like me to put it on you?"

I felt my hand fly up to my bare neck. "Sure."

"Here, let me help you. Can you move your ponytail out of the way?" We both stood up, and she placed the strand around my neck. When she was done with the clasp, she pointed toward one of the enormous mirrors. "There you go. Have a look."

I walked over to check out my reflection and couldn't help but smile at what I saw. "Wow, it's beautiful, Ava. Thank you."

"It looks lovely on you." Then she nodded toward Andie, who I knew hated pearls almost as much as she hated exercising. Back in high school her mom had made her wear them for every special occasion, which blunted her efforts to be the trendy girl. "Come to think of it, pearls would look lovely with that bridesmaid dress, don't you both think?"

Andie and I exchanged a look that said we understood each other.

"Yes," we both answered with a smile.

• • •

Once we were back in the car, Ava turned to me and Andie.

"I have a little surprise for you."

"A surprise?" At that point all Andie and I wanted to do was go lie out by the pool, but it looked like that might not happen.

She nodded. "We're headed to Sugar Chef."

Our blank stares indicated we had no idea what she talking about.

"You've never heard of it?"

We shook our heads.

Bee gave her a look. "Ava, they don't live in Florida."

Bee was cool.

Ava adjusted the rearview mirror. "Well, it's a very popular bakery. And I've made an appointment for us to taste some wedding cakes!"

Say what?

We were going to taste wedding cakes?

If there was *one part* of the wedding I actually wanted to take care of myself, it was selecting the cake.

Actually, unless it was solid chocolate, I wasn't all that interested in cake. If it were up to me, I'd be celebrating my nuptials privately with a yummy plate of chocolate—for two, of course. But I knew better than to hope for that.

And if I *was* going to go cake tasting, I wanted to do it with Jake, not his mother.

Sigh.

His mom was so excited that I couldn't bear to let on how I really felt, so I held my tongue as we pulled up at the bakery. She introduced us to the owner, who soon brought out a huge selection of cake bites for us to taste. Over the next hour, we tried every type of cake I'd ever heard of, plus several I hadn't. Red velvet. Carrot. Raspberry cream. Vanilla custard. Lemon chiffon. It was endless.

By the time we'd finished, I wasn't sure I'd be able to fit into my wedding dress anymore.

"I feel sick," Andie said as we climbed back into the car.

Ava was delighted. She thought the raspberry cream was the best choice, and I just didn't have any strength left to tell her that the only flavor I wanted was about as far away from that as it gets. So I just smiled and thought about spending our last hours in Florida relaxing at the hotel. Andie and I weren't leaving until this evening, so we still had time to enjoy the sun.

Pool, here I come.

We'd barely left the bakery parking lot when Ava called over her shoulder to us in the back seat. "Would you two mind if we stopped at the mall for a few minutes?"

I looked at Andie. *The mall?*

She shrugged, her eyes already half closed.

"Um, okay," I said.

"Bee needs to pick up some eye cream before she heads back to Miami, and there's a Jordan Brooke right on the way to your hotel."

My ears perked up. *Jordan Brooke?* That was one of our biggest accounts at Waverly's Honey Shop.

"Sure, no problem." I looked over at Andie again, who was nearly asleep.

Eventually we pulled into The Gardens mall. I nudged Andie awake.

"You okay?" I whispered to her as we approached the entrance.

She yawned. "Good as new. I'm a champion, remember?"

"I'll just be a few minutes." Bee looked at her watch. "Meet me here in fifteen?"

"Sure," Ava said. "I'll have a peek at the shoes."

As Bee wandered away, Andie said, "Maybe I'll visit the makeup counter too. I could use a new lipstick."

"Okay." I gestured toward the directory. "I'm going to check out the second floor. Jordan Brooke is one of our biggest accounts."

"Excuse me, dear?" Ava said.

I cleared my throat. "Um, Jordan Brooke is one of our biggest accounts."

"Biggest accounts for what?"

"For my, um, my Honey products."

"Your Honey products?"

Andie put a hand on her arm. "You don't know about Waverly's Honey Shop?"

Ava raised her eyebrows. "Waverly's...Honey Shop? No. What's that?"

Andie waved her forefinger in the air. "Shame on Jake for not telling you. Waverly created an entire line of products based around *Honey on Your Mind.*"

Ave looked a bit stunned. "You did?"

I smiled and nodded.

"But how?"

I cleared my throat. "Um, out of my apartment?" *What is up with all the throat clearing?*

Andie shook her head. "Not out of her apartment anymore. She's big-time now. Let's go have a look, shall we?" She pointed to the escalator, and Ava and I followed her up. When we reached the second floor, she beelined to the first employee she saw.

"Excuse me, where do you sell the Waverly's Honey Shop line?"

The young woman smiled and pointed to her left. "On the other side of lingerie, right before you get to juniors."

"Thanks."

Andie motioned for us to keep following her. "Ladies, if you will."

We passed through a sea of bras and underwear, and soon I saw my Honey products. The small display was much like the one Paige and I had used to present the line at trade shows, back when we were trying to land our first account. Honey Tees, Honey Totes, Honey Eye Pillows, even a few packs of Honey Notes. It wasn't a big selection, but there it was, my imagination come to life under a blue-and-green sign that said WAVERLY'S HONEY SHOP: SOMETIMES WE ALL NEED A SPOONFUL OF HONEY. The line wasn't in the Manhattan Jordan Brooke yet, so this was first time I'd seen them on display like this.

Ava picked up a light-blue eye pillow that said DREAM.

"These are...your products?"

I smiled. "Looks like it."

"You came up with these on your own?"

I nodded. "Originally, yes. I have some help now."

"And you do this in addition to your work on *Love, Wendy*?"

I nodded again.

"How in the *world* do you find time to do both?"

I smiled. "I'm still trying to figure out how to be in two places at once, but for now, I just race around a lot and drink a lot of coffee."

"She's a rock star." Andie put her arm around me. "I'm sure you already know it, but you're quite lucky to have this one joining your family."

Ava turned to set the eye pillow down, and as she did so, Andie nudged me. I looked at her, and she mouthed the words *That should shut her up about Holly.*

"Waverly, is that you?"

Startled, I turned to my left. The woman's face was familiar, but I couldn't place it. Her dark-blonde hair was pulled back in a messy bun, the kind that didn't look messy on purpose, just... messy. And a little dirty. She wore a navy-blue suit with what looked like a coffee stain on the lapel.

"That's me," I said with a smile. *And you are?*

"It's me, Rebecca Clark."

The look in my eyes must have been blank.

"Becca Clark? I'm the buyer here?"

Oh my God! Rebecca Clark from Jordan Brooke! My memory flashed to the year before, when during a life-changing brunch meeting (for me at least), she had decided to carry Waverly's Honey Shop products at hundreds of Jordan Brooke stores across the country.

"Oh yes, Rebecca, of course. I'm so sorry. I just...wasn't expecting to see you here. You live in Ohio, right?" I could feel my cheeks flush with embarrassment. How had I not recognized her?

She nodded with a smile, and I remembered how friendly she'd been to me and Paige that morning. "Please, call me Becca. And yes, I live in Cleveland, but I'm on the road a lot checking on the merchandise. I see you've found your Honey products."

"Yes, I was, um, just showing them to my friends." I gestured to Andie and Ava. "This is Andie Barnett, and this is my, um, my fiancé's mother, Ava McIntyre." I stumbled over the word *fiancé*, and all I could think was, *Davey was so right.*

Becca eagerly shook their hands. "You're getting married?"

I nodded. "In February. I live in New York, but he's from Florida, so we decided to get married down here. Ava threw me a beautiful shower yesterday."

"The wedding's at the Breakers," Ava added with a polite smile. I cringed and wanted to yell *Who cares!*

Becca, probably used to South Floridians like Ava, politely ignored the superfluous comment and nodded her head toward the product display. "We just love Waverly's products. They're so creative, don't you think?"

Andie nodded. "They're amazing. Waverly's amazing."

Ava nodded slightly but didn't speak.

Becca crossed her arms in front of her chest. "So how's Paige? I haven't heard from her in a while."

I hesitated. We hadn't told any of our buyers about Paige's pregnancy. Or imminent departure.

Stay composed, Waverly. You don't need to share that information.

"She just had a baby," I blurted.

Oh, crap.

A look of compassion and concern crossed over Becca's face. "A baby? Really? I had no idea she was pregnant."

I wanted to kick myself. *What is wrong with you?*

I swallowed "Um, yes, well, she was. She um, she had a little boy named Graham. He's super cute." I remember Becca had mentioned her kids in the meeting Paige and I had with her in Cleveland, so I hoped this news was no cause for alarm.

I was wrong.

"Who's taking over for her while she's out? And how long will she be gone?" she asked.

Out of the corner of my eye, I could see Andie and Ava watching this uncomfortable conversation unfold. I was mortified that they were witnessing it and wanted to shoo them away, but I couldn't see any way to do it without making everything worse.

I thought about how to answer Becca's question.

Should I lie?

I didn't want to lie.

Plus I'm a terrible liar.

So I opted for the truth.

Or mostly the truth.

I forced a smile. "I think we've found the perfect person to transition into the position. In fact, I'm about to offer her the job tomorrow."

She raised her eyebrows. "You didn't find someone before Paige had her baby?"

I willed myself to keep smiling. "Oh, believe me, we tried. But dynamos like Paige don't come around every day, as you can imagine. Plus she was working up until the day she gave birth, so we didn't want to jump the gun." *Jump the gun? Ugh.* I hated when clichés flew unexpectedly out of my mouth.

Becca nodded, but concern was written all over her face.

In block letters.

As it should have been.

She was a bit rumpled, but she was no idiot. She knew Paige had been running the show.

"It will be fine, I promise. Paige put everything in excellent order. Encyclopedic, actually. Your account managers will hardly notice that she's...um...not there." I couldn't bring myself to use the word *gone.* I could only hope she wouldn't press the *When is she coming back?* issue, because no amount of clever semantics could gloss over the meaning of *never.*

Becca nodded again. "Okay, I guess we'll see. But in the future, please keep me in the loop about these things, okay?" Her warm smile from earlier was nearly gone.

"Okay, I promise." I felt my face and neck get hot at the reprimand. I wished I could crawl inside one of the nearby clothing rounders and hide like I used to do as a kid.

She put a hand on my arm. "I like your products, Waverly, I really do. I'd hate to see them get lost in the shuffle because of logistical mishaps. That happens quite often with young companies, and it's such a shame to see them fail."

I nodded. "Got it." My voice was shaky. The word *fail* hung in the air.

"Good. I'm glad we understand each other." She gave my arm a little squeeze, then turned to Ava and Andie and offered a genuine smile. "Well, I've got to run, I'm afraid. It was lovely meeting you both." She gave me a quick hug. "Waverly, congratulations on your engagement, and please give Paige my best. That's wonderful news for both of you."

I forced a smile. "Thank you, Becca."

She turned on her heel and was gone. I felt myself begin to shake as I watched her walk toward the escalator.

As soon as she was out of sight, I started to cry.

Not floods of tears, but enough to qualify as…crying.

"Waverly, dear, are you all right?" Jake's mom put her hand on my shoulder.

I coughed and wiped my cheeks. "I'm…trying to be."

Andie looked at Ava. "She's been under a lot of stress trying to find a replacement for her business partner. Good help is hard to find, you know."

"I can't believe I didn't know anything about this," Ava said to Andie. "I thought *Love, Wendy* was her only job."

Andie shook her head. "Nope. Rock star." I was so grateful to have her there.

"It's just...incredible," Ava said, then turned to me. "You have all that to manage, and you still came down here for a bridal shower?"

I nodded through my tears. "I knew it meant a lot to you."

"And don't forget it's her birthday weekend too," Andie said.

Ava put a hand on her heart. "I...I don't know what to say."

"Waverly tries harder than anyone I know to please everyone around her," Andie said. "Sometimes it gets her in trouble, but that's why her friends love her so much."

"Thank you, Waverly," Ava said quietly. She still looked stunned.

I smiled. "You're welcome, Ava."

I looked at Andie and spoke with my eyes. *Thank* you.

chapter twenty-one

"You really ran into the buyer at your biggest account while you were in the store?" Jake handed me a steaming mug of hot chocolate and sat down next to me on the couch.

I laughed weakly and cupped the mug with both hands. "Can you believe it? What are the chances? There are like a zillion Jordan Brooke stores out there. Given my lack of coordination, you'd think I'd have a better chance of literally running into a wall than into Becca Clark at one of them."

I'd just arrived home from the airport and finished recounting the weekend to Jake, who'd arrived at my apartment just a few minutes after I'd called him. I loved that he lived close enough to come over so quickly. Next step was for him to move in, which *should* have been a wonderful and exciting event to look forward to, but somehow it had turned into yet another burden on a growing to-do list. How had I veered so off track from what was really important to me?

"But other than that, the weekend went okay?"

I smiled and tried to focus on the positive. "Surprisingly, yes. We got a *lot* of loot at the shower, by the way." I looked around the living room. "I have no idea where we're going to put it all when it arrives, but we scored big time." At least we'd checked *register* off our to-do list.

He brushed a loose strand of hair out of my eyes. "Let's worry about that when the time comes. I know you've got enough on your mind already. Did my mom behave?"

"I love your word choice. As if she were a dog or something."

He laughed. "Well, did she?"

I nodded. "She had her moments, but overall she was really nice. Bee was too. That lady's got a bit of spunk in her."

"Bee? You got that right. There's more than meets the eye with that one."

I put my hand on the pearl necklace. "Oh, check out what your mom gave me for my birthday."

He leaned forward to have a look. "My mom gave you that?"

"She and your dad. She said it was from both of them."

"Pearls? Wow. She loves her pearls, so you must have really won her over. Nice work, wife-to-be."

I took a seated bow. "Why thank you, husband-to-be. Actually, she did something above and beyond this necklace that makes me think I've finally won her over."

He scratched his eyebrow. "Above and beyond a strand of pearls? Did she buy you a car or something?"

I laughed. "Maybe next year."

"What did she do?"

I hesitated for a moment, then smiled. "She…she asked me to call her Ava."

"Really?"

"Really."

"Well, it's about time."

"Hey, she got there eventually."

He laughed. "And good she did. Do you know how many times I've told her how absurd it is to let you call her *Mrs. McIntyre* when my dad is begging you to call him Walt?"

"You told her that?"

"Of course. She knew what she was doing. It was completely unnecessary."

"Well, thanks for sticking up for me, I guess." I wasn't sure how I felt about that.

"I'm not happy about having to do it."

"Well, thanks anyway."

He gently touched my cheek. "I love my mom, and I know she means well, but I also know she can be a bit frosty."

"So I've learned. But you know something else?"

"What?"

I held my palms out in front of me. "That episode with Becca was flat-out *mortifying*, and your mom witnessed the whole thing, which could have added insult to injury. But the way she reacted, Jake, she was...*kind* to me, really kind."

"She was?"

I nodded. "And instead of making me feel worse, the way she reacted made it, I don't know, comforting to have her there. Almost nurturing."

"So I'm guessing you're going to offer the job to the woman you mentioned the other day? What was her name?"

"Eunice. And yes, I've decided to offer it to her tomorrow. I guess we'll see if she accepts. After what happened with Courtney, I'm not holding my breath."

"Sounds like the right call, even if it's not ideal."

I sighed. "She's good enough. Actually, she's very good, even though she's not what I'd envisioned, if that makes sense."

"You mean to join your sorority?"

I smirked. "Very funny. But, yes, in a way I guess you're right. Through this whole interview process I've realized that the *people* behind Waverly's Honey Shop are what I really love about the company, you know?"

He nodded.

"I know it sounds silly to hear from a business owner, but I want to have fun at work, and Eunice just doesn't seem to have that work-and-play spirit. I mean, at *Love, Wendy*, I may not adore *every*one in the office, but I get to spend my days chatting up all of New York City. And you know how much I love to chat."

"That's not silly, Waverly. Sounds pretty healthy, actually."

"Plus I've learned that while I have lots of creative ideas, I don't exactly shine on the business side of the coin, which is why having Paige was so great."

He nodded again.

"But I can't keep searching for that perfect someone to replace her forever. I mean, I already found *you* for my love life. I was bound to strike out eventually."

"You're comparing me to a job applicant?"

I stood up and smoothed my hands over my skirt. "You have to admit, the screening process for a romantic partner is similar."

"How so exactly?"

I started counting on my fingers. "Time-consuming, exhausting, disappointing. Do you want me to go on?"

He held up his hands and shook his head. "Please don't."

I picked up our mugs and walked into the kitchen. "Don't worry, though. You have job security," I called over my shoulder.

"Is that right?"

"Yep. *That* position has definitely been filled. You get benefits too."

As I was washing the mugs in the sink, he walked up behind me and slid his arms around my waist, then nuzzled his lips into my neck. "Benefits? I like the sound of that."

• • •

The next morning I taped a *Honey on Your Mind* segment in which I asked harried commuters in Grand Central Station what was on their minds as they began the work week. I expected the many variations on *I'd rather be on a beach* and *I wish I were still in bed* I got, but not some of the more earnest responses that came my way. Maybe it was because it was a chilly Monday morning at the tail end of a lovely warm fall, but many people were brutally forthcoming with angst-ridden answers, many of which were followed by a gasp and a *Please don't use that on TV!*

"When I was little, I always swore I wouldn't turn into my parents, but here I am, working too hard at a job I hate. How did that happen?"

"I'm so glad to be out of my house. I really need to leave him. I don't even love him."

"My boss is a cruel and heartless person, but I can't bring myself to quit. What is wrong with me?"

After the following reply, I had to stop:

"I have to fire a good man today, and he has no idea it's coming. I hate my job."

I dropped the hand holding the microphone to my side and looked at the camera man.

"Will, this isn't working."

He laughed. "You think?"

"Everyone is so *depressed*."

He laughed again. "You're just realizing that now?"

I sighed. "I clearly need to come up with a better topic. I know Justin isn't a fan of veering off course, but I have to call an audible here."

"I agree. Justin will understand."

"How about we get some coffee and brainstorm?"

He shrugged. "Sure, sounds good."

We packed up and were walking toward the stairwell when I noticed a display in the window of one of the more expensive shops in Grand Central. It said: HAT'S, GLOVE'S ON SALE.

I stopped in my tracks.

Hat's and *glove's*?

I looked at Will and pointed at the sign. "Do you see that?"

He shrugged. "No one cares about grammar anymore. I hear high school kids these days write their essays in all lowercase."

I raised my eyebrows. "Hey, maybe I should do a segment on grammatical errors. I could point them out all over the city!"

He laughed. "Good luck making friends doing that."

"Good point. Okay, let's hit the food court."

Downstairs we found an unoccupied table near Zaro's Bread Basket. Will sat down with his equipment while I went to order, and as I waited in line I pulled out my phone to check my messages.

There was just one text, from Davey.

Lunch today? Interesting news to discuss with you.

I typed a quick reply.

Can we do tomorrow? I'm at a taping then have to go hire someone.

I bought two large coffees, and on my way back to the table my phone buzzed with a new message.

Don't hire anyone before speaking with me. This is important.
Meet me at noon at Junior's? West 45th and Broadway.

I stared at my phone and reread the message.
I typed a quick reply.

OK, see you there.

• • •

Twenty minutes later Will and I were back in the main terminal of Grand Central, ready to try again. With a new approach and a fresh jolt of caffeine coursing through my bloodstream, I was ready to go. The morning rush in New York City lasts for hours, so even though it was well after nine now, the station was still packed with people on their way to work.

I began approaching random men and women with a smile and the following question: *If you could have your dream job, what would it be?*

I got the usual brush-off by many people rushing by, but this time several stopped when they heard me. Their eyes lit up as they smiled and eagerly answered.

Some examples:

"I'm an accountant, but I've always wanted to open a little corner bookstore like Meg Ryan had in You've Got Mail. *I'd probably eventually go out of business too, but I still think it would be fun."*

"My dream job? I'd love to have a bakery, one that makes only wedding cakes. Don't ask me why, because I'm twice divorced and will probably be in therapy for the rest of my life, but for some reason that's my own little fantasy. I think each day would be a treat."

"*A friend of mine from college runs a bungee jumping business out in Whistler. How killer is that? Damn, I'm jealous of that dude. He even has a little pug dog named Bungee. I'm an attorney, which means I'm at the office too much to own a freaking fish.*"

"*Navy SEAL captain. How badass would* that *be?*"

After a dozen or so interviews, I still needed a bit more footage of women, so I approached a blonde fortysomething in jeans and a crisp black blazer carrying a black leather backpack.

"Excuse me, ma'am, could I ask you a quick question? I'm Waverly Bryson from *Love, Wendy*."

She gave me a confused look, but she seemed friendly. "Who? And from what?"

I smiled. "*Love, Wendy.* It's a popular daytime show on NBC."

"I'm sorry, I don't watch daytime TV."

I laughed and glanced at the camera. "It's okay, I didn't expect that many people I'd meet at Grand Central at nine thirty in the morning would. Anyhow, I work for the show, and I was wondering if I could ask you the following question: If you could have your dream job, what would it be?"

She shifted her backpack from one shoulder to the other. "My dream job?"

I nodded.

She smiled and looked like she was about to reply, but then she hesitated. "I'm so sorry, what did you say your name was again?"

"Waverly. Waverly Bryson."

"Well, Waverly, I've got to tell you, I already have it."

I raised my eyebrows. "You do?"

She nodded. "About ten years ago I quit my finance job and started my own business."

"You did? What kind of company?"

"We make dark chocolate. Have you ever heard of Lauren's Chocolate?"

My eyes got big. "You run *Lauren's Chocolate*?"

She nodded. "I founded it. I'm Lauren Flaig."

"I eat those chocolate bars all the time!" I blurted, then immediately covered my mouth with my hand. *Oops.*

I glanced sheepishly at the camera. "I'm, um, I'm a big fan of chocolate, especially dark chocolate. They sell Lauren's Chocolate at a little shop I go to in Dumbo." *Oh, sugar, shut up already, Waverly!*

Lauren laughed. "I'm glad to hear it. Dark chocolate is good for you, you know."

"And thank God for that. It's such a pleasure to meet you, Lauren." I turned to the camera. "And for those of you watching at home, I can't say enough about how delicious those chocolate bars are. If you haven't tried them yet, you simply must. Wendy, back to you." For God knows what reason I saluted to the camera, then dropped the microphone to my side when Will gave me the signal that he'd stopped filming.

"You think we got enough footage to make a good segment?" I asked him.

He nodded and set the camera down. "Definitely. Where did that salute come from?"

"I have no idea." I laughed and turned to Lauren. "It's a real pleasure to meet you, and not just because I love your chocolate bars. You're the first person I've interviewed who isn't fantasizing about what they'd *like* to be doing with their lives. Sounds like you're actually *doing* it."

She smiled. "I guess I am."

"It's very inspiring. I know our viewers will love it. Who doesn't love a good American dream story?"

She glanced at her watch. "Well, I'm far from filthy rich, but it's fun, and I'm happy, which is more important to me. And unfortunately, I'm also late to a meeting. Please let me know when this airs, will you? I'd love to see it." She reached into her back pocket and handed me her business card. Then she opened her backpack and pulled out a chocolate bar. "Would you like one?"

I snatched it out of her hand. "Now, that's a rhetorical question if I ever heard one."

She laughed. "I'm glad you're a fan. Bye, um..."

I laughed. "Waverly."

"I'm sorry. I'm just terrible with names. If I hadn't named my own company after myself, I'd probably forget that too."

I smiled. "No worries. I'm terrible with a *lot* of things."

As I watched her disappear into the swarming crowd, it struck me that nearly every person I'd interviewed had responded with a variation on the same answer.

Everyone's dream job is something other than what they are currently doing.

Did everyone hate their jobs? I certainly didn't. I had a ball working at *Love, Wendy*.

I stood there thinking about what Lauren had said. Did everyone want to own their own business? Was that the key to happiness? Or was it a matter of simply being able to do something you think is...fun?

"Waverly, you okay?"

I blinked. "What?"

Will gave me a funny look. "You're just staring into space, like a zombie."

"I'm sorry, I spaced for a moment. You ready to go?"

I nodded.

"Let's hit it," he said.

As we left the station, I looked at the chocolate bar in my hand and wondered how many times I'd bought one just like it at the little shop across the street from Waverly's Honey Shop.

My other job.

The company that *I* started, but which was controlling me right now more than I was controlling it.

The grass is *always greener.*

• • •

"So, what's the big news? The last time you called me like this, you announced that you'd eloped to Vegas." I slipped into a booth across from Davey and was about to reach for the menu when he blocked me with his arm.

"I took the liberty of ordering you a turkey sandwich with fries and a Diet Coke. You still love turkey sandwiches with fries and a Diet Coke?"

I nodded. "Your memory is impressive."

He looked at his watch. "Actually, I need to get back to the office for a meeting at one, so in the interest of time, I rolled the dice."

I laughed. "You always were a master of efficiency. So what's going on? Why didn't you want me to hire anyone? Have you changed your mind about working with me?" I gave him a hopeful grin.

"Bryson, if you knew the borderline obscene amount of money I'm being paid, you probably wouldn't ask me that."

I shrugged. "Good point. So, what, then? Did you think of the perfect person to take the job? And by the way, after that comment about your salary, you're paying for this lunch."

He spread his hands on the table. "Something happened this morning."

"Uh-oh."

Just as he was about to speak, the waiter appeared with our meals and set them down on the table.

I picked up a fry and tossed it into my mouth. "Do I want to hear this?"

Davey took a big sip of his iced tea, then looked at me. "Your JUST SMILE Honey Tote arrived."

"Oh no, did Lindsay see it or something? Did I send it to the wrong address?"

He shook his head. "No, it arrived at the office, just liked I asked. Thanks, by the way. Anyhow, I went straight from the mailroom to a meeting with the entire marketing team."

"Okay..."

He poured ketchup over his fries. "The purpose of the meeting was to come up with promotion ideas for our various product lines, and we were discussing gift bags."

"Sounds fascinating." I pretended to yawn.

He pointed a fry at me. "Save it. Did you know that Blush has a small line of products that are honey-based? Face creams, cleansing masks, body scrubs and lotion, that sort of thing. It's called Honey Blush."

I nodded. "I think I've seen them. I can't *afford* them, but I've seen them."

"Well, as we were discussing promotion ideas for that line, I opened your package. Everyone else in the room was female, so they of course asked what it was."

I took a bite of my sandwich and nodded.

"So I showed them the Honey Tote."

My mouth was full, so I said *And?* with my eyes.

"And they loved it, Waverly. *Loved* it."

I washed down the food with a gulp of soda. "Really?"

He nodded. "Totally. They all wanted to know where I got it, so I explained how I knew you from my days at JAG, and how you're a big star on *Love, Wendy* now, and how you also have a whole line of products called Waverly's Honey Shop. I even showed them your website on my iPad. They thought it was adorable."

I narrowed my eyes. "So let me guess. You asked me here because you want to give away your Honey Blush promotional items inside a Honey Tote."

"No. Well, yes, but no."

I narrowed my eyes even more. "Do you want to include a *different* Honey product with the promotion? Like a Honey Tee or something?"

He shook his head.

I leaned back against the booth. "Then, *honey*, I'm afraid you've lost me."

He hesitated and looked around the crowded diner, then leaned forward and lowered his voice. "Waverly, just by chance, the chief of global product development happens to be in town, and she was at the meeting."

"The who? Of what?"

"Francine DeVaroux, the chief of global product development. In other words, the woman who makes the ultimate decisions on what products Blush is going to make and sell."

"She saw my products?"

He nodded. "She loved them, Waverly. I'm talking head over heels."

I swallowed. He had me on the edge of the seat, but I still couldn't begin to guess where this was going.

"And?"

"And…"

"And *what*, Davey? What are you trying to tell me?"

He keep his voice low. "This is just me speculating out loud here, but I think if you were to plant a seed, Blush and Company might be up for buying Waverly's Honey Shop to fold into the Honey Blush line."

My jaw dropped.

"What?"

He leaned back against the booth. "You heard me."

"Blush would *buy* Waverly's Honey Shop?"

He nodded and took a sip of his iced tea. "I think you could probably make it happen. If you wanted to, that is. Would you even want to sell?"

I sat there for a moment, not sure how to reply. Despite the anxiety Paige's departure was causing me, *selling* Waverly's Honey Shop had never even crossed my mind.

"I...I...I guess I never really thought about it," I finally said.

"Well, it's time to start thinking about it. You could probably make a lot of money, Waverly."

I sat there too stunned to speak.

Davey was nearly done with his hamburger before I finally found my voice again.

"I...don't know what to say," I finally said.

"The thing is, Francine is at our office only until the end of day tomorrow. If you want me to plant that seed for you, I will. If not, we can pretend this conversation never happened. It's totally up to you."

"End of day tomorrow?" I whispered.

He nodded. "Tomorrow morning she's off to San Francisco for a couple days, and then back to our headquarters in France and then God knows where else. So if you want to act, now is the time. Otherwise, she's so crazy-busy with other things that I think the window will be shut."

"Okay," I said, still dazed.

"So you'll let me know what you want me to do?"

I nodded slowly. "I guess so."

"No pressure or anything. Just looking out for you, Bryson." He finished off his fries.

I kept nodding. "I know. Thanks, Davey."

He covered his plate with a napkin and signaled for the check. "Oh, and later this week I'm going to need to order five hundred Honey Totes for the gift bags. Who should I call about that?"

I looked at him and sighed. "Honestly? I'm not sure."

chapter twenty-two

I didn't call Eunice that afternoon.

Or Davey.

Or anyone.

Instead, after lunch I went to Dumbo, alone, to mull things over. I opened the office door, turned on the lights, and took a seat at the conference table. Tasha and Beth weren't due to arrive until later in the afternoon, so I had some time to myself.

To think.

And think.

I felt like Dorothy in *The Wizard of Oz*, trapped in the Wicked Witch's castle watching the grains of sand slide through the hourglass. Only I knew there was no Toto—much less anyone who could *talk*—to rush in and tell me what to do before time ran out. The decision was mine and mine alone.

Should I hire Eunice to keep Waverly's Honey Shop running?

Or should I try to sell it to Blush?

If I sold it, would I regret giving it up?

I closed my eyes and thought of the woman from Lauren's Chocolate. Despite my skepticism regarding fate, it seemed like more than a mere coincidence that I'd met her today.

Lauren Flaig, out of nearly two dozen people I'd interviewed, was the only one who seemed truly happy with her professional life.

Was that because she was running her own business?

Or was it because running her own business was a choice of her own making, and *that* was what made her happy?

I sighed.

I'd gone to my office to figure out what I wanted, but now I was more confused than ever.

I don't want to give this up.

But I know I can't do everything.

I know Eunice isn't the perfect fit.

But she can do the job.

And I have to do something.

I closed my eyes.

I have to do something.

It's time for me to take control of my destiny.

I kept my eyes closed for a few moments, then stood up and walked across the still-undecorated office to the window. I gazed across the East River toward Manhattan, then to the bridges on my left and to my right. Dumbo offers a rare close-up view of both the Brooklyn and Manhattan bridges, two formidable structures that allow for quick travel between the two boroughs in a way that hadn't been possible before, all because someone had thought of a better...solution.

Then I thought about something Jake had said about Paige's decision to move to Tennessee. I'd wondered aloud if she was giving up too much, and he'd disagreed. "She's compromising, not sacrificing," he'd said to me. "There's a difference."

As usual, he was right, because even though she was leaving New York, Paige was happier than I'd ever seen her.

I closed my eyes.

Jake was saying healthy relationships are about compromise, not sacrifice. Just like Davey and Paige have been telling me I can't live my life for other people.

Compromise, not sacrifice.

Compromise, not sacrifice.

They'd been talking about personal relationships, but the more I thought about their words, the more I realized they could apply to more than just that. They could also apply to how I'd been—

I interrupted my own thoughts with a new one.

Oh my God.

I know what to do now.

About everything.

I hurried back to the conference table and reached for my purse.

I had a few phone calls to make, and each one was going to begin the same way.

Hi, it's Waverly. I really need to talk to you.

chapter twenty-three

I looked in the full-length mirror and adjusted my dress.

Then I leaned in close to inspect my hair and makeup, my fingers gently rolling over the strand of pearls draped around my neck.

Then I tried to convince myself this was really happening.

This is it.

I'm really getting married.

To Jake.

I took a deep breath.

I turned around and held my arms out to the side. Andie was sitting on the couch, playing Angry Birds on her phone.

"Well?" I held out my arms.

She looked up and smiled. "Wow, you look beautiful."

"Really?"

She nodded and stood up. "Prettier than I've ever seen you. Now let's get a move on, or we're going to be even later than we already are."

• • •

"Are you ready?"

I smiled and nodded. "Very."

"I'm *so* happy for you, Waverly."

I felt my eyes well up with tears. "Thanks, Mackie. I'm so happy for me too," I whispered.

"You look stunning, by the way. I just love your dress. It's so *you*."

I put my fingers on the spaghetti straps and looked down at the plain ivory bodice that flowed in a slight A-line cut to about an inch above the knee. "Thanks. I know it's simple, but simple just feels...*right*, you know?"

She squeezed my shoulder. "Waverly, everything about you and Jake feels simple and right, just the way it should."

I leaned over and hugged her as much as I could, given how enormous her belly was becoming. "Thanks so much for coming. I know traveling is a huge pain right now."

"I wouldn't have missed this. Plus this way the baby can say he was at Auntie Waverly's wedding."

"He?" I raised my eyebrows.

She laughed. "Or she."

"Okay, just checking."

Just then Andie walked over and handed me my bouquet. "Okay, women, enough hugging, it's showtime." I could hear the soft harp music in the distance.

McKenna put her hand on my shoulder. "Are you ready?"

I nodded. "More ready than I've ever been."

Andie clapped her hands together. "Chop chop. Let's get this show on the road. You've got a couple of anxious men waiting for you, starting with that handsome one right there." She gestured toward my dad, who was quietly standing a respectful distance away. He knew how important it was that I have this moment with my best friends.

I swallowed and nodded again. "Okay, I'm ready. Let's do this." Then I looked at my dad and waved him over. "Mr. Bryson, you ready too?"

"Baby, you just say the word." He walked over and held out the crook of his arm, a grin on his face that bordered on silly. *Is he really that happy for me?* My dad was hardly the emotional type, and I was touched to see him this way.

McKenna and Andie walked away, leaving the two of us standing there on the grass.

"I'm just overjoyed for you, baby," he said. "You look beautiful."

I smiled. "Thanks, Dad. And thanks for going along with this. I know it's a bit…well…a bit unusual."

He shook his head. "Not at all. I get to walk my daughter down the aisle *twice*. What father wouldn't want to do that?"

"I think the better question is probably, *What father would?*"

He laughed. "I guess it depends on how you look at it."

I smoothed my hair with my hand. "And I apologize for the short notice. I just knew if we waited any longer, it would be way too cold to do this outside." It was already chilly, but for once I didn't care.

"Not to worry. So are you ready?"

I smiled. "Yes, I'm ready."

My bouquet in one hand, the other wrapped around my dad's arm, we slowly walked across the grass, my low heels squishing into the soil. I could hear the music grow louder as we approached the secluded area where Jake had proposed to me. As we rounded a big tree, I squeezed my bouquet and lifted it to my face.

I closed my eyes to breathe in the fragrance of the flowers.

Casablancas.

Celebration.

Then I opened my eyes and saw him.

He was standing about twenty feet away, staring at the ground, his hands clasped behind his back. Next to him was Nick, who through the magical powers of the Internet had recently become an "ordained minister" to perform the ceremony.

When I saw them together like that, the full force of what I was about to do hit me. I caught my breath and froze.

I can't believe this is finally happening.

I can't believe this is real.

I can't believe how happy I am.

As if reading my mind, Jake looked up and smiled at me. As soon as we made eye contact, everyone and everything around me disappeared, and my anxiety melted away. I knew Andie and McKenna were there, and Jake's parents, and Betty, but I couldn't see anyone but Jake. I could feel myself holding onto my dad's arm, but I could no longer see him either. I didn't even hear the music of the harpist just a few feet away.

I kept my eyes firmly locked on Jake, who was all that mattered.

I hesitated for a moment, then took a deep breath and prepared to take my first step down the aisle.

My first step toward my future as a married woman.

I was just about to move when Jake mouthed the words *I love you.*

And everything was right.

I smiled at him and tried to lift my foot.

Only I couldn't.

Because my heel was stuck in a soft patch of soil.

"Are you *kidding* me?" I looked down at the ground, then held on to my dad's arm and yanked my leg up.

The heel came free, unleashing a swirl of grassy dirt with it, and everyone laughed. Even Jake's mom. She hadn't been thrilled when we'd told her about our plan to have two weddings, but in the end she'd come around, especially after I told her I'd have the second wedding in a church—officiated by Father McMillan. With Jake at my side I'd finally stood up to her, but with respect for her feelings, and she'd responded in kind. I gently touched the pearl necklace and smiled. Jake and his dad had been right all along. She could be a handful, but her heart was in the right place. His siblings were completely on board but were following McKenna's lead and planned to attend just one event, families in tow.

"You okay, baby?" my dad asked.

I laughed too, then stood up straight and smoothed my hair with my hand. "I'm fine. Now let's do this."

Then I walked down the aisle, where Jake McIntyre was waiting to become my husband.

• • •

"Here's to the married couple." Andie held up her glass for a champagne toast. It was about thirty minutes later, and the entire wedding group, all nine of us, were at the picturesque Central Park Boathouse to celebrate.

I held a finger up to my lips and laughed. "Shhh, that's a secret until after the eighteenth of February."

Jake, Andie, McKenna, Nick, and I were sitting in the lounge area, sharing a bottle of champagne. My dad and Betty were outside, admiring the scenery and chatting with Jake's parents.

"What if one of your fans spotted you and already posted something on Twitter?" Andie said. "Then the jig would be up."

I briefly panicked and looked around the room. "Oh Jesus, do you really think that could happen?"

McKenna laughed. "Waverly, please. First of all, that's highly unlikely. And even if it did happen, do you really think any of

Jake's mom's friends are following the Twitter feeds of random housewives from Nebraska?"

"Good point," I said

"So why all the secrecy, anyway?" Nick handed me a fresh glass of champagne. "If you wanted a small wedding, why didn't you just have a small wedding?"

I took a sip and smiled at him. "Thank you. And if you hadn't noticed, I *did* just have a small wedding."

He gave me a look. "Given that you're *also* having a monster of a wedding in February, I believe you are missing the point of my question."

I looked at Jake and spoke with my eyes. *Help.*

"We decided this was a good compromise," he said. "A way for Waverly to be in two places at once, if you will."

I nodded. "Compromise, not sacrifice. That's our motto."

Andie shrugged and drank some champagne. "I don't like to compromise. I like getting what I want. Always."

I smiled. "And somehow, you always do."

Nick put his arm around her and smiled proudly. "Damned straight she does. She got *me*, didn't she?"

My smile turned into a laugh. "Yes, she did, and she's a lucky girl for it." Nick and Andie weren't engaged, but they were still together, which was good enough for me.

"Have you ever noticed that I love you?" I said to Nick.

Andie rolled her eyes. "Don't encourage him. So we really have to go through another wedding in February? The whole nine yards?"

I nodded. "You, yes. Mackie, no. She gets a pass."

McKenna smiled at Andie and put her hands on her bulbous stomach. "I'll be thinking of you in your floor-length, navy-blue bridesmaid dress. I hear it's just gorgeous."

"I hate you," Andie said. "Do you know how much gaudy gold jewelry is going to be on display that weekend? God knows how much alcohol I'm going to consume to get me through the spectacle." Then she looked at Jake. "No offense, of course. Nothing against you and your people."

Jake laughed and raised his hands. "None taken. I know it's going to be a scene."

I leaned over and kissed Jake on the cheek. "I'm actually looking forward to it. Now that I have all I really wanted, which was to marry this amazing man in front of my closest friends, I can relax and enjoy a big fancy party at a gorgeous hotel. What's not to like?"

Andie looked at McKenna. "Her dress weighs like a hundred pounds. Did she tell you that?"

McKenna laughed. "Only a hundred?"

"Weak," Nick said to me. "You could handle more."

I laughed and took a sip of my champagne. "I admit it's going to be a bit over-the-top for my taste, but it will be beautiful, and it's going to make Jake's mom really happy, which makes *me* happy. Plus it will be so fun to have all my friends together in one place." I knew Davey and Lindsay were coming, and Shane and Kristina too, and of course Tasha and Beth. Even Paige and Gary were planning to fly down from Nashville. And despite his crazy schedule, Scotty had said that he and Tad wouldn't miss it. They all knew that Jake and I would already be legally married, but they didn't care.

Quickly realizing my omission, I put my hand on McKenna's arm. "All my friends except for *you*, of course. We'll miss you dearly."

She put her hand over mine. "I'm so happy you decided to do it this way. It would have crushed me to miss seeing you and Jake get married. I'm just sorry Hunter couldn't make it, but someone had to stay home to watch Elizabeth."

I nodded. "Compromise, not sacrifice, right?"

Andie rolled her eyes. "You'd better be careful with all these life lessons you're spouting out, Mrs. Bride. Pretty soon you're going to start sounding like an after-school special."

"Do they even have those anymore?" Jake asked.

McKenna shook her head. "I doubt it. Kids today spend their free time uploading cell phone videos of *themselves*, not watching movies about other kids."

We all laughed, and Jake took my hand in his. "Did you get your passport renewed?"

McKenna looked at me. "Passport?"

I nodded. "Paris. Just for a few days for business. And Jake's coming along, so we're calling it our practice honeymoon."

Jake raised an eyebrow. "Is that what *we're* calling it?"

I grinned at him. "I just made that up, so...I guess...yes, *we* are. We're *married* now, you know."

He put his arm around me and squeezed. "Yes, *we* are. And it's about time."

McKenna put her hand on my arm. "So what's going on in Paris?"

"Yeah, since when do you go to Europe for work?" Andie said. "Is it some special thing for NBC?"

I glanced briefly at Jake, then shook my head. "It's not for *Honey on Your Mind*, actually. It's for Waverly's Honey Shop."

McKenna's eyes got big. "Really? Are you going international?"

I swallowed. "Sort of. You know Blush and Company?"

"The cosmetics company? Of course," she said.

"Never heard of it," Nick said with a shrug.

Andie looked at him. "They're enormous. Waverly's old boss works there now."

I nodded. "Yes, um, well, I'm sort of…selling Waverly's Honey Shop to them."

"*What!*" Andie said.

"You're selling it?" McKenna said.

"When?" Andie said.

"Why?" McKenna said.

I cleared my throat. "Well, as you know, Andie's cousin Paige is moving to Nashville."

"But I thought you'd found a replacement for her," Andie said. "Isn't that what you said?"

I nodded. "I did find one, and I did say that. But my new boss at *Love, Wendy* wants me to start doing more segments each week, and the more I thought about it, the more I realized that I just couldn't do both anymore if I wanted to do both well. It's too much stress. I realized I was letting my jobs run me, and if I wanted to be happy, it was time to make a choice."

"You're really giving up the Honey Shop? After all that work?" McKenna looked disappointed, which hurt me to see.

I held up my index finger. "Well, that's where the *sort of* comes in."

"Say what?" Andie said.

I smiled. "What I mean is, *yes*, I sold it, but I didn't give it up entirely. As part of the contract, Blush is going to keep the Waverly's Honey Shop brand name, and I'm going to act as a creative consultant."

Jake nudged me. "Tell them about Dave and the interns."

"Is that a new band?" Nick asked.

I smirked at him. "Maybe. I guess we'll see, because I'll be working with all of them."

"Say what?" Andie said again.

I smiled. "Waverly's Honey Shop is going to be housed within a line of products that Davey oversees, so technically I'll be working for him again. *And* I got him to bring my interns, Tasha and Beth, on board as part of the deal."

"Keeping the band together. I like it," Nick said.

I nodded. "I'm pretty excited about the arrangement. I know it sounds glamorous to run your own company, but I've thought a lot about it, and for *me*, this is the best solution. I really enjoy working at *Love, Wendy*, and while I'm extremely proud of Waverly's Honey Shop, in my heart I'm just not a businessperson...I'm a *people* person. Trying to be both is exhausting, and it doesn't make me very good at either."

"And the replacement you found for Paige just wasn't your type of people?" McKenna asked.

I pointed at her. "Bingo. It just didn't feel right to do whatever it took to keep the company up and running on my own, which is what society says I should do. To me, being *happy* is what's important, and working with Davey again will be a pleasure, not an obligation or step backward."

"You and your newfound rejection of societal pressures," Andie said. "Isn't that what you said after you lost your engagement ring?"

I shrugged. "Apparently I have become a poster child for unconventional lifestyle choices."

"So what does all this have to do with Paris?" Nick asked.

"Blush and Company is based there, so I guess this is what you'd call...an orientation," I said.

Nick raised his eyebrows. "You mean a boondoggle?"

I shook my head. "No."

Jake laughed. "That's what I'm calling it."

I laughed too. "It's not a boondoggle! Well, okay, maybe it is a little bit, but I really do need to learn some things while I'm over there, so why not enjoy the sights while I'm in town, right?"

Nick coughed. "Boondoggle."

Andie playfully tapped the back of his head. "Save it for someone who cares. You know my whole trip to New York has been a boondoggle."

"And thank God it's coming to a close." He put his arm around her. "Not to get too sappy, little one, but you have been *missed*. Now, who wants some more champagne?"

We all raised our empty glasses, and with my free hand I silently reached for Jake's.

"Did someone order cake?"

The sound of my dad's voice made us all turn our heads. He was standing behind us, holding a pink box from the Prolific Oven, my favorite bakery in the entire world. Jake's parents were next to him. Ava looked a little uncomfortable, but Walt was smiling.

As soon as I saw the box, I turned and gaped at McKenna. "Is that what I think it is?" *A double chocolate?*

She nodded. "You bet it is."

I felt a lump form in my throat. "You brought that all the way from California?" I squeaked the words out.

She nodded again. "You bet I did."

I tried not to cry. "This is officially the best day of my life," I squeaked.

Jake laughed and leaned over to kiss me. "It took the *cake* to make it official? I will try not to take offense at that."

I glanced up at his dad, who winked at me.

"Speaking of making it official, that reminds me!" Nick set his glass down and started to unbutton his shirt.

"Oh God, I'm not sure I want to see this." I pretended to shield my eyes.

"Come on now, where's the love? I had this one custom designed." He opened his dress shirt to reveal a light-blue T-shirt underneath:

I OFFICIATED THE AMAZING WEDDING OF MR. AND MRS.
WAVERLY BRYSON, AND ALL I GOT WAS THIS STUPID T-SHIRT.

chapter twenty-four

After a group dinner at the Boathouse, topped off by wedding cake and coffee, Jake and I walked over to the Plaza, where he'd surprised me by booking a room. When we checked in, I was flooded with memories of the only time I'd stayed there before, the weekend I'd participated in that singles auction.

Two years later, here we were again.

On our wedding night.

I think I'm the one who won that weekend.

Jake had dropped off an overnight bag before the wedding. A few minutes after the bellman brought it up, the doorbell rang again.

"Will you get that?" Jake asked.

"Sure." I walked over to the door and opened it.

A different bellman was standing there. This one was holding a small plate covered by the hallmark silver lid of room service.

"Mrs. McIntyre?" he asked with a smile.

Mrs. McIntyre?

I looked over at Jake. "Is your mom coming over?"

"I think he means you, Waverly."

"Oh yes, of course...oops."

I took the covered plate from the bellman, then shut the door and walked across the room to set it down on the table. When I removed the lid, I gasped.

It was a plate of chocolates.

From Lauren's Chocolate.

Just enough for two.

I looked at Jake. "Who sent this?"

He held his palms up.

I slowly pointed at him.

"Was it…you?"

He smiled. "Maybe."

"You ordered us a plate of chocolates on our wedding night?"

He scratched his eyebrow. "I know you like it more than cake, so I thought it would be fun to share some with you tonight, sort of a private wedding celebration."

I squinted at him. "Do I talk in my sleep?"

He laughed and shook his head. "I know you better than you think I do."

"And you still love me?"

"Forever."

"Even though my last name is still Bryson?"

He nodded slowly. "*Forever.*"

I picked up a piece of chocolate, then walked over and handed it to him. "Thanks for becoming my husband, Jake McIntyre."

He took the chocolate and set it down, then wrapped his arms around me. "Thanks for *wanting* me to be your husband, Waverly Bryson."

I leaned against him and whispered into his chest. "I love you more than you could ever know."

"I love you even more than that," he whispered back.

epilogue

Late the next morning Jake and I took a cab back to Brooklyn, our first official trip across the bridge as a married couple. He dropped me off at my apartment, then went home to Cobble Hill to pack. He'd already given notice on his place and was finally moving in.

Once inside, I removed my coat, then took off my dress and tossed it into the hamper. After a long hot shower, I pulled on some jeans and a shirt and dug my suitcase out of the hall closet.

I was on my way to the bedroom to begin packing when I stopped, set the suitcase down, and looked at the plain platinum band on my left hand. I kissed it, then gently removed it and carried it over to the bookcase. I pulled down my mom's wooden box and opened it, then carefully set the wedding ring alongside the photographs of my parents. The plan was for me and Jake to store both our rings here until the second wedding in Florida.

I was nearly done packing when I realized that I'd mistakenly tossed my dress from this morning into the hamper—a *dry clean only* dress that had no business being there. I opened the lid and fished out the dress. I was about to close it when I noticed something flickering at the bottom.

No way.

I got down on one knee, reached my arm as far as I could into the hamper, and slowly ran my fingers across the wicker grooves.

And then I felt it.

Wedged tightly between two strands, safe and secure, was my engagement ring.

thank you!

Since the last Waverly Bryson novel (*Honey on Your Mind*) came out, I've been overwhelmed by the fan mail I've received from all over the world. Despite my chosen profession, I can't seem to find words to adequately express how much I appreciate each and every message. Hearing from readers is my favorite part of being an author, and I sincerely hope you fans out there enjoyed this book as much as (and ideally more than) the others in the series. As I always say, if you enjoy my novels, the best thing you can do to help me keep writing them is to tell your friends!

Speaking of friends, soon after beginning *Chocolate for Two*, I once again turned to the people in my own life for inspiration. Not surprisingly, they didn't disappoint. This time around I owe a great deal of thanks to: Nicole Allen, Steph Bernabe, Kim Bishop, Jennifer (Brusha) Bressie, Lauren Lyons Cole, Andrea Dershin, Rosie Gonzales Ibrahim FitzGerald, Deron (DJ) Haley, Mike Krieger, Iris Lancaster, Alison Marquiss, Kara Mele, Monica Murnane Morey, Brett Sharkey, Michele Murnane Sharkey, and Ithti Toy Ulit. Super fan Megan DiPasquale also sent me a fantastic dating story that was so off the charts I had to include it. Thank you, Megan, for giving me permission to do so.

On the editing side, I can't say enough about Christina Henry de Tessan, whose uncanny ability to look at the big picture is something that awes me each time I have the pleasure of working with her. I also want to thank my amazing mother (Flo

Murnane, a.k.a., Mommy Dearest) for her impressive proofreading skills, as well as my dad, Mike, a.k.a., Pa, for just being there. And I'd be lost without Alberto Ferrer, who wasn't afraid to give me some tough feedback that led to two significant changes at the eleventh hour. His honesty makes me proud to be his friend.

I also want to give a special shout-out to Garett Vassel. I hope it isn't apparent to anyone reading this book, but I've never been to south Florida and relied on him to help me paint a realistic picture of what upper-crust life there is like. I'm forever grateful for the patience he demonstrated in convincing me, a California girl whose parents once drove a VW bus, that ritzy Southern women of a certain generation really are named after small animals and snack foods.

And to Alex Carr, Jessica Poore, Sarah Tomashek, Vicky Griffith, and company at Amazon Publishing: I don't think you'll ever understand how grateful I am to you for believing in me. Thank you thank you thank you for making my dreams come true.

about the author

Maria Murnane left a successful career as a public-relations executive to pursue a more fulfilling life as a novelist and speaker. Her own "story behind the story" is an entertaining tale of the courage, passion, and perseverance required to get the first Waverly novel, *Perfect on Paper*, published. (*Chocolate for Two* is the fourth in the series, following *It's a Waverly Life* and *Honey on Your Mind*.) Maria graduated with high honors in English and Spanish from the University of California–Berkeley, where she was a Regents' and Chancellor's Scholar. She also holds a master's degree in integrated marketing communications from Northwestern University. She currently lives in New York City.

For more information about her books, her speaking engagements, and her consulting services, please visit www.mariamurnane.com.